DED

To Brandon, Nick, James, and Charlee

Hope you enjoy it Lorna

Joan Donaldson-Yarmey

Whistler's Murder

By

Joan Donaldson-Yarmey

PUBLISHED BY:

Books We Love Publishing Partners (BWLPP)
192 Lakeside Greens Drive
Chestermere, Alberta, T1X 1C2
Canada

Copyright 2011 by Joan Donaldson-Yarmey
Cover art by Michelle Lee Copyright 2011

All rights reserved. Without limiting the rights under copyright reserved above, no part of this publication may be reproduced, stored in or introduced into a retrieval system, or transmitted, in any form, or by any means (electronic, mechanical, photocopying, recording, or otherwise) without the prior written permission of both the copyright owner and the above publisher of this book.

Prologue

The woman stood near the climbing wall, waiting, listening. The dim light from the building a short distance away shone faintly making the dark outside her vision even darker. She was quickly regretting that she had been talked into meeting at this time of night. She should have insisted on a better lit place or even scheduled it for during the day. She realized now that they didn't have to do all their catching up in one day, they had years ahead of them for getting to know each other.

She heard a noise and turned quickly, her heart skipping a beat. She peered into the darkness and waited but no one stepped up to her. No one called "Hi" giving her a feeling of relief. She looked at her watch to see what time it was. They were supposed to meet at eleven-fifteen and she knew she had gotten here early but it felt like she had been waiting half an hour. According to her watch she'd only been here fifteen minutes. She pulled her cell phone out of her purse and checked the time on it. Yes, fifteen minutes.

She stepped to the side of the wall and leaned her back against it. This put her into the darkness as well as giving her only three directions to watch. She had no reason to be afraid of the person she was meeting but she did fear the bears and other nocturnal animals that could be roaming around. She had been warned to keep to the known areas during the day and to make noise if she did go into the bush. No one had said what to do at night.

Another noise and she tried to pinpoint where it came from and what may have made it. Was it someone walking, an animal prowling? Should she call out letting whoever or whatever it was know she was there? It felt better to remain quiet although her stomach was churning and her hands sweating. She was sure that if it was her sister she would have come up to her by now.

Which made her wonder, where was her sister? After all, she was the one who had wanted to meet here and at this time, claiming she wanted so badly to have a long talk. And she herself, at the time, wanting to talk also.

Maybe her sister was running late or something had

happened but if that were true, why hadn't she called to tell her?

A rattling sound like pebbles being rolled across concrete to her right. What could have caused that? It hadn't sounded natural but then she wasn't from here and didn't know what natural was.

Her fear was getting the best of her and she wanted to head back to her room. She wanted to get into the light, where she could see what was around her. She knew she wasn't supposed to run if she encountered a bear during the day but she wasn't sure what was out there and her instinct was to run to the steps, down them, then across the bridge, along the sidewalk and to her car.

Would her mad dash startle the animal enough that it wouldn't follow her? She would have to take the chance because staying here just wasn't an option anymore. She pushed herself away from the wall and hurried over to the concrete steps. She heard the scrape of shoes as the person jumped out of the darkness and her peripheral vision saw them but she had neither time to think about why they had hidden beside the steps and why they had leaped out just as she was going by. Her mind registered the pain in her head and the sense of falling and then went blank.

Chapter 1

"Wow, so this is Whistler," Sally Matthews said, looking around at the green tree-covered mountains outlined against the bright blue sky.

"Yeah, it looks different in the summer than what we see in the photographs of it in winter," Elizabeth Oliver said, as she drove along the Sea to Sky Highway through the town. "It would be nice to come for the skiing sometime."

"I don't think we could afford to come here in the winter," Sally said, ruefully. "It's expensive enough now during the off season."

Elizabeth and Sally were best friends, had been since grade school. They were both in their thirties, medium height with Sally slightly taller, and slim. Elizabeth's hair was light brown, straight, and hung to her shoulders. She usually wore it in a pony tail. Sally's was blonde and curly. The summer before, Sally had enrolled in a two week long science fiction/ fantasy retreat in Whistler and had invited Elizabeth to come along for a holiday.

Elizabeth hadn't hesitated in accepting. Whistler, B.C. The name was iconic with downhill skiing and snowboarding, excitement, fun, money, and the 2010 Olympics. She had immediately Googled Whistler and learned, to her surprise, that there were also summer activities.

Over the past few summers she'd written travel articles for magazines, doing the travelling and researching while on her holidays. After learning about Whistler she'd sent off a proposal to one of the magazines she contributed to and suggested an article on the resort town, tentatively titled Whistler--A Summer Vacation Spot. The idea had been accepted and she'd made her plans.

Both Elizabeth and Sally worked at a long term care facility as nursing attendants. Wanting to make sure they got their holidays at the same time, they'd booked them early in the year.

They'd left Edmonton the previous morning and spent the night in Chilliwack. After a leisurely breakfast to miss the rush hour traffic, they'd followed Highway 1 through some of the cities that made up Greater Vancouver. Just before the Horseshoe Ferry Terminal they'd taken the Sea to Sky Highway, also known as Highway 99, to Whistler.

As they'd driven the highway, stopping at attractions along the way and Elizabeth realized what a wealth of material there was for travel-related articles she'd e-mailed the magazine editor about doing a second article tentatively titled, <u>The Journey to Whistler</u>, which could be published at the same time or maybe the month before.

Elizabeth drove her Tracker past Village Gate Boulevard and at the second set of lights turned right on Nancy Greene Way.

Sally glanced to her right just after the turn. "Down that driveway and behind those tall trees is where the Whistler Sci-Fi and Fantasy Retreat and Convention begins tomorrow," she told Elizabeth. "Now, just follow this drive around and it becomes Ambassador Crescent." Sally looked at the set of directions she'd been sent. "SnowBound Bed and Breakfast should be on the left part way down."

Ambassador Crescent was a narrow street with no sidewalks. Elizabeth drove slowly. Ahead they could see a large backhoe in a yard and a crowd of people standing on the street. They passed three other bed and breakfasts before spying the large sign that was shaped like a mountain and had snow painted on top. It was just beyond the yard where the backhoe was tearing down a house.

Elizabeth inched along the road and the crowd grudgingly moved out of her way. She pulled into the small, paved parking lot in front of the white, three storey house where they had rented a suite for the two weeks.

Elizabeth and Sally stepped out of the Tracker. Elizabeth grimaced at the roar of the machine's motor and the cracking of the wood. They looked over and were just in time to see the operator direct the bucket out so its teeth dug into the roof of the old, wood-sided house, pulling off some more of the shingles and plywood. The next time it broke some of the rafters. The crowd was silent as the watchers stared at the progress.

"I wonder what's so fascinating about demolishing a building?" Sally asked.

"Yeah, you'd think in Whistler B.C. there would be more interesting things to do."

Elizabeth reached in and picked up Chevy, her cockapoo dog. She didn't want him running off because of the noise. They went around to the back of the vehicle and Sally opened the door. She pulled out her two bags.

"I'll come back and get mine once we've checked in," Elizabeth said.

It was a short walk along a path through some low bushes to the office. Beside the door was a sign to just walk in. They pushed open the door, which rang an overhead bell. The room they entered was large and looked like a living room, dining room, kitchen combination. There were tables to the right and left, a small kitchen in the far right corner, and a living room with a fireplace to the far left. Ahead was a hallway with doors opening off it and a set of stairs at the end. A woman came out of one of the doors and smiled when she saw them.

"Ms. Matthews and Ms. Oliver?"

"That's us," Sally said, setting down her bags.

"Good." The woman walked up to them and held out her hand. "I'm Beverly Sanders."

They shook hands. "And this must be Chevy." She held out the back of her hand to him. He sniffed it then struggled to get down.

"What's happening next door?" Sally asked, while Beverly led them down the hall into a small office.

"The owners of that house have decided to tear it down and build a bed and breakfast."

"Another bed and breakfast?" Sally said. "We saw three along this street just getting here."

"And there are more further along the crescent. Our street's nickname is B&B Crescent."

"So, why the crowd out there?" Elizabeth asked.

"Well, it seems that years ago the mother of a previous owner disappeared and rumour has it that her daughter killed her and buried her body in the house somewhere." She handed each of them a card to fill out.

"Oh, no," Elizabeth muttered under her breath, as she wrote her name, address, and vehicle licence number on her card.

Sally turned to her with a smirk. "And you thought you were going to be able to relax here."

Beverly looked at them, a puzzled expression on her face.

"My friend here is quite renowned for solving murders," Sally said, handing back the card. "She has four to her credit already."

"Well, if there is a body, then the murderer will probably have been the daughter, like the story," Beverly said. "And if there is no body then the rumour will be put to rest."

"How come it took so long to tear down the house and see?" Sally asked.

"Because the police really had nothing to go on other than the woman's disappearance. And her daughter said she had run off with her boyfriend. She even had a letter from her to prove it. So nothing was done until today and for an entirely different reason."

They followed Beverly up two flights of stairs to their suite on the top floor. There was a kitchen to the right, a dining room table and chairs in the middle, and a couch and two overstuffed chairs facing a television on the left. Beside the table an open patio door led to a balcony that had a bistro table and two chairs. Beverly hurried over to close the door blocking out most of the noise from the demolition.

"The two bedrooms are exactly the same," she said, opening a door off the kitchen. Inside was a double bed, dresser, desk and chair and an en-suite. She dug in her jean pockets. "Here are keys for each of you to the front door and for the suite. The front door is unlocked all day but we do lock it at 10:00pm."

"Thank you," Sally said, pocketing hers.

Elizabeth did the same.

"The pool is covered until after the demolition," Beverly said, as she went out the door. "I'll be downstairs if you need anything."

Elizabeth went over to the patio door. She looked down on

the rapidly disappearing house. Though the door was closed it did little to muffle the noise. She also saw the pool. She planned on spending a lot of time swimming and sun tanning.

"I'd better go get my things," she said. She hated the idea of having to go down where the machine was so loud, but she also wanted to get unpacked.

"I'll stay here with Chevy," Sally called from her bedroom. She was already hanging her clothes in her closet.

At the vehicle Elizabeth grabbed her suitcase and laptop then locked the door and hurried back to her room. She entered the other bedroom, which was off the living room. After she'd hung her clothes and put her suitcases away she set her tape recorder and computer on the desk. She used her computer with its voice activation to record the distance between attractions, what streets or roads her readers would take to get to the sites, and what she saw from her vehicle as she drove. Her tape recorder was for when she entered buildings, went on hikes, and read interpretive signs. She also used it when she interviewed people. On the days when weather or some other problem prevented her from travelling, she spent her time entering the data she'd recorded onto her laptop.

She'd just finished organizing her room when the backhoe finally shut off. Both she and Sally went out on the balcony to look down.

"Well, no one seems excited so it looks like there's no skeleton," Elizabeth said.

"Are you disappointed? Because there's still the basement or crawl space, or whatever is under it," Sally grinned.

"Oh, stop it." Elizabeth stepped inside and picked up Chevy's leash with two plastic bags tied to it. This set him jumping at her leg and barking. "I'm going to take him for a walk then we can go buy groceries."

Chevy was her companion on her research trips. He supplied company and a reason to go for walks to keep in shape. While she did get out to visit sites and attractions, she also spent a lot of time driving from place to place. By the end of the day she felt the need to get rid of her excess energy.

* * *

I'm up earlier than usual. I quickly shower then get my suitcase out and open it on my bed. It's time to pack for my stay in Whistler. I am at the closet when an image appears and blocks out my closet door. It disappears before I can recognize it and I see the door again. Another shape replaces the door. I turn to my dresser and then my bed. More images flit in and out of my sight overlying anything I am looking at. Then the short flashes of light, almost like small lightening strikes, begin.

I know what's happening. I hurry to my case and unpack my laptop, quickly turning it on. I wait impatiently. It's taking so long. I wonder who is contacting me this time. Is it Mikk relating his story about his experimental freezing and thawing of bodies or Gwin telling about her experiences as a convict sent to this planet during its very early history.

The words come. It's a continuation of Mikk's story. I type as fast as I can. I know I miss words, sometimes whole sentences but I can't help it. I've tried writing it out by hand but that's even slower.

* * *

Mikk pushed open the door to the test room and entered. He glanced at the man strapped to the bed and nodded. He didn't have to look to know that the eyes of the man followed him as he walked over to the table beside the bed. On it was a button, a chart, and a syringe. Mikk picked up the chart and read the notations of the night staff.

"Your glucose levels have remained within our target range for the past week."

"Yippee for me."

Mikk ignored the sarcasm. All the volunteers were all like that, eager to join the test group at the beginning but over time.... " Looks like you spent another restful night."

"What else am I going to do being chained to my bed day and night?"

"We have to protect our staff." His eyes ran down the chart. "You had your final meal of potatoes this morning."

"If I survive this I'll never eat potatoes again."

Mikk put the chart back and picked up the syringe. He uncapped it and held it up to the light, checking the dosage.

"You understand what's going to happen," Mikk said.

"Yeah, yeah. You've told me enough times."

"I just want to make sure you are aware that this is an experiment and there is no guarantee as to the final results."

"I know. I may wake up and I may not. What are you trying to do? Ease your guilt at using a human being for your experiments?"

"The choice was yours."

"Yeah, and some choice. Either stay in the Orbital Prison for the rest of my life or be frozen solid for awhile and hopefully still be alive when I'm thawed."

"If you're alive you get to return to your family on Megalopolis Two with a pension."

The man snorted. "Just get on with it."

Mikk stuck the needle into the man's arm and injected the sedative. He threw the syringe in the garbage and checked his watch. It should take effect in a few moments.

Mikk was a scientist and one of his assignments was space cryonics. The Space Organization hoped to eventually send frozen explorers to other galaxies, thawing them once they'd reached their destination. For the past two years he'd been working on a way to freeze living bodies and then thaw them without harming their cells.

He'd tried various unsuccessful methods before reading a history book about a species of reptiles that had once lived on the planet. In winter they would burrow into the ground and freeze; come spring they would thaw with no ill effects. Scientists at the time believed that the glucose in the reptile's cells prevented ice crystals from forming and bursting those cells.

He'd asked for Orbital Prison volunteers and had spent weeks feeding them various foods and measuring their glucose. With all the foods the level had risen after eating but had lowered again within ninety minutes. Even having them eat often throughout the day hadn't kept their count up for more than the ninety minutes.

Working with a planet scientist he'd devised a synthetic glucose solution which he administered to the volunteers intravenously. It had increased and maintained the glucose for up to three hours after the intravenous was removed. But that still wasn't long enough, so he and the planet scientist had injected the solution into potato plants. When the volunteers ate the potatoes over a three week period the glucose in their cells increased and remained at that level for a few days after their last potato. He hadn't been sure how high a quantity of glucose was needed to ensure a safe frozen state and eventual thawing, and unfortunately all of the Orbital Prison volunteers used so far had died.

He now hoped he had the right amount, for time was running out. A group of fellow space scientists were beginning work with a segmentation machine, which, they hoped, could separate the mind from the body. Once separated, the scientists planned to transport the "person" to another planet and implant it into a body there. The mind then would direct that body and through it explore the planet, gaining an understanding of the life on it.

Mikk watched the eyes of the man as they slowly closed. As in the others, he saw fear replace the hostility they'd all exhibited throughout the pre-freeze analysis. Their final thoughts were that they might not return.

Mikk checked the man's pulse and found it slow and steady. He lifted the eyelids. The eyes stared back at him, unseeing. There would be no problems. He pushed the button which summoned two attendants with a trolley bed. While he waited he undid the straps.

When the bed arrived, Mikk had the attendants lift the man onto it and strap him in, this time so that if he had a seizure he wouldn't fall off. Mikk led the way from the test room to his freezing laboratory.

They wheeled the bed over beside a long, oval shaped chamber. Various hoses and wires ran from the glass lid to a large machine. Mikk opened the lid, taking care to position the wires so the electrodes on the ends didn't touch. The attendants stripped off the man's clothes and rubbed the oil used to prevent freezer burn all over his body. They placed the body in the chamber and after washing their hands, left.

Mikk checked the man's vital signs which were still good. He hooked up a pulse instrument to the man's wrist and neck. He taped electrodes to the man's forehead just above his nose, behind his right ear, over his heart, on his left testicle, behind his left knee, and just above the ankle bone on his right leg. He picked up a long, needle-sized thermometer and inserted it through the stomach into the inner body. The hole would be stitched up if the man survived the process.

Mikk turned on the tracing machine and checked that the thermometer and each electrode was sending back a signal. When he was satisfied, he closed the glass lid and fastened it securely. Beside the tracing machine was an instrument panel with dials, switches, and gauges. Mikk twisted two dials watching to make sure their pressures were the same. He watched two gasses swirl together under the glass.

He checked the gauges. The temperature inside the chamber had to drop gradually giving the body time to adjust to the cooler conditions. He studied the readouts on the tracing machine. So far the temperature of the whole body was falling at the same rate. Mikk looked through the glass lid. The body was shivering, a natural response as it tried to keep warm. By noon the temperature hovered just above the freezing mark. Mikk shut off the gasses. It was time for the final body function check.

The pulse instrument showed a very weak, very slow movement. The glucose helped maintain a state of life until the actual freezing. The tracing machine displayed the body temperature as being uniform and the thermometer indicated that the inner temperature had dropped. Everything was proceeding normally.

Mikk turned the dials again and the gasses stirred. He increased the pressure, mindful that the temperature couldn't drop too fast. The objective was to steadily take the whole body down to just under the freezing point. The gasses slowly created a layer of frost on the lid blocking Mikk's view. When the gauge registered five degrees below freezing, Mikk slacked off the pressure. He now would have to spend the rest of the day minutely adjusting the dials until the temperature remained constant.

* * *

That's it. I sit back drained. My back hurts. My arms ache. While I'm typing I don't move. Again, I wonder when this will all make sense, what the full story will be when it has all been told. I wish I could tell someone what's happening to me, but they wouldn't understand. I look at my watch and jump up. Where did the time go? The retreat starts tomorrow and I have to drive to Whistler yet today.

Chapter 2

The demolished house was now just a pile of splintered wood, drywall, and shingles. Elizabeth was surprised to see some people still grouped in front of it. Chevy stopped to smell a small bush and Elizabeth smiled at a couple who glanced her way.

"What's going up now?" she asked, even though she knew the answer. A question was always a good icebreaker.

"Another bed and breakfast is one of the stories we heard," the woman said. She had reddish blonde hair and was wearing blue capri pants with a matching blue top. She looked to be in her early forties.

"There are a lot of them on this street," Elizabeth said.

"And they are full up all winter and most of the summer."

Although she had solved other mysteries, Elizabeth had initially been reluctant to get involved in each of them. Since she was already talking with these people it wouldn't hurt to learn more about this one. She was unsure, however, how to broach the subject about the old rumour.

"Well, I guess we can go," a man said. "Doesn't look like they will be doing anything more today."

"Yeah," another man agreed. "They won't find any bones until they start to remove all that rubble."

"Bones?" Elizabeth asked, giving a mental sigh of relief. It's nice when people cooperate.

"Haven't you heard?" the woman asked.

Elizabeth shook her head wondering if, by not actually saying the word "No," she was still telling a little white lie. "My friend and I just arrived from Edmonton. We're staying in that the SnowBound Bed & Breakfast. My name is Elizabeth Oliver."

"I'm Alison and this is my husband Rick. We live in that house across the road." She pointed to a gray, two storey place with a multi-coloured stone parking area.

"So, what was this about bones?" Elizabeth asked.

"Back in the 1980s a woman who lived in this house

disappeared and has never been seen since," Alison said.

"Right," Rick agreed. He had gray brown hair and was dressed in shorts and a golf shirt. The Maui Jim sunglasses he was wearing hid the colour of his eyes. "She was living with her daughter and from what we've heard she was hard to get along with and they fought all the time. Everyone thought that the daughter had killed her."

"What did the daughter say?" Chevy had grown tired of the bush and wanted to go into the yard. Elizabeth held firm onto his leash causing him to turn and look at her.

"She denied it, of course." Alison said.

"Were the police notified?"

"Yes, but they had nothing to go on. The daughter said the mother had left with her boyfriend."

Elizabeth was disappointed that she hadn't learned anything new. "Did you know either the mother or daughter?"

"No, we just moved here three months ago. But our neighbour, Cynthia, did and she's the one who told us the story."

Chevy pulled on his leash. Elizabeth knew he was anxious to begin exploring his new surroundings. She looked at the pile of splintered wood. The backhoe operator hadn't been too careful at knocking the place down. Obviously, he and the present owners didn't believe the story.

For a little dog, Chevy had a lot of pulling power. Elizabeth's arm stretched out and her upper body leaned forward. "I'd better go," she said. "He has a one track mind when he's on his walk and that doesn't include me stopping and talking."

She walked to where Ambassador Crescent intersected with Fitzsimmons Road South and crossed it. She passed three houses on the left and reached some large boulders across the road. Ahead was a berm with a wire fence at the top. The gate in the fence was open. Elizabeth climbed the berm and was thrilled to see the rushing waters of Fitzsimmons Creek. She let Chevy off his leash and he headed to the nearest fence post where he lifted his leg. What looked like an old road ran along side the river and she began walking down it. Chevy, his nose to the ground, zipped from rock to rock.

* * *

I thought the story was finished for today but the images and flashes of light begin again. I haven't replaced my computer in its case so I leave my packing and return to the keyboard. It's Gwin's story this time.

She'd had a career as a space explorer on Terrene and she'd been part of a three-person team that had gone in search of a suitable planet to colonize with the prisoners of Terrene. They'd found three which had the right atmosphere to support a colony. On the last planet, Gwin had done some exploring on her own and had seen some inhabitants who stood on two legs and wore animal skins. Their interaction with each other had been gentle and they seemed content with their lives. The first thing that entered her mind was, what would the arrival of murderers and cigarette pushers from her planet do to those people?

At the meeting of the Global Alliance the other members of the team had stated that in their opinion the last planet was the best. Gwin hadn't told anyone else about her sightings but she'd read a statement at the meeting citing reasons for why she thought the first planet they had visited would be better. She'd been invited back to present her evidence. However, other people had had their own lucrative plans that involved the settling of the last planet, and to stop her from influencing the decision they had framed her for murder. Found guilty, she was sent to the Orbital Prisons. Her ship was one of three that were being sent to establish a settlement on the new planet.

Also, she'd been engaged to Mikk.

* * *

When they arrived at the planet the ships had landed near a large clearing by a river and Gwin recognized the site immediately. She and her co-explorers had stayed here for three days during their exploration.

It was deemed that all prisoners would sleep and be fed on the spaceships until the dormitories, warehouses, and kitchens were built. Lots were laid out and decisions made as to where each building would go. However, the prisoners had been raised in the Megalopolis. They had no idea what to do with the equipment and tools sent and few had any willingness to learn. The project supervisors were equally in the dark. They had a rudimentary understanding of what the tools were for but no experience in using them.

However, some of the convicts realized that their existence depended on setting up the colony. Eventually, the sides of the dorms and warehouses were completed. To speed up construction canvas was stretched overhead for a makeshift roof. The prisoners were moved into the dorms and the supplies stacked in the warehouses. Pens were erected for the animals that had been brought. Ground was dug up with the tools that had been sent and seeds planted.

When this was done two of the space ships were readied to fly home.

Gwin didn't consider herself a convict. She hadn't committed a crime as the others had. So she didn't feel the need to help with the building of the colony. Instead she set about trying to find a way to get off the planet and back to Terrene to clear her name. She watched for a favourable time to sneak aboard one of the ships before it took off. But she wasn't the only one with that idea. It seemed that most of the prisoners wanted off the planet.

Guards with their weapons ready were stationed at the ships and five prisoners were shot when they attempted to climb aboard during the night. No one made it on the ships before take off.

One space craft was left. It housed the police and guards until their barracks were built and was also there to travel to the nearest supply planet in an emergency. Since she knew how to fly it, Gwin waited for an opportunity to board. But it was heavily guarded so she had to bide her time, watching for any opening in their routine that could be to her advantage.

Leaving the planet wasn't the only thing that occupied Gwin's mind. When she could, Gwin snuck away to look for any planet people in this area.

"Where are you going, Gwin?" Sari, another prisoner, asked one day when Gwin was heading into the nearby bush.

Damn. She'd tried to disappear quietly into the trees each time she went and so far had been successful.

"I see you have some food," Sari continued. "Are you setting up a cache somewhere?"

"No, actually, I'm going for a walk. Do you want to come?"

Sari had been one of the women in her cell on the voyage over. They had fought for the first few days then had reached a mutual agreement to leave each other alone. Gwin knew that if she tried to hide anything, Sari would be the first to begin digging into what she was doing.

"No," Sari shook her head.

As Gwin headed through the bush she pretended to be interested in the flowers she saw. At the same time she kept an eye out for Sari. She'd been curious enough to ask and Gwin didn't trust her to just walk away. So, instead of taking her usual route, Gwin wound her way through the trees, making a show of eating the food as she went. Then she hurried back to the settlement.

The next day she took a round about way along the river to go into the bush. When she was sure that no one had seen her she crossed a large meadow into more trees. Here, on a previous search, she'd found a well-worn path. She wasn't sure if it was from animals or the inhabitants. She'd already checked through the trees to see if there was a camp or a sign of habitation and hadn't found any.

She'd decided to extend her search towards some hills in the distance. Maybe they lived in a valley or a cave. She was so intent in scrutinizing the trees and open areas that she wasn't prepared when one of the inhabitants stepped out in front of her on the edge of a clump of bush.

Gwin stopped cold, staring at him. Her heart beat faster. After all the rehearsing she'd done for this moment she couldn't think of anything to do. So far, she'd assumed that any of them she met would be friendly, but now looking at what she supposed was the male of the species she realized just how stupid that thought had been.

He stood on two legs and had two arms. He was taller than she was and very sturdily built. He had long shaggy hair on his head and shorter hair on his chest, arms, and legs. He wore an animal skin around his waist and it hung half way to his knees. He carried a tool with a long handle and what looked like a pointed end made of rock. He had two blue eyes, a nose, two ears, and a mouth. He was carrying a small dead animal.

He was exactly like the ones she had seen on another part of the planet during the exploratory visit.

Gwin calmed enough to smile at him and hold her hand with the food in it towards him. He looked at it then back at her. Thinking he might not know what it was, she took some and put it in her mouth. She chewed and swallowed it, then offered him the rest. He made no move to take it.

What did she do now?

Suddenly another man stepped out of the trees. Behind him were a woman and child. The second man was much the same as the first while the woman was shorter and her skins covered her from shoulder to knee. The hair on her head was just as shaggy but she didn't have as much body hair. The child was small with only hair on his or her head.

They stared at Gwin. None of them made a sound nor moved their hands in any type of greeting. They turned and went back into the bush. The first man waited a few moments before taking off after them.

It looked like they were on a path and Gwin decided to follow it. She'd just started into the trees when the first man stopped and turned back. He shook his hand with the tool in it at her. She stopped. It looked as if he was warning her not to continue.

She hesitated then smiled and waved to the man before retreating. She would try again in a few days. That may give them time to get curious about her and maybe be friendlier.

* * *

Unfortunately, these episodes come at their whim not mine. I quickly finish packing then grab my suitcase and laptop and head to my car.

I didn't enrol in the retreat for the instruction on how to write science fiction and fantasy. I enrolled for the one-on-one session with the instructor. I've already e-mailed her the first few chapters so she can read them before our meeting. That way she will be able to give me some ideas on how to pull this together. I've already decided that I'm not going to tell anyone where this is coming from and about the images and lights. They might think I'm crazy.

Chapter 3

"I saw you talking to the people in front of the demolished house," Sally said with a grin when Elizabeth and Chevy returned to the room. "Did you learn anything more about the possible body?"

Elizabeth shook her head. "They told the same story as Beverly. The only new thing I learned is that the person who lives next door to them knew the woman who disappeared."

"Well, while you were gone I got directions to the nearest grocery store from Beverly and I made a list. Have you phoned your dad and Terry and Sherry yet?"

Elizabeth took out her cell phone. "I'll do that now." She dialled the numbers for her younger twin siblings and left messages on their machines then called her dad's number. Her mother had died a few years ago from cancer and she and Sally had moved into his basement suite to keep him company. When he answered the phone she told him they had arrived okay.

"Did you stop in and see your Grandmother on your way through Vancouver?" Phil asked.

Her maternal grandmother lived in a condo on False Creek near Granville Island. When the final arrangements had been made for the trip, Elizabeth had called her to let her know she was coming to Whistler. She'd agreed to contact her when she arrived so they could get together.

"No," Elizabeth said. "Sally wanted to get here and set up. But I called her and I'm going to see her next weekend."

"Good."

Her last phone call was to Jared, the man she had met and fallen in love with last year. He was in a wheelchair due to an accident and because of that had trouble with his bowels. He'd already had one operation for an obstruction two years ago and had had a colonoscopy three weeks ago. The doctors had found precancerous polyps and were going to remove part of his large intestine tomorrow.

She'd been willing to cancel her trip to be with him for his operation but he'd insisted she go. He understood how important her writing career was to her. "Besides," he'd said. "I'll be spending my convalescence at Paul's. We're still adjusting to our new family dynamics."

Elizabeth had nodded. Last year, at Jared's request, she'd helped him discover who had murdered his mother but in the process they had found out that Paul, the man who had raised him and whom he called Dad, was not his biological father. She was glad that he was coming to terms with that because the knowledge had destroyed the family concept he'd thought he'd belonged to.

In the grocery store, Elizabeth and Sally pushed the cart up and down the aisles not sure what to purchase. They'd be having breakfast at the bed and breakfast and Sally's lunches were included in her package. They didn't know how their schedules would work for supper so they'd decided to wait until each evening arrived. Either they would fend for themselves, or they would buy something to cook in their kitchen, or they'd go out.

So, really Elizabeth just needed something for her lunch. She stocked up on sandwich meat, bread, butter, and mustard and grabbed a carton of Pepsi. She didn't drink coffee, getting her caffeine jolt from the pop. Sally added vegetables and fruit for her snacks, and juice containers. They also threw in a pizza for their supper and some crackers, cheeses, and salsa.

When they'd unpacked the groceries, Elizabeth went to her bedroom to set out her research equipment. Besides her laptop and tape recorder she also had her digital camera with its four rechargeable batteries, charger, and extra memory cards for pictures. She plugged in the charger to made sure the batteries were topped up for tomorrow. As a precaution in case she took a lot of pictures she carried regular batteries as backup.

She had begun planning her research for Whistler by looking up the town's web site on the Internet. Then she used Google Map to see all the streets. Since she could only see small sections of the town at a time, she'd bought a Whistler map so she could lay the whole town out at once and see how the streets interconnected. She wasn't sure if she was going to begin the article with the reader arriving in the town or if she was going to start at the Whistler village and spread out from there. She would have to gather her information first and see which worked best.

* * *

After a shower and a quick early morning walk with Chevy, Elizabeth joined Sally and they headed downstairs to the dining room for breakfast. She liked staying at bed and breakfasts while doing her research because the owners were always friendly and usually gave her information for her article.

In the dining room there were three round tables that each accommodated four and one that sat two people. They all had white crocheted tablecloths over a multi-coloured underlay. The chairs had cushions to match the underlay. There was a couple at the smaller table so Elizabeth and Sally chose one of the larger ones. The plates, cutlery, and cups were already in place. On the table was a candle burning in a holder.

While they waited Elizabeth looked around the room. The *Whistler Question* and the *Vancouver Sun* newspapers were on a small table by the hall entrance. Beside the table was a yellow sideboard with a coffeepot, kettle, teapot and various teas, a pitcher half full of orange juice and matching glasses, a vase with a single artificial rose, a bowl of mints, and two burning candles. On the wall above it hung four Anne of Green Gables collector plates.

The living room consisted of a couch, a loveseat, and two

chairs arranged in front of a fireplace. On the mantle of the fireplace were four old-style oil lamps. Along one wall were three cabinets with shelves full of books, and a roll top writing desk. Floor length windows with sheer drapes made up the opposite wall. Just about all the space on the other three walls was covered with photographs or paintings or needlework.

The guest kitchen had an apartment sized fridge and stove, and a glassed-front upper cupboard full of cups, glasses, and dishes. On the counter was a microwave, toaster oven, paper towels, and various other utensils. The bottom cupboards were closed but Elizabeth imagined they held pots and pans for cooking. She doubted that she and Sally would be using them very much.

A man in his early forties and then a woman in her mid-thirties came down the stairs. They each chose to sit by themselves at the other tables.

Beverly entered the room with two, three-tiered trays. On the top tier were grapes and strawberries, the second one contained bran and fruit muffins, and the third held butter and various jams. She set one each on the two other occupied tables and headed back down the hall. She returned with two more.

"Your breakfasts will be ready shortly," Beverly said, as she placed them on the tables. "Help yourself to some orange juice or coffee. The kettle has hot water in it for tea."

While Sally went to get some coffee, Elizabeth headed over to look at the newspapers. The *Whistler Question* was dated last Thursday so it must come out once a week. The *Vancouver Sun* had today's date. She returned to her table. She wasn't interested in the Vancouver paper and would read the local paper later when she came back this evening.

Breakfast was a plate with a shish kebob of sausage, tomato, onion, and mushroom, and scrambled eggs and toast. Each plate was delivered to the tables by Beverly.

The room was quiet as everyone ate. The meal was very good and Elizabeth ate extra because she knew it would be a long time until lunch. After breakfast they returned to their room and Elizabeth made her lunch while Sally put her retreat papers into her backpack, then stepped out onto the balcony to enjoy the sunshine. Elizabeth gathered up her research equipment said goodbye and she and Chevy headed to her vehicle.

On the way she stopped in at the kitchen to see Beverly. "On the highway coming here I noticed the Village Gate Boulevard goes to the visitor information centre. Is there any parking there?"

"There is," Beverly said. "But you have to pay for it. If you get back onto Highway 99 from Nancy Greene Way and turn left onto Lorimer and then right onto Blackcomb Way you will find some large parking lots. Some of them are free and if you park there you can walk across Blackcomb Way to the Village.'

"How do I get to the Upper Village?" She'd looked at the maps she had but hadn't been able to figure out the way there.

"Go to parking lot #1 and just as you enter it you will cross a walkway. If you follow the walkway to your left you will reach the village."

"Thank you," Elizabeth smiled. Again the bed and breakfast owner had come through for her.

As she loaded her stuff she could see that a crew with a front-end loader had come in to start cleaning up the site next door. She felt a twinge of disappointment that no body had been found but then grinned. That was good. It meant that she wouldn't be trying to solve anything during her research and thereby having to put off her article writing until she returned home. She would get her research done and her article written in the first week she was here. And once that was completed she would be able to relax by the pool and catch up on her reading while Sally was at her retreat. Her holiday would go as planned.

She started her Tracker and headed to her first stop, the Village.

* * *

I'm barely out of bed when the images and flashes of light begin. I quickly bring up my Terrene file.

* * *

Mikk left his apartment early each morning, arriving at work an hour before everyone else. As soon as he entered the building he headed to the sixth floor to check on the chamber even though an alarm was set that would ring on the pager he had strapped to his arm if something went wrong with the instruments. It wasn't that he mistrusted the alarm, it was that this was his project and he wanted to maintain control over it. He didn't want a machine deciding to shut it down or to change settings.

On this morning Mikk turned the two dials and watched the temperature of the chamber rise to the freezing mark. The frost gradually melted off the glass and he could see the prisoner lying in the frozen state. He now had to slowly raise the temperature in the chamber so the body thawed evenly.

He looked at the tracing machine hooked to the electrodes on the outer body and the body thermometer he'd inserted through the belly button before freezing. It showed that the body temperature inside and out was at the freezing point. This was the crucial time. He'd learned that the temperature had to rise so minutely as to almost not move at all. It would be another 24 hours before the prisoner's body temperature would be normal.

As the day wore on Mikk could feel the tiredness creep up on him. He needed some sleep and something to eat but there was no one he trusted enough to work the dials. He'd had a cot installed after the first successful thawing but, because of the one flaw in that thawing, during the second experiment and this one he seldom took the time to relax or sleep on it. He went over to the cot now and stretched out. He had time for a short nap before he had to raise the temperature again.

But he didn't get to sleep. As soon as his mind was off the chamber his thoughts turned to Gwin. How was she doing? Was the colony being established as planned? Had she really murdered that person and if so, why? There were so many questions he needed answered.

According to the law, no one could visit a prisoner once they had been charged. Everything was left up to the courts to sort out and then make a decision. If the person was found guilty they were immediately sent to the Orbital Prisons. After a year of good behaviour they were allowed visitors.

He hadn't been able to see Gwin because just after her conviction, she'd been sent to the colony planet. He knew the Space Organization was receiving messages from the spaceship Lederer that had been left with the colony. He'd contacted them many times under the pretext of finding out how the tools he'd helped design were working. They'd only been able to tell him that the construction of the buildings and the planting of seeds was progressing. There was nothing about anyone specific.

He'd even asked about any space ships flying to the colony planet but had been told that none were scheduled. There just wasn't any way that he could contact anyone there or even fly there himself. He felt so powerless. He missed Gwin so much and he wanted to do something to find out what happened and to bring her back. There must have been a mistake, for he never believed that she could kill someone.

All he could do now was hope something happen either here or on the colony planet to make a flight necessary. Then he would apply to go along.

An hour later Mikk rose and adjusted the temperature again and he did it every hour until the body began shivering. Once the shivering started he raised the temperature at a faster rate until the body was at its normal state. He'd been instructed to contact his superiors just before the awakening so they could watch the final moments of the prisoner returning to life. He let them know the moment was imminent and they hurried over.

According to the pulse instrument and the body temperature gauges the prisoner should be opening his eyes soon. Mikk leaned over the chamber to watch for movement. He'd finally hit on the amount of glucose needed to keep the body from dying while frozen and the last two bodies had return to life just the same as before the freezing. The pulse, breathing, heart rate, and bodily functions were normal. The problem had been that their minds were dead. Their bodies had nothing to direct them. He'd made some adjustments after the first but the same had happened in the second thawing. This was his third attempt and he hoped this one worked.

"How is the research going on separating the mind from the body and transporting it?" Mikk asked his superiors as they hovered over the chamber.

"They haven't been able to overcome the mind fighting that goes on when it enters another body."

Mikk still felt that he had been right to pursue his idea of freezing the whole person. He just had to get the mind to thaw intact, though. When that finally happened they'd only have to make sure the temperature of the compartment sent to a far off planet could be controlled from here. That way it would only thaw when the space ship had securely landed. But that part had nothing to do with him. It would be up to the technicians to build a chamber that would fit in a spaceclipper.

Mikk undid the latches on the chamber and lifted the cover. He felt the body and it was warm. He removed the electrodes and probe but the contact failed to make the prisoner move. Mikk had a sinking feeling as he lifted the lid of one of the eyes. Behind it was a blank stare, the same as the first two volunteers. Mikk let it close.

He turned to his superiors. "It didn't work. The body thawed but his mind is lost."

"What do you mean lost?"

"It's gone. The body is alive but there is no mind to operate it."

"So you won't be able to freeze a scientist and sent him to explore another planet?" one of his superiors said.

"His body will make it but his mind won't."

"So what are you doing now?"

"I'm still trying but I don't think I can do much more."

"Perhaps you can offer your help with the mind separation experiment."

* * *

Again Gwin continues her story.

* * *

The leaves on the trees had begun to turn a bright yellow and orange colour. One day, while most of the other prisoners wandered aimlessly up and down the streets, Gwin decided to search for the inhabitants she had seen. Making sure no one was watching her she headed into the bush. When she reached the spot where she had seen them she stopped unsure if she should wait to see if they came or follow the path. They had acted as if they didn't want her to go any further the first time, however, her curiosity won out and she walked into the bush. Some of the leaves had begun to fall from the trees carpeting the forest floor and sending up a pungent odour. Gwin inhaled deeply, liking the smell.

She came to a meadow and could see where the trail meandered through it to the hills beyond. There was still no sign of activity.

"If they are in the hills, they'll see me coming," Gwin mused. "And they'll either come to meet me or hide."

As she walked her nerves were on end, expecting them to jump out of the grass at any time. This is getting spooky, she thought. They should have seen me by now. She followed the path up the slope to the crest of the hill and looked down on a lovely valley. In the middle, the waters of a small lake shimmered. Golden grass waved softly in the breeze. Wild animals, which were small in the distance, grazed contentedly. The trail continued along the slope to a cave in the hillside.

Gwin looked around but could not see any of the inhabitants. She headed to the cave. As she drew nearer she could see where rock had been placed to form a small terrace in front of the opening. A large pit with ashes in the bottom was to one side and a huge pile of bones lay halfway down the slope.

"Hello," Gwin called. "Anyone here?"

There was no answer.

She stepped closer to the cave opening and called again. No reply. Gwin walked up to the opening and peered inside but because of the sun all she could see was darkness. She stepped in and waited until her eyes adjusted to the dim light. She saw many small hearths with wood beside them and ashes in them. There were animal skins spread out on the floor and various tools, some similar to the one she'd seen in the inhabitant's hand, leaned against the wall. Baskets wove from grass or carved from wood sat near the hearths. Long bones shaped as spoons rested in the baskets. The cave didn't look abandoned. It looked as if the inhabitants had left but expected to return soon.

Gwin didn't touch anything. When she stepped out she looked down at the valley, shielding her eyes against the sun with her hand. Far in the valley where the wild animals had grazed, she could see figures with long spears in their hands chasing one of the animals. As she watched one of the people threw his spear and hit the animal in the side. The animal stumbled and that was enough for the other figures to crowd around it stabbing with their spears. When that animal was dead, two others hurried over and began to remove the hide. The hunters headed after the herd again.

The skinners were fast. They had the hide off and the animal gutted in minutes. Another group began to cut up the meat as soon as they were finished.

They were hunting for food. That was why the place is empty. Gwin watched for a while then headed back to the colony.

* * *

I look at my watch. Geeze, if I don't hurry I'm going to be late for the first class.

Chapter 4

After breakfast with Elizabeth, Sally got out the map of Whistler that had been supplied with all her papers and looked at it again. It was a four block walk from their bed and breakfast back to Nancy Greene Way and the private school where the retreat was being held. She could go that way or she could wander through the neighbourhood. Today, just to make sure she got there on time she decided to go the route she knew. She placed the map in her backpack with her notebook and the bare bones outline for her course.

When she'd received the information, she'd been given the choice of four different sections: writing novels and short stories, writing scripts for movies or television series, designing games, or writing plays for theatre. Since she'd already started a novel, she'd chosen novel and short story writing.

There would be lectures in the morning with the afternoons left free to write, to work on assignments, or to explore Whistler. Each of those who had sent in their short stories or the first three chapters from their novels would have their one-on-one time with the instructor in the afternoon. She hadn't signed up for that. She was new to this and just wanted to sit back and gather information for now.

The course ran from Monday to Friday. The first weekend was left for the students to do as they pleased. The second weekend was reserved for a large SciFi/Fantasy Convention to end the retreat. During the day on Saturday there would be a number of panels with science fiction or fantasy writers who would talk on different subjects. These panels were included in the students' package but were also open, for a fee, to anyone of the general public who was a science fiction or fantasy fan. There would also be two agents to answer questions about how to send query letters and proposals to an agent.

Saturday evening was for a supper followed by a dance where everyone who wished to do so could dress up as their favourite hero or alien. Prizes would be given for the best costumes in different categories. Sally had gone looking for a costume to rent but found that there weren't many for women unless she wanted to wear a mini dress with metallic trim, or a two piece Amidala with a sexy top, or a red or blue Star Trek mini dress. She decided against a costume. She wasn't sure if she even wanted to go to the party. Sunday was reserved for a final class with the instructor giving each student suggestions on how better to approach their writing.

Sally turned right when she got out onto Ambassador Crescent and walked to the end where it curved and became Nancy Greene Way. She passed Toni Sailor Lane and came to the crossroad where Fitzsimmons Road North and South met, then crossed Fitzsimmons Creek. Finally after passing Blackcomb Way, which she had noticed seemed to wander through much of Whistler, she reached the entrance for the retreat. She stopped and looked down the driveway. The building wasn't visible from the street but she could see cars parked in a lot.

"Don't be afraid," a voice said behind her.

Sally jumped and turned to see a tall man with graying hair smiling at her. She tried to think of a quick come back but nothing suitable came to mind so she just smiled back. "Are you going to the retreat?" she asked. It was obvious that he was but she couldn't come up with anything else.

"Yes." He held out his hand. "My name is Michael Wolf."

"Sally Matthews." She shook his hand, which felt very soft. She wondered what he did for a living.

They started down the driveway.

"Have you been to a retreat before?" Sally asked.

Michael nodded. "This is my second one. You?"

"My first."

When the trees ended they came upon a large two storey building with plenty of gables. Some covered small patios, others windows and doors, and one seemed just for decoration. The lower storey was gray brick while the second one was white siding. Two people were having a smoke and talking at the far corner of the building.

Michael opened the door for her.

A polite man, Sally thought as she thanked him.

In the foyer was a map showing the four rooms where the different sections of the retreat were being held.

"What part are you taking?" Michael asked.

"Novel and short story," Sally answered. "What about you?"

"Script writing."

"I thought about that but figured I should have a story first."

Michael nodded. "I took the novel writing course here with Kat Mac two years ago. I finished my novel and have found a small press to publish it. Now I want to make it into a screenplay."

They studied the map. Sally's classroom was down the hall to the right while Michael's was upstairs.

"Congratulations on getting published and success with your script writing," Sally said, when they parted.

The classroom, with tiered platform seating, was almost full when Sally arrived. She stopped inside the door and looked around. Tables with chairs behind them were set on the raised sections so that three people shared a table. She climbed to the top and took an empty chair at the end of a table. There was a man at the other end and a woman in the middle. Both appeared to be about her age. From where she sat she could look down on the heads of the rest of the students. She figured she could watch what was happening without getting too involved. Usually the ones who wanted to interact with the instructor sat in the front row.

It was a mixture of students with twice as many males as females. Some were introducing themselves to the ones next to them. Others were organizing their laptops or their notebooks and pens on the table. Some were like her, observing. She recognized two of them from breakfast at the bed and breakfast. When the instructor entered the room, all noise ceased. They looked at her expectantly.

She was dressed in a calf length multi-coloured peasant skirt and matching vest with a long sleeved white blouse. Her dark blonde hair was knotted in a braid that hung down her back.

"Good morning and welcome to my class," she said. "My name is Katherine MacKenzie and I will be your instructor for the next two weeks. You may call me Katherine, Ms MacKenzie, or even Kat Mac, which is the name I write under. If you looked at the material I sent you, you will have noticed that I didn't give you any idea of what my lectures would be about. That's because I didn't want you rushing to the Internet looking it all up. I wanted you to come here with an open mind so that you listen to what I have to say."

Then my mind is exactly what you are wanting, Sally thought. There hadn't been time in her busy schedule to look at much more than the map and the list of places to stay.

Kat Mac looked around the room. "We will start this morning with introductions and then get right into the course. I want to cover as much as I can in the short time we have."

Sally had thought two weeks was a long time, but then again, she didn't know much about writing and even less about writing science fiction.

Kat Mac eyes settled on Sally. "We'll begin with the last row and work our way down to the front. Would you please stand, give us your name and a brief bio about yourself and why you are here?"

Sally stood slowly. She hated that the instructor had called upon her first There were twelve other writers in the group and she didn't know how brief was brief. Were these introductions supposed to take ten minutes, five minutes or just thirty seconds?

"My name is Sally Matthews. I'm from Edmonton, Alberta. I love to read science fiction and some fantasy. I'm in the beginning stages of writing a novel and I'm here to learn as much as I can about the creative process for science fiction. Uh… this is my first retreat." Sally sat down her face reddening. She turned to the woman who sat beside her.

The woman stood. "I'm Lisa Zhang. This is also my first retreat. I've almost finished a novel. I live in Chilliwack, B.C."

The man at their table was Luke Johnson from Lillooett, B.C. and he had completed his novel. He was really here because he needed the time away from work and family to edit it.

"My name is Bonnie Stone and I don't know if any of you have noticed but there are thirteen of us and that is an unlucky number to have in a class."

"I'm number fourteen," Kat Mac said.

Bonnie shook her head. "The instructor doesn't count. There are thirteen students. That's a bad sign. I might not be able to stay." She sat down without saying anything about herself.

So Bonnie was the woman she'd seen at breakfast, Sally thought. She waited to learn who the man from the bed and breakfast was.

"This is my third retreat," Russ Peters from Vancouver said. "I didn't learn much at the other two, so I'm still working on the same novel. I'm hoping this one will be the charm."

And so it went around the room. Sally marked down names and the places they were from so she knew who they were. She didn't trust her memory. Most were from the province but one man, Reggie Shaw, was from Hinton, Alberta. She put a tick beside Daryl Cannon from Victoria because he was the man she'd noticed at the bed and breakfast.

For many this was their first retreat. Most had already started a novel, while a few were hoping to begin one during these two weeks. One man, Kirk West, had come because he had a story idea and thought it might fit into the science fiction genre. He was wanting to learn all that he could.

"I am going to speak in my regular voice at my regular speed," Kat Mac said, at the end of the introductions. "If you want to record my lecture, you may do so but I will be moving around as I talk so my voice will be quieter or louder depending on where your recording device is. I do not allow them on my desk."

Sally had checked the Internet to find out what there was in recording technology that would make it easier for her to take notes during the lecture. She had found microphones for investigators to wear on their body, which she'd laughingly shown that to Elizabeth and suggested she might need it for her amateur sleuthing. There was a bionic ear that would allow her to hear conversations up to thirty-five metres feet away. That would help her hear the lecture but not write it. Then she'd read about the super high sensitivity microphones that were good for anyone attending a large conference. They came with up to thirty-five metres of cable and attached to a recorder. One with an eight metre cable cost about one hundred dollars plus shipping and handling and relevant taxes. When she'd read that she'd opted for the old-fashioned art of writing it out by hand and then she'd use the new technology and read it back into her computer via the voice activated software.

"With that out of the way I now have a surprise for you," Kat Mac continued. "On the last Friday there will be a publisher here to give a speech on what his publishing house is looked for in manuscript ideas."

There was a gasp from some of the students. They began talking to her and to each other.

Kat Mac held up her hand. When it was quiet, she continued. "After his speech each of you will have ten minutes with him in order to pitch an idea for a book, tell him about your book and ask if it would be a fit for his publishing house, or just ask him questions. The choice is yours."

This set the room a buzz again. Everyone was talking excitedly. Sally didn't take part in it. She wasn't sure how she felt about this. She was working on a story and had written the first three Chapters but she didn't know if she wanted to share it with anyone, especially a publisher. If he said he didn't like it, what would she do, and if he did like it then the pressure would be on for her to finish it and she wasn't even sure how the next Chapters would go or even how the story was going to play out. Maybe by the end of next week she would have a better idea.

Kat Mac waited a few minutes then brought the room back to order. "Science fiction and fantasy are sometimes called speculative fiction because the writer allows their imagination to wander outside the realm of our reality," she said, getting right into her lecture. She paused and looked around the room. "I don't know how familiar you are with science fiction or fantasy writing so this morning I will give you an overview. Later we'll discuss them in length.

"Over the years there have been many definitions given for science fiction and fantasy depending on who you ask. Rod Serling, host of the late 1960s, early 1970s television show, *The Twilight Zone*, is supposed to have said. '*Fantasy is the impossible made probable and science fiction is the improbable made possible.*'"

She was pacing up and down the room as she talked, stopping occasionally to look at the students. It was easy to see that she was passionate about her subject.

"Science fiction writing comes from each writer's conjectures based on present events or on inventions in science or technology. They take that event or invention and project it into the future, modifying it to suit the circumstances of their story. But the story's abstract components are possible within the laws of nature as seen by the scientific establishment.

"Science fiction writers should have a basic knowledge of the world around them, some understanding of science, and a good imagination. In the case of fantasy writing, usually magic, the supernatural, or mythology is the basis for the themes, plots, or settings. It stays away from the scientific technology but follows the 'Laws' of whatever its theme is. If the theme is magic, then the story must be contained within the rules of magic. Myths, fairy tales, and legends are thought to be some of the first fantasy stories."

Sally tried to write as fast as Kat Mac was talking but it was impossible to write what she had heard and listen to what was being said. She quickly looked around the room and saw the most of the students were like her, bent over their notebooks pens flying across their pages. Now would have been to good time to know shorthand, she lamented.

"Science fiction writing dates back to the 2nd century with Lucian of Samosata's *True History*," Kat Mac continued. "It is about space travel, aliens, and space wars. Some of the Arabian Nights stories are science fiction as are Jonathan Swift's *Gulliver's Travels*, Voltaire's *Micromegas*, and Kempler's *Somnium*. Mary Shelley, Jules Verne, Edgar Allan Poe, and H.G. Wells were four of the most famous 19th century science fiction writers. And of course we have Carl Sagan, Isaac Asimov, Frederik Pohl, and Judith Merril in the 20th century."

Doesn't she ever pause for a breath, Sally wondered writing furiously.

"Fantasy is believed to have begun with the poem from Ancient Irag called *The Epic of Gilgamesh*, versions of which date back to 2150 BCE. Over the centuries there have been *The Odyssey*, *Beowulf*, the Authurian tales, and the *Devine Comedy*. Modern fantasy literature is said to have begun with George MacDonald, who wrote *Phantastes* in 1858. One of the most famous modern fantasy writers was J.R.R. Tolkien author of *Lord Of the Rings*. And who hasn't heard of J.K Rowlings' Harry Potter."

Finally, Kat Mac called for a break and everyone swarmed out of the room. Some headed to a small atrium with stuffed chairs, a coffee machine, and a vending machine while some went outside. A few gathered around the instructor as she walked away.

Sally went to the atrium and poured herself a coffee. She stood listening to the others talk about the lecture so far.

"I'm not sure if I should be in this class," Kendra Logan said, with a smile. "I got lost once she started mentioning the different writers and their works of science fiction." She appeared to be the outdoor type dressed in jeans, shirt, and hiking boots. Her blonde hair was cut short. "So far I haven't understood much of what she has said."

"Oh, I'm glad you said that," Lisa Zhang said. She was short and slender with dark hair pulled into a pony tail. "I've never heard of most of them and yet she made them seem as if they were very important to the genre."

Sally nodded her agreement.

"Obviously, you three are not true science fiction fans," Daryl Cannon said, a touch of arrogance in his voice. "So far she has given one of the best introductions to science fiction and fantasy that I have heard. If you don't like it you shouldn't be here." He walked away.

Sally remembered that he was from Vancouver and this was his third retreat. He had on jeans and a blue t-shirt. His hair was dark and curly and his blue eyes had burned into hers. She didn't like his attitude, mainly because as far as she could tell, Kat Mac had hardly said anything in depth about either genre. She'd just been touching on certain features of them and the people who wrote them explaining that she would go into them more extensively later.

Kirk West, piped up. "I'm afraid I agree with Kendra. I hope Kat Mac starts talking about how to write soon."

Sally noticed that one man, Reggie Shaw, just stood to one side with a coffee in his hand. He seemed to be listening but didn't try to make a comment. She wished he would because she thought he was cute in a mature sort of way and, although she usually went for older men, it wouldn't hurt to get to know him while here.

Bonnie was the one who interested Sally the most. She was dressed in brown slacks and cream blouse and she wore large glasses that had gone out of style years ago. She also stood on the fringes, not taking part in the conversation. If they were staying in the same bed and breakfast together they might as well get to know each other.

"Do you really think the class is unlucky?" Sally asked her.

Bonnie looked at her and nodded. "Something bad is going to happen. I can feel it."

"Bad in what way?" Kendra asked. She was twisting and turning her body and stretching her legs.

Bonnie shrugged. "I don't know, but thirteen always brings bad luck."

"It probably means I'm going to fail the course," Lisa laughed.

"It's not funny," Bonnie said sombrely. "If my feeling doesn't go away within the next few days, I'm dropping out." She walked away.

"Wow, she takes her superstition seriously, doesn't she?" Kendra said.

Back in class after the break Kat Mac continued her outline of science fiction and fantasy for the rest of the morning, then just before noon she ended with. "There are many subgenres to science fiction such as military SF, which is based on interplanetary or interstellar wars. Another is time travel, which is used to correct some event in the past or to see into the future. The subgenre I want you to think about today is apocalyptic. This deals with the end of our civilization through some disaster or with our world after such as disaster."

She looked around the room with a smile. "So your first assignment is to write, in one thousand words or less, a different ending to the movie, Armageddon, which starred Bruce Willis. You are to assume that the asteroid that was about to hit the earth was not averted and describe the aftermath of its slamming into our planet. I would like it by Thursday morning."

Chapter 5

Elizabeth pulled into one of the free parking lots and parked in the row that was sheltered by the trees. She rolled her windows partway down for Chevy, gathered her camera and recorder, and walked to where steps took her up to the street level. There were pedestrian crosswalks from each parking lot. She went to the closest one and pushed the button to turn the traffic light red. By the time that happened and the cars were stopped, there was a crowd of people to cross with her.

She went down the steps, crossed a little bridge, and wandered through the village on the wide, brick Village Stroll. There were a number of cafés and restaurants and coffee shops with outdoor tables, a spa, a cinema, a pharmacy, a grocery store, bike shops, and many, many hotels. She walked into some of the stores, most of which handled clothing and souvenirs and looked for something to take back to Jared, her father, and her siblings. She saw a Cuban cigar store but no one she knew smoked cigars.

Elizabeth took pictures of the shops, the hotels, and the stone flower beds, which held trees and bushes and an array of flowers. In one bed a dog lay in the shade of a tree waiting for his master.

She noted that there was no parking in the village. There were even signs stating it was a pedestrian village and people were supposed to walk their bikes and skateboards. She tried to imagine the village in winter, with snow covered roofs, tiny lights in all the trees and on the buildings, crowds of people bundled in winter jackets, toques, and mitts, and carrying skis or snowboards.

It would be so romantic to be here with a friend or family, walking these streets on a winter evening, discussing how you zipped down the slopes, and going into a café or a bar for a nightcap. Maybe she'd make it back sometime in the winter.

She found the tourist information centre and got a map of the village. The person behind the counter showed her where the

Peak 2 Peak Gondola was since that was definitely one adventure she wanted to try.

"I'm working on an article about Whistler in the summer," Elizabeth said. "Is there anything about the village or the people here that is different or unusual, something that would make the readers go 'Hey, I didn't know that.'"

The woman thought a while. "Well, we did have someone buy a winning lottery ticket from one of our stores a few years ago. The store that sold the ticket had a sign up for a year stating the fact that they had sold a winning ticket." The woman sniffed. "Like their store was lucky or something."

"Do the winners still live here?" Maybe she could do an interview to find out what life after the lottery was like as a sidebar.

"I don't know that they even did. No one from here ever came forward and said they were the winners. But that's not surprising. Hundreds of people come here every week. It could have been one of them buying a ticket before heading home. The winner could have been from Saskatchewan or Nova Scotia."

Elizabeth thanked the woman and followed the map to the Whistler gondola. On one side of the square was a ski lift for mountain bikers. She watched as the bikers quickly put their bikes on a bike lift then ran ahead and got on the person lift, so that when they reached the top they would be able to grab their bikes. She looked up the hillside beneath the gondola wires and watched as bikers wound their way down the trails to the beginning of the lift again.

On the other side of the square Elizabeth saw where the passenger gondolas were loaded. She watched as the gondolas left the end of the building on their way up the mountain. Her stomach felt queasy just at the thought of the movement of the gondola plus being so high off the ground. She knew she couldn't do the ride today. She'd wait until Sally was able to join her. She told herself that it was because Sally could take her picture to use in the article or she could use a photograph of Sally. But, she knew deep down that it was her fear of heights combined with motion sickness that kept her from going up today.

She went to Parking Lot #1 and followed the sidewalk Beverly had talked about towards the Upper Village. On the way she reached a large map on a sign that showed her the area. She continued on the sidewalk until she came to a crossroads. To her left was a path for Lost Lake Trails. On her right was a covered bridge over Fitzsimmons Creek. Just before she crossed the creek to her right was a small area with three picnic tables and four chairs overlooking the creek. On her left she saw a sign for Rebagliati Park, which she knew was named after the Canadian snowboarder who won the first ever Olympic gold medal for that sport at the 1998 winter games in Negano, Japan. She crossed the creek, went under a traffic bridge, climbed some steps, and was in the Upper Village.

She took a few pictures, noting that the Upper Village, with its climbing wall, trampoline, luge, a miniature golf for families, and horse back riding, was mainly for children.

* * *

I am so excited. Kat Mac asked me to stay after class. She told me that so far she likes my story and she asked if I have any more chapters for her to read. I told her I would e-mail them. I skip lunch and hurry to my room. I bring up the chapters on my laptop that I managed to edit before coming. I send them all to her.

Then I go through my files. I already have the assignment done. The story is what happened to the planet of Terrene. It was dictated to me months ago. I just have to change the name of the planet to Earth. So far I haven't included it in my manuscript because I wasn't sure if it should be a Prologue or integrated throughout the story. I'm sure Kat Mac will be able to help me on that. I find it and read it over.

* * *

Two asteroids collided out in space. Both were bumped out of their orbits and one broke into pieces. Two of those pieces soared towards one side of the Earth. One hit land throwing a thick layer of dust into the air, and starting countless raging fires which consumed towns and cities. The other landed in an ocean creating massive tidal waves on most shores. The waves submerged islands and swamped half the land on the continents, drowning all people and animals in its path.

The dust formed a blanket and the plants on the land not hit by the waves died for lack of sunlight and moisture. People who survived the fires and tidal waves had choked to death or died of starvation. When the water finally subsided it exposed the islands, now bare, and left huge salt water lakes on the continents. It took months for the untouched countries on the other side of the planet to assess the destruction. One-third of the planet's former landmass was under water or covered by a dust mantle and half of the planet's population had died.

During that time the true horror of the catastrophe done by the asteroids was revealed. The bump occurred when the planet was in its equinox and that was how it stayed. The middle section or equator permanently faced the sun as it rotated. Over the next few years the hotter rays burned off the ozone layer at the equator. The sun shone with a brilliant white light and the land for long distances on both sides of the equator could no longer support life.

Great masses of people trekked north and south looking for a new place to live. Fences, patrolled by armed guards, were erected around the towns and cities in their paths but they were hungry and angry and could not be stopped. Thousands were killed as they swarmed through the towns and cities, looting stores for food and water and clothing, and setting fires. But when that was over there was still no place for them to go and no food for them to eat and hundreds of thousands starved to death before tent cities could be set up and meagre rations of food distributed.

Fear, and the knowledge that this may be their only chance, drove all the countries of the planet to join as one large Global Alliance. Leaders worked together looking into the best way to save their species. To the north and south, where the ozone layer was thicker, the weather was more temperate. The alliance decreed this land was to be used to grow grains, vegetables, and domesticated animals sufficient to feed the people of the new mega cities.

In what became known as the Great Change, twenty Megalopolises were built on huge sectors of arid land close to the farmland. They consisted of levels built into the ground and ones rising above ground. Once they were completed, all the people who weren't farmers were moved to the cities where they were given jobs and provided with rent-free apartments until they could afford to buy.

Most of the villages, towns, and cities were then demolished so the land could be turned into more farmland. Special forests were planted for the cultivation of medicinal plants as well as for the small percentage of air purification they provided. It took years for the farmers to kill the remaining plants and work the land for seeding. They went as high up the mountain sides as trees had been able to grow and claimed the edges of the deserts through irrigation. What was too rocky or had substandard soil was turned into feedlots or pasture for the animals. Any other species of animal not of direct benefit to the human race was exterminated.

Scientists developed new strains of grains and vegetables that grew faster and larger so that six crops could be planted in a year. Animals were fed growth hormones and were ready for market in half the normal time. Great fishing farms were set up in the oceans and lakes.

At the same time there were purges. The Leaders decreed that everyone must have a job. So began the Tech Purge. Technology that had been developed over hundreds of years, first to make life easier and then to increase company profits by eliminating the worker, was banned. Walled-in industrial parks were erected beside each Megalopolis and any company that wanted to move there had to convert back to people power. Soon, the equipment that had taken over assembly lines, the apparatuses that had mixed and built, the computers that had done the thinking were thrown into Tech Dumps. People ran the looms that made cloth, cutters cut the patterns, seamstresses made the garments. People were on the assembly lines, used pens to fill ledgers, made the bread.

When a walkway in the megalopolises had to be repaired, workers mixed the compound by hand and others carried it in buckets to the repair site. When walkways needed sweeping, sweepers armed with brooms were out in force. When a new level was to be built, construction workers mixed and poured and built the apartments. Everyone capable of working had a job and everyone earned enough to look after his or her needs. It was only where the lift and carry was too heavy or the distance of transport was too far, that limited machinery was used.

Some remnants, such as telephones for communication and television for in home entertainment, had been kept. Education, especially the subject of history, was encouraged.

During the Corruption Purge, it was decided that those who committed a crime were not to be tolerated. Anyone in the Megalopolises who committed murder or sold tobacco, the two worst crimes, was automatically jailed in the Orbital Prisons. These were old interplanetary ships that were no longer suitable for long distance flight. They hovered in space above the planet.

All first time convicted criminals of other crimes were sent to the Fringes, former cities left near the megalopolises, for five years. What they did there was of no concern to the justice system, but if they were caught back in the giant cities during their term, their sentences were doubled and they were sent to the Orbital Prisons.

Present life on the planet was good. The population was growing slowly; the food supply increasing. The one drawback, though, was the crime. It, too, was on the rise and they were running out of room to house their convicts in the Orbital Prisons.

* * *

I count the words. I have to pare my story down by ninety-one.

* * *

After lunch Sally headed back to the bed and breakfast. She

walked slowly along the street wondering how she was going to do her assignment. She had no idea where to start her story. She hadn't seen the movie and resented that the instructor would assume that everyone had.

"Kat Mac should have asked us first and then tailored the assignment to our answers," she muttered. "Or at least she should have told us to watch it before we came."

As she neared the bed and breakfast she saw that there were three RCMP cars parked in front of the demolished house and one officer was taping off the yard. She stopped and watched for a few minutes. When she'd left this morning a crew had already started to do a clean-up of the site. She wondered if they'd found something. There was no one else on the sidewalk and she doubted the officer would answer her questions so she headed into the bed and breakfast. Beverly would probably know.

"A mummified body was found under the partial basement," Beverly said.

"Oh, won't Elizabeth be excited to hear this," Sally said, gleefully.

Beverly looked at her. "I know you said Ms. Oliver had solved murders but are you serious?"

Sally nodded. "It seems each time she strikes out to work on a travel article, she comes across a murder and she manages to solve it."

"Really? Is she a private detective?"

"Oh, no." Sally shook her head. "She's strictly amateur. She just seems to have a knack for figuring out the clues."

Up in her room Sally opened a juice box then using the wireless Internet of the bed and breakfast, she looked up the movie Armageddon to see what she could learn. She found many different descriptions of the movie and sorted through the bits of information.

A huge asteroid is headed towards earth and will hit in eighteen days. Scientists decide that the only way to divert it is to blow it up. An oil well drilling crew is brought in to fly into space to drill a hole in the asteroid and insert a nuclear warhead. Of course, after many heart-stopping disasters, the crew completes the mission.

    Sally leaned back in her chair. Her assignment was to figure out what would have happened to Earth if the crew had not been able to blow up the asteroid. This is where the science fiction comes in, she thought. And I have no idea where to begin.

    She wondered if Bonnie and Daryl were hard at work in their rooms. Probably. Or maybe Bonnie was packing getting ready to leave. Sally got up and walked out of her bedroom and over to the balcony. The police were still at the place next door and a few people were on the street. She thought about going down to the pool for a swim then changed her mind. She'd spent a lot of money to come to this retreat and she wanted to work as much as possible on it, or at least until Elizabeth got back.

Chapter 6

When Elizabeth returned to the bed and breakfast in mid-afternoon she saw the police cars and the yellow tape. Another crowd had gathered to watch. She stared at them a moment then, with an impish smile, she climbed out and went up to Alison and Rick who were part of the group.

"What happened?" she asked. "Did someone get hurt?"

"No, a mummified body was found under the dirt floor of the partial basement," Alison said. "The story is true. The woman was killed by her daughter."

"How did they find it? They are still removing the wood?"

"I guess one of the workers saw a hand or what was left of a hand sticking out of the dirt."

"So where is the daughter now?" Elizabeth asked.

Rick shrugged. "No one seems to know. From what we heard she sold the place and moved away about ten years ago."

"Have the same people owned it since then?"

"Yes, but they live in Vancouver and have been renting it out."

At that moment a news van pulled up and a man with a microphone climbed out. A cameraman quickly followed and they looked for a place to film their story with the remains of the house behind them.

Elizabeth turned away. There really was no mystery. The body belonged to the missing mother and the police would probably be looking for the daughter. She got Chevy out of the Tracker and went to their room where she dumped her camera, laptop, and recorder on one of the chairs. She went out onto the balcony and could see that most of the floor had been ripped up. There was a pile of concrete and wood pushed to one side and police officers were bent over an area in one corner. Nothing to see, she thought as she re-entered the suite.

Sally came out of her bedroom. "So how was your research?"

"The village is a great place," Elizabeth said, getting a Pepsi from the fridge. "I spent all this time just walking around it looking at the shops and gathering information. We'll have to go there when you get a chance. Plus, I want you to ride the Peak 2 Peak Gondola with me."

"What's that?"

Elizabeth filled her in then asked. "How did your day go?"

"Well, we have our first assignment and I have no idea how to do it." Sally flopped in the other chair.

"Sounds like being back in high school," Elizabeth grinned, popping the tab on her can. "What's it about?"

"We have to change the ending of the movie Armageddon starring Bruce Willis."

"In what way?"

"The asteroid is supposed to hit the earth and we have to describe what happens to life as we know it in one thousand words or less."

"Sounds like fun," Elizabeth said dryly. "How much have you got done?"

"Two paragraphs." Sally stood. "But, I'm not going to spend another minute on it. I'm going to change into my bathing suit and head to the pool. Are you coming?"

"That sounds exactly like high school, too," Elizabeth laughed. "Sure, I'll join you."

She went into her bedroom, changed into her swim suit, then grabbed Chevy's leash. "We're just going to the pool," she said, when he began to get excited. "We'll go for a walk after supper."

On the way down to the pool, Sally told her about Bonnie and Daryl from the retreat also staying in the bed and breakfast. "They were the two single people who came down this morning for breakfast."

A tall hedge separated the pool area from the lot next door. Elizabeth put her towel on one of the lounge chairs and Chevy laid under it out of the sun.

"Did you hear about the body?" Sally asked, as she threw her towel on another chair.

"Yes." Elizabeth said, taking off her sandals.

"Are you sorry that there's no mystery?"

Elizabeth shook her head as they sat on the edge of the pool. "I'll admit that I have been thinking about it but at the same time I was really looking forward to relaxing and enjoying my research and then to having a holiday."

"Good," Sally reached down and sprayed Elizabeth with a handful of water. She lowered herself into the pool.

Elizabeth gasped at the coolness of the water then stood up and dove in. When she surfaced she saw a man staring over at Sally who was floating on her back. His expression bothered her. She wasn't sure if he was mad or ogling her but his full concentration was on Sally. Elizabeth swam over and floated beside her.

"That Daryl you were talking about is staring at you," she whispered out the side of her mouth.

Sally opened her eyes and began to tread water. She glanced around. When she spotted him, she smiled and waved her hand. "Come on in," she called. "The water is perfect."

He stepped closer. "You should be working on your assignment."

"Maybe I'm finished," Sally said.

He seemed a little taken aback by that. He gave her a scowl and turned away walking back into the building.

"He wasn't very friendly," Elizabeth said. "What was that about?"

"Well, there are some of us who weren't that enthused with the lecture today and he basically told us we shouldn't be in the class."

"A bit serious, is he?"

"Very. And stuffy, too. But I wish I'd kept my mouth shut."

"Why?"

"Because, now I have to get my new ending done for Armageddon." Sally went back to her floating.

"Are all the students like him?" Elizabeth asked, slipping onto her back beside Sally.

"Some are, some are like me, and then there is Bonnie who

thinks something bad is going to happen because there are thirteen students in the class."

"She's superstitious?"

"Very. She says she might have to leave."

Elizabeth swam away and put in some laps in the short pool until she tired.

After their swim, they drove to the grocery store and bought a grilled chicken, roasted potatoes, and salad for their supper. They stored the leftovers in their fridge.

"Now, it's time for a walk," Elizabeth said to Chevy. He immediately headed for the door. "Do you want to come with us?" she asked Sally.

"No, I'd better get back at my assignment. I don't want to be the dunce of the class."

On her way out of the building, Elizabeth met Beverly. "Did you hear about the body?" Beverly asked.

Elizabeth nodded. "The rumours have proved to be true."

"Well, not exactly. According to the news this evening the body belongs to a young woman not an older lady."

"Oh?" Elizabeth said, and in that one word could feel her plans begin to fall apart.

* * *

Elizabeth was having a relaxing morning so Sally went down for breakfast on her own. She saw Bonnie sitting at a table. She helped herself to a coffee then went over.

"Do you mind of I join you?" Sally asked.

"Not at all," Bonnie smiled. "Where's your friend?"

"Oh, Elizabeth is working on an article about Whistler and she can't go to some of the places she wants to until they open, so she's taking her time about coming down." Sally pulled out a chair and sat. So far they were the only ones in the dining room.

Beverly brought out the muffin and jam tray then went back for the breakfast plates.

"Do you still have a bad feeling about the course?"

"Yes, but I've checked my Angel cards and so far they

haven't advised me to leave."

"Angel cards?" Sally said, reaching for a muffin. "What are they?"

"They're along the same idea as Tarot cards in that they tell me what to expect but the messages are from Angels. If I'm upset or confused or just want a little reassurance that my life is going as it should I ask them for their guidance. They tell me what the outcome will be so that I can relax and let it happen."

Beverly came in with breakfast. "Is Elizabeth off working on the mystery?" she asked as she set down their plates containing an omelette, English muffin, and hash browns.

Sally grinned. "Oh, I'm sure she's thinking about it but her article comes first. She'll be down later for breakfast."

"So, where are you from?" Sally asked Bonnie, as she cut up her omelette. During introductions at the retreat, Bonnie have not given her last name nor her hometown.

"Well, that's up in the air right now."

Sally raised her eyebrow, not sure what to say.

"My husband and I are still living in the same house together but we're going through a nasty divorce. I'm not sure which of us will break down and move out first."

Sally noticed that she still hadn't answered her question. She decided to leave it alone. After all, what difference did it make? She tried the hash browns. Delicious. This was a perfect meal.

"What's this about your friend and mysteries?" Bonnie asked.

Sally waved her hand. "Elizabeth seems to have a knack for getting involved in finding murderers and since that body was discovered yesterday Beverly is wondering if Elizabeth is working on it."

Bonnie leaned forward. "How many murders has she figured out?"

"Four."

"Wow, that's a lot."

"For an amateur it is," Sally agreed. She pushed her plate back. It was time to go.

"Do you want a ride?" Bonnie asked.

"Thank you, but no. I prefer walking and I'm taking a different route today so that I can see a bit of the area."

"Meet you there, then." Bonnie grabbed her case and left.

Sally went up to her room, retrieved her backpack, and headed out to the street. She turned left on Ambassador Crescent. She counted four more bed and breakfasts down this way. There were a number of people walking on the street ahead of her. She didn't recognize any of them from her class so assumed they were taking one of the other courses offered. She looked at the houses as she passed them. There certainly was a variety, anywhere from small cabins to huge mansions. What she did note was that there were no sidewalks and that the bigger the house the better the landscaping although very few of the yards had any flowers or grass. Most of the front was taken up by paved driveways and the grass and weeds in those that were not paved were left to grow wild. Tall trees usually acted as fences between houses.

Also, the houses to the left, which included their Bed & Breakfast, backed onto a hill while the back yards of those along the right were flat.

She turned right onto Fitzsimmons Road South and stopped to admire the yard of the second house on the right. It was full of colourful flowerbeds: along the sides of the lawn, in a circle in the centre of the driveway, in boxes hanging from the deck railing and the windowsills, and around the pond near the street. A man in his early sixties was in the flower bed closest to the street. He looked up and smiled at Sally.

"What a lovely yard," Sally said.

"Thank you." He bowed slightly, then grinned. "Although, there isn't much to compare it to, is there?"

"No," Sally admitted. "Why is that?"

He shrugged. "I think because the people who own the houses can't be bothered. It's easier to pave than pull weeds. Plus, the season that's important here is skiing and many people only use their homes in the winter. They have managers look after them in the summer."

Sally thought how different that was from Edmonton where

the summer cabins were closed down in the winter.

"You are probably wondering why I have all these flowers when others don't."

"You're a mind reader."

"When I left my job my daughter decided that I needed something to occupy my spare time. So she began going to the greenhouse in Squamish and buying me the left over flowers and plants. She said I needed the challenge of trying to save the plants from dying. Soon our yard was full and I had to build the boxes for the windows and deck."

"You certainly have done an amazing job with leftovers."

"Are you going to that science fiction/ fantasy retreat?"

Sally nodded.

"Writing a book?"

"Working on a story but I'm not sure if it will ever become a book."

"I've been thinking of taking the course but I've heard mixed reviews from others attending it. What do you think of it so far?"

Sally wasn't sure how to answer that. Did she give the opinion of an avid reader but rank amateur at the art of writing science fiction or did she tell him what other, more serious fans said.

"I've only been there one day so I really can't give you an honest opinion yet."

"Did you understand much of what was said yesterday?"

What? Had he heard what she'd told Elizabeth? "Not really. But I'm new to this. Others think our instructor gave a great talk."

The man nodded. "Every year it's the same. Some like it, some don't. I guess I will have to enrol in order to find out who is right."

"Well, if you do, you sure won't have to drive there," Sally grinned, looking at the car and the van parked in the driveway. "Nice meeting you," she said, and continued on her way.

When she reached Nancy Greene Way she turned left and quickly reached the driveway to the retreat. She was earlier today and many students were outside. Sally did a quick head count and then multiplied that with what she'd paid. Running a retreat could be quite lucrative.

She went up to where Kendra, Kirk, Lisa, and Bonnie were standing in a circle. Bonnie was telling them about her Angel Cards. "They have been warning me that something bad is going to happen here and that I should be careful," Bonnie was saying.

"I don't know about those things," Kirk said. "It sounds like they are the same as getting your tea leaves or palms read."

"Oh, they are better than that. The Angels are looking over us and after us. We all have Angels even if we don't know it. I've actually seen one of my Angels."

Sally looked around and saw Reggie Shaw leaning against the building watching them. Should she invite him to come over? Maybe she should go up to him and just ask him a question, get to know him. After all, she still thought he was cute. As if he understood her thoughts, Reggie turned and walked through the doors.

A trifle disappointed Sally again focused on the conversation. "I'll show you how the cards work after lunch," Bonnie was saying. "I can give you each a short reading."

The smokers of the group butted out their cigarettes and began heading towards the doors. Soon the others were on their way to their classes also.

Sally slid into her seat and took out her notepad and pen. The room slowly filled and Kat Mac began her morning lecture.

"If you go on the Internet and bring up Wikipedia's list of science fiction writers you will find hundreds of names. Today we will talk about some of the great men and women writers."

Sally listened to Kat Mac as she droned on and on. She had thought that she'd come here and be given the outline on how to write a SF book much like she'd heard there was an outline for romances. By page such and such there had to be a kiss, by page such and such there had to be a disagreement.

She didn't understand much of what Kat Mac was saying and she didn't know many of the people she was mentioning. She did listen with interest, though, when Kat Mac told the class where the writers got their ideas and how each of them approached the task of taking those ideas and turning them into a story. Maybe she could try some of their methods.

At last Kat Mac called for a break. Everyone streamed out of the room, some to go outside for their smoke, some to go to the atrium for coffee.

"Tell us more about the Angel Cards," Lisa said, as a group gathered with their coffee cups.

Bonnie pulled a box with an Angel on the front out of her backpack. She opened it and removed a deck of thick cards and began to shuffle them. She stopped and turned the top one over. A group gathered around to listen.

"See this is Bridgette," Bonnie said. "Her first words are 'Caution is warranted.' She has been coming up every time I do this since I came to the retreat."

"What else does she say?" Sally asked.

"Look deeper into this situation before proceeding further," Bonnie read.

"That does sound ominous," Kendra said.

"Yeah, if you believed in those things," Daryl scoffed and walked away.

"I guess he doesn't," Sally smiled, trying to lightened the mood. She wasn't sure if she believed in the Angel cards but Bonnie sure did. And others seemed to be on the verge.

"Can you do a reading for me?" Kendra asked.

"After lunch," Bonnie promised.

* * *

Elizabeth tried to put the news she had received the night before from Beverly out of her head. She had to stick to her plan, had to get her research done so she wasn't pressed to get the article written when she got home. Besides, she wasn't here to solve anything. That was up to the police. She resolutely drove to Highway 99 and turned right. She started to record the kilometres from there but had to quickly turn onto Spruce Grove Way. She immediately turned onto Mons Road go to Scandinave Spa. When she reached the parking lot she got out and walked up the hill on a pea gravel trail through tall trees. At the end of the trail was a sign "Welcome to our Haven of Peace and Quiet."

She walked into the huge foyer and went to the desk. Once she explained what she was doing to the woman behind the counter, she was allowed to take pictures of the hot baths, the cold baths, and the grounds.

"We have many people come from town and from the nearby campground to spend the day at the spa," the woman said.

Elizabeth looked at the surrounding mountains and thought about how very relaxing the place was. Maybe she and Sally would have to come here for a treatment before they left. She went back to Spruce Grove Way turned left and then immediately went left again on Kirkpatrick Way. A short drive took her to the parking area for Spruce Grove Park. She put Chevy on a leash and they walked past the field house, then came upon a sign that gave advice as to what to do if you met a bear.

She recorded the information for her readers. "First stop and assess the situation. Remain calm. If the bear does not detect you quietly leave the area. If the bear does detect you, do not run. Back away slowly facing the bear. Talk in a soft voice so the bear can identify you as human. If the bear approaches you wave your arms and talk louder to assert your dominance. Continue to back away and leave the area."

She and Chevy walked between two of the three baseball diamonds to a centre area, then went left towards the hillside. There was a steep climb up to a hiking trail. A sign stated that this as a dog walking trail during the winter because of a conflict of dogs on the snowshoe and cross hiking trails.

She knew this was part of a vast web of trails that went from the Upper Village to Green Lake. When she'd looked on the map she'd laughed at the names of some of the paths: Donkey Puncher; Pinocchio's Furniture; Gee I Like your Pants; and Johnny Can't Read. The trails were marked and she had a map but she didn't want to go too far the first time. It looked like it would be quite easy to get lost if you weren't used to the region.

She reached the White Gold Traverse Trail which also ran

behind the SnowBound Bed and Breakfast, followed it a ways so Chevy could have a walk, then returned to her vehicle.

Back on Highway 99 Elizabeth reached Nicklaus Road where she turned to go to the Nicklaus North Golf Course. She had researched that this 18 hole par 71 course was designed by Jack Nicklaus and opened in 1996. She stopped to take some pictures and then carried on. She wasn't a golfer so she didn't envision coming here with Sally.

On the highway again she crossed the Golden Dreams River and turned right onto Alpine Way and then right again to go to Edgewater Stables on Green Lake for horse back riding. She found some horses and a barn but no one was there. She continued to Eco Tours which offered canoeing or kayaking on the lake. In the log building she inquired about their rates. She wanted to spend some time enjoying the attractions here after finishing her research.

She learned that she could canoe on Green Lake for an hour or she could start at Alta Lake with a guide and canoe down the River of Dreams for three hours to Green Lake. Another adventure for her and Sally, she thought. Sally had already agreed to do the Peak 2 Peak Gondola with her so if this kept up Sally wasn't going to have much time for her writing assignments.

Before Elizabeth left she asked about the Edgewater stables and was told that she could book a ride at the Outdoor Adventures in the Village.

She glanced at her watch. She'd gotten a later than usual start this morning and it was now past four o'clock. Because the area she was writing about was small, there wasn't the need to work until dark like in other years. Sally was probably ready for a break in whatever she was working on for her course. Maybe she'd go discuss the adventures she had found for them to do and see if Sally thought she would have time for any of them. If not, then Elizabeth would have to do them herself.

On her drive back to the bed and breakfast she congratulated herself on not once thinking about the decomposed body.

Chapter 7

Just before the end of the class Kat Mac said. "Now, for your second assignment I want you decide if you think space aliens should be part of science fiction writing or fantasy writing. Tomorrow we will divide into two groups, those who pick fantasy and those who decide on science fiction, and we will have a panel discussion. You can bring whatever material you wish to back up your decision."

"Oh, no," Sally groaned. Now what was she going to do?

She packed up her notes and headed to the lunch room with the rest of the class. Going to the buffet she picked an egg salad sandwich, a salad, and milk, and Jello for dessert. She sat at a table and was soon joined by Bonnie, Kendra, and Lisa.

After she ate, Bonnie pulled out her cards. "Who wants to be first?"

"Me," Kendra said, eagerly.

"First, I have to clear the cards," Bonnie said, taking a crystal out of her bag. She spread the cards out and rubbed each of them with it. Then she stacked them and placed the crystal on top. She closed her eyes for a few seconds, then opened them again.

"What did you just do?" Lisa asked.

"These are my cards and my energy is imprinted on them," Bonnie said. "In order for me to do a reading for someone else, I have to remove my energy from them. Now they are ready for Kendra to touch."

Kendra reached over and tentatively picked up the deck.

"Shuffle them and ask a question in your mind or state a concern you have about your life," Bonnie said. "When you feel you have done enough, stop and set them down."

Everyone waited until Kendra had shuffled and set them on the table. Sally noticed that Kirk West, Russ Peters, and Reggie Shaw from their class and a few from other classes had sauntered over to see what was happening. She was glad to see Reggie had joined the group. Maybe, she would get a chance to speak with him.

"Now, tell me what you thought about, just the general idea, like money or health or career," Bonnie said to Kendra.

"I want to know what my future holds," Kendra answered.

"Okay," Bonnie said. "You are looking ahead, so take the top three cards, or you can fan them out and take whichever three you want, and just lay them side by side face up."

While Kendra did that Bonnie picked up her guidebook and opened it to page sixteen. "The first card will represent the present." She looked at the card. "Merlina. She says that you do not have enough information right now to make an informed decision. Before you do anything you should do more research or ask an expert."

"Wow," Kendra said, looking around at the others. "That is so true."

"How?" asked Sally.

"I was actually thinking of dropping out of the retreat because I am very confused right now. None of it is making sense to me." She looked at Bonnie. "What does the next one mean?"

"The second one is for the immediate future and it is Daniel. He is the angel of marriage."

"Oh," Kendra gasped.

"What?" demanded Lisa.

"My boyfriend asked me to marry him before I came here. Part of the reason I was going to drop out was to go back and tell him no."

"No?" Kirk asked.

Kendra nodded her head. "We fight all the time. I'm not sure if I want to do that for the rest of my life. What is the third one?"

"The third one is for three months ahead." Bonnie said. "Opal looks after your children here on earth and in heaven if they die."

"My children?" Kendra exclaimed. "My children?"

"Yes," Bonnie nodded. "Do you have any?"

Tears formed in Kendra's eyes. "Yes, I have two sons."

Suddenly she stood up and hurried away.

No one spoke for a few moments. Was something happening with her sons, Sally wondered? Were they sick, dead? Sally watched Kendra leave the building.

"Who wants to be next?" Bonnie asked, clearing the cards with the crystal.

Reggie stepped forward and picked up the deck of cards. "I want to know if I will be rich."

"Okay," Bonnie said. "When you have finished shuffling lay seven cards out in the capital letter H. One, two and three down the left side, four five and six down the right and the seventh card in the centre."

Reggie did as he was told. "The first card will explain what you learned about money when you were a child." Bonnie opened the guidebook to the Angel and read the meaning.

Others wanted to have a reading. Bonnie cleared the cards before each one and delivered the message from the Angels in a composed, unemotional voice. Some joked about their outcome, while others seemed to take it seriously. Out of the corner of her eye Sally saw Daryl, accompanied by Henry Freisen and Luke Johnson, coming up to the group. Daryl looked angry.

"Why don't you people spend your time working on your stories or assignments instead of listening to this crap," he demanded, waving his hand in Bonnie's direction.

"Hey, lay off," Kirk said. "we're just having some fun here."

"That's the problem with you dabblers," Daryl seethed. "You don't take this seriously. You're only here to have fun, to have a holiday away from work and family. Not to write."

"We are all here for our own reasons," Sally said quietly. "If they don't happen to meet your approval, then that's your problem."

"No, it's your problem," Daryl jabbed his finger at her. "There are lots of good writers out there who would love to come here but because you dabblers sent your money first, they have to wait."

"We have as much right as anyone," Russ Peters said.

Daryl shook his head. "You don't get it, do you? It's got nothing to do with who has the right and everything to do with who is going to do the actual writing. Dabblers all want to write a book but they don't want to put in the time and energy it takes get the words on the pages."

"I think you should leave," Russ said.

"You are all wasting your time thinking you are going to write a book," Luke Johnson said. "You never will." The three men turned and stomped out of the building.

"What got into them?" Kirk asked.

"I don't know," Russ Peters answered. "But Daryl is starting to sound like a fanatic."

"Yeah," Lisa agreed. "I hope he cools down soon. I don't like the idea of taking the class with him anymore."

"And it looks like he has some followers," Kirk said.

There was an awkward few moments broken by Lisa asking. "Could you read my cards?"

Bonnie hesitated.

"Oh, go ahead," Sally said. "Don't let Daryl or his buddies spoil our enjoyment."

"Okay," Bonnie said, handing the cleared cards to Lisa to shuffle. "What do you want to know?"

"I want know if my dream will come true."

Lisa laid out the cards and Bonnie began to interpret. "Azure says that what you wish for will occur in the near future. Archangel Gabrielle tells you that you will be involved in communication and the arts and to not let your insecurities stop you. Merlina cautions you to seek expert help and Patience says to enjoy being a student and learn as much as you can."

"Are you sure that's what they say?" Lisa asked.

"Read them for yourself," Bonnie said, giving her the booklet.

"Wouldn't it be nice if this all came true," Lisa breathed, handing it back.

"It will if you believe and work at it," Bonnie said.

As everyone began to leave. Sally leaned over and said to Bonnie. "If Kendra's and a few others are so dead on, I think you should heed your cards and be careful."

"I know," Bonnie said, as she slowly put her cards in their box.

* * *

I shouldn't have stayed after lunch. I should have come to my room and had a nap. But I didn't and the aura starts again as soon as I close my door. I rush to my computer.

* * *

Gwin noticed more yellow and orange leaves in among the green ones on the trees and bushes. She thought the trees were so beautiful with their new colours but wondered, as a few others did, why they had changed.

The tall grass in the fields and meadows turned a golden yellow. The birds that had been singing in the trees gathered in flocks and flew away. There was a lessening of daylight hours and the air turned cooler.

One day she saw dark clouds forming in the distance. They slowly advanced towards the colony, a cold wind preceding them. Soon they blocked the sun and the blue sky, and as they moved overhead it began raining lightly. The drops spattered the dry ground sending up miniature dust clouds.

The prisoners, who hadn't experienced rain on their former planet, ran in it, tilted their heads to feel it on their faces, and opened their mouths to taste it. However, as the centre of the storm moved closer the clouds grew darker and wind blew stronger. Lightning streaked across the sky followed by the heavy rumblings of thunder. The flashes and noise scared the convicts and they scurried into their dormitories.

Gwin stood in the doorway and watched the rain. Soon there were large puddles in front of the buildings and the water flowed in a stream down the middle of the streets taking a lot of the dirt with it. The canvases used for roofs sagged as the water gathered in them.

The evening meal was cold because no fires could be lit. During the night the storm passed and in the morning the prisoners got up to slick, muddy streets. By the next day, though, almost everything was dry again.

But soon the storms returned in force. The air turned cold and the rain poured. After the first day the canvas roofs could not contain all the water and began to leak. Gwin, like most of the other prisoners could not sleep because of the constant dripping of the water on her bed. On the second day, the canvas roofs, whipped by the increased wind, began to tear. The rain and wind pelted the people huddled in their wet blankets.

The third day it was so cold Gwin could see her breath. The dirt floors of the buildings were now thick, slimy mud. Everyone in her dormitory slowly sloshed through it and went outside to stand in the mud there. The fourth day, the snow began and soon coated everything in white. The cold increased. People doubled up in their bunks to keep warm.

Gwin felt disappointed and slightly betrayed. When she and her team had been here they hadn't seen any of this bad weather. Of course, they hadn't had time to fly over the whole planet but what they did see had been green and lush and warm and idyllic. She'd stood in front of the Leaders and asked them not to send the prisoners here because she hadn't wanted its beauty and its people spoiled. She'd been framed and sent to the Orbital Prisons because of her stance. And now the planet had changed. The beauty was gone, replaced by cold and rains and snow. It was as if the planet had turned on her.

When the sun returned it was not as hot as it had been. The snow partially melted. Everyone shivered in their damp clothes. No one had eaten in days. The prisoners were starving and unwilling to wait for the cooks to clean up the stoves and prepare something. They rioted, heading en mass to the warehouses. The guards attempted to beat them back but sheer numbers dictated that the prisoners would win. The guards ran to the space ship letting the prisoners ransack the warehouses.

The freezing convicts then stormed the space ship, wanting a warm place. The ship lifted off and hovered overhead for a few days. When it was clear that it would be unsafe to land, the ship left.

Gwin could not describe her fear as she watched it leave. She knew they were all destined to die. Slowly. For the supply ship would never make it back with food before they starved.

She wandered around looking at the damage. All of the canvas roofs were torn. The stoves were useless. Most of the animals had died due to the cold or flooding in their pens. The planted fields were underwater.

She knew her only hope was the inhabitants.

* * *

I just barely finish and Mikk starts in. He had heard about the change in weather on the new planet and the rioting, and has been frantically trying to find out about a rescue flight to the settlement planet so that he can go and bring Gwin back. So far, none is scheduled and his worry increases. Can she and the other prisoners survive without some sort of immediate help? To take his mind off her for a while he visits the Separation Room.

* * *

Mikk joined Bob and Shar in the Separation Room. A prisoner with a shaved head was brought in escorted by two guards. She stood silently as Shar ran through the warning.

"You have volunteered for an experiment that has had some favourable results and some that are not so favourable. If it works you will be given your freedom and a pension for the rest of your life. This is your last opportunity to change your mind." She looked at her expectantly.

"I'll go for it," the prisoner said. "At least it gives me a chance to get out of the Orbital Prisons."

"Then if you would lie on this table, we will get started," Bob said.

The guards remained until the prisoner's body, arms, legs and head were strapped securely to the table. "Where are you sending me?" She could only stare at the ceiling.

"To a planet called Zedor," Bob said, as he rolled the prisoner's sleeves up and attached electrodes.

"Where is that?"

"It's in our galaxy."

"What am I going to do there?"

"You'll be transplanted into the head of an occupant of the planet and will see and hear what it sees and hears."

"And then what?"

"After a week you'll be brought back to your body and you'll be able to tell us what is on that planet."

"Don't you already know what's there?"

"Yes, but we want you to tell us so we know the experiment worked."

"Are you sure I'll come back?" A note of fear appeared in her voice.

"There's always an element of risk," Bob said, taping more electrodes to her shaved skull.

Mikk watched as part of the prisoner's head was frozen and a piece of her skull removed. Then the procedure began that would separate the mind from the brain. The prisoner lay still as if waiting for some sort of strange feeling in her brain. Suddenly she emitted a dreadful scream. Mikk jumped and looked over at her in time to see her eyes close and her body go limp. Neither Bob nor Shar seemed concerned.

"Why did she scream like that?" Mikk asked.

Bob shrugged. "They all do at the moment of separation."

"Does it hurt?"

"I don't know. None of the minds have come back so far."

"Why not?'

"We believe they aren't strong enough to take over the mind that is already in the host body on the planet and so they are killed."

"Why do you continue to send them?"

"We're hoping eventually we will find the right technique that will give our minds greater strength."

"How will her mind locate a body on the planet?" Mikk

asked, as he watched Shar unstrap the prisoner then go to the door and signal two attendants to enter the room. They guided a bed to the side of the table, moved the body onto it and then pushed it out of the room.

"She just searches for a host and tries to enter it," Bob answered.

"So it doesn't necessarily find an intelligent being."

"No. But we've been studying the inhabitants of Zedor and with our changes, we're hoping that this time she will be able to determine intelligent life from animal life. When that intelligent life is found then the mind will enter it."

"What makes you think that it will be able to enter easier?"

"Animal minds are fierce and merciless. They have developed their competitive skills in order to beat other animals to prey. They are totally focussed on hunting and on raising their young and their instinct is to fight savagely to maintain their lives. We are hoping that our minds and those of the people of Zedor are similar and that the Zedor mind won't be as brutal in protecting itself."

"When will it reach the planet?" Mikk asked.

"It's there already."

"How does it enter the host?"

"All species breath so it enters through their breathing passages and goes directly to the brain.

"When will you know if her mind has entered someone?"

"The mind will send a signal to our computer as soon as there is contact." He walked over to where Shar was seated in front of the computer. She punched a few keys then shook her head.

"And what happens on contact?"

"We hope that the new process works and her mind is stronger than the inhabitant's mind so she can overpower it."

"What will she do then?"

"She'll be able to use the body to explore the planet and will come back here with vital information about it."

"How is your experiment with freezing coming along?" Shar asked.

"The freezing and thawing works on the body but it kills

the mind."

"So if we separated the mind first, you could send both it and the body to a planet," Bob said speculatively. "There they would reattach and could then explore."

Mikk thought about it. "But how would you get them both back?" he asked. "There wouldn't be a separation machine handy."

"We'd have to find a way of removing the information from the mind while it is on the planet."

"And then just leave the person there?"

Bob inclined his head. "Sometimes the knowledge is worth more than a few lives."

"We received a signal," Shar said.

"Already?" Mikk asked, surprised.

"It doesn't take long," Bob said, going over to where Shar sat at the computer. "What did it say?"

"It was scrambled like the other ones."

"You mean her mind lost the fight," Mikk said.

"I'm afraid so." Shar nodded.

"What are you going to do now?"

"Well, our only hope is to look for an unformed mind on that planet," Bob said. "One that hasn't been instilled with any teachings or instincts."

"And where are you going to find one of those?"

"We have no idea yet, but we'll keep searching."

Chapter 8

When Elizabeth returned to the bed and breakfast she saw that there was a For Sale sign in front of the house next to Alison and Rick's. Were they the first of the neighbours to want to get away from the stigma of living close to where a murder had taken place?

She saw Alison sitting at a small table on her porch with another woman. Alison beckoned her over. Elizabeth put Chevy on his leash, then went across to see her. On her way over she noticed that someone had put a bouquet of flowers in front of the lot. Had it been a family member or a stranger moved by the story?

Alison introduced Elizabeth to Cynthia Newcomb, her neighbour. Cynthia was in her early sixties with brunette hair laced with gray and brown eyes. She was casually dressed in slacks and short-sleeved blouse.

"Have you heard anything new about the young girl found across the road?" Elizabeth asked, once she was seated.

"Just what I've heard on the news," Alison said. "The police were here questioning us but they just wanted information. They didn't give any out."

"Yes," Cynthia agreed. "They came to see me, too."

"Would you ladies like some iced tea?" Alison asked, standing.

"I'd like some," Cynthia said, while Elizabeth declined.

When Alison had gone into the house Cynthia looked over her shoulder, then leaned towards Elizabeth. "I hear that you're an amateur detective," she whispered.

Elizabeth grinned self-consciously. "I have worked on a few mysteries." She also lowered her voice although she wasn't sure why.

"Could I hire you to work for me?"

"Oh, no," Elizabeth protested, holding her hands up in front of her. "I'm not that type of detective."

"But you've helped solve murders," Cynthia said. "Beverly

told me."

"Yes, but..." Elizabeth didn't know where to begin an explanation of how and what she had done. She'd basically stumbled into the first two, and then there was Jared's mother's murder that the two of them had solved last year. So it wasn't as if she'd sought them out. "I really don't know anything about how to conduct an investigation."

"Well, you must know something or you wouldn't have been so successful."

"Why don't you hire a professional private investigator?" Maybe that would satisfy her.

"There aren't any here," Cynthia said. "And if I get one from Vancouver then I have to pay his travelling time to come here, plus accommodations."

"I'm sorry..." Elizabeth started to say.

"Aren't you even interested in hearing what I want you for?" Cynthia asked, quickly looking towards the house again.

Elizabeth really wanted to shake her head and say "No," but that was impossible. "Okay," she said. "Tell me."

"I want you to find out who that young girl was who was buried in the basement across the road."

"You do?" Elizabeth blurted out. "Why do you want to know who she is?"

Before Cynthia could answer the door opened and Alison stepped out carrying a tray with a pitcher and three glasses on it. She set it on the table and poured her and Cynthia each a glass. "I brought an extra one for you in case you changed your mind," she said to Elizabeth. "Now what were we discussing?"

"The death of the young girl," Cynthia said. She looked directly at Elizabeth. "I'll bet her family would like to know what happened."

"I read in the newspaper this morning that there are already three families who have come here to see if she is their missing daughter," Alison said.

"There will probably be a lot more before this is solved," Cynthia said.

"I hear you're a travel writer," Alison said to Elizabeth.

"Yes," Elizabeth admitted. "I'm working on an article about Whistler in the summer."

"Where have you been so far?" Cynthia asked.

"The village, the Scandanave Spa, Green Lake, and I just finished walking some of the trails behind here."

"Ah, yes," Alison nodded. "Are you going to the Whistler Olympic Park?"

"I saw the sign on my way into Whistler," Elizabeth said. "What is there to see?"

"It's privately owned and the owners offer tours once a day. For just under $100.00 you get to see where the luge and some of the ski runs took place during the 2010 Olympics, plus you get a lunch."

"Can't I drive there?" She hadn't asked the person at the information centre about it because she'd just assumed it was open to the public. That's what assuming gets you, she thought.

"No," Alison said. "It's about a five kilometre drive from the highway to a gate across the road. And you can't see anything from the gate. However, if you want to get pictures of bears that road is a good place to find them."

Elizabeth stood. "I better get back to work," she said. "Thank you for the information." She turned to Cynthia unsure of what to say. It was obvious that she didn't want Alison to know what they had talked about. "It was nice meeting you."

"I'm sure we'll see each other again soon," Cynthia said with a smile.

* * *

Sally was working on her laptop when Elizabeth and Chevy entered. She looked up and grinned.

"Now, I can take a break," she said, standing and stretching her arms over her head. "I said I would stick at this until you came back."

"Is it that hard?"

Sally smiled ruefully. "I think that Daryl might be right about me being at the retreat. I'm still totally lost."

"How is your assignment going?"

"Not very well and now we have another one. Apparently, I'm supposed to have an opinion about whether space aliens should be part of science fiction or of fantasy. Tomorrow we will be taking sides and having a debate about it."

"What do you mean?"

"Well, the way I figure it is, if you believe they are real, then writing about them falls into regular writing or science fiction. If you don't think they are real then stories about them should be called fantasy writing. It would be like writing about a horse vs. a unicorn."

"I'm not sure I follow," Elizabeth grinned. "But I'm not about to ask any more questions."

"Good, because I don't have the answers."

"Let's share a cooler on the balcony while I tell you about my news."

Sally grabbed a cooler from their fridge while Elizabeth got two glasses. "So, tell me," Sally said, as she divided the drink into the glasses.

"I told you about the couple I met who live across the street, the ones who told me about the rumour."

Sally nodded.

"Well, just now when I came back, Alison was on her patio with another woman and they beckoned me over. I went and it turns out this woman, Cynthia, wants to hire me to find out who the girl was under the house."

"She wants to hire you? Pay you money?"

Elizabeth grinned. "That's what she said."

"What did you say?"

"No, of course."

"So, did she tell you why?"

Elizabeth took a sip of her drink and explained the meeting to Sally.

"So, you're not interested in finding out who the young girl is and what happened to her?"

"Of course I am," Elizabeth laughed. "But I have no idea where to begin looking. As I told her I am not a professional with training. Besides, I think the police will uncover who the young woman was and how she died soon enough. All Cynthia has to do is wait."

When their cooler was finished they ate their supper on the balcony. It was a warm evening and the sun gave a soft light as it was setting over the mountains. It seemed strange to have twilight so early. In Alberta it didn't get dark until around 10:00pm during the summer.

"I've found two more attractions that I think you might like to go on with me," Elizabeth said.

"Okay," Sally nodded. "What are they?"

"The first is a three hour canoe trip down a creek from one lake to another."

"That sounds like fun."

"And the other is a treatment at a spa surrounded by mountains."

"Ohh, I could go for that. Do I have to give you a definite time for any of these?"

Elizabeth shook her head. "Whenever you can spare the time."

"Well, according to Daryl, I should have the next week and a half off."

"What do you mean?" Elizabeth asked.

Sally shrugged and explained the encounter with Daryl. "He really got mad at us today because some of us were having our Angel cards read and he thought we should be working on our assignments."

"What's it to him, what you do in your spare time?"

"He's just taking this all too seriously. I'm thinking he's afraid that somehow we are going to wreck his retreat."

When supper was over and clean up done, Sally went back to her laptop. Elizabeth looked down on the now-empty lot. The wood from the old house had been hauled away. The only things to see were the hole from the partial basement, the lawn, and a few shrubs. An older couple stood on the sidewalk looking at the yard. Elizabeth wondered if they were parents here in search of answers about a missing daughter or if they were just curious neighbours.

Elizabeth put the leash on Chevy and went down the stairs. She'd learned that people like to talk to or pet dogs. She headed out onto the street and walked slowly towards the couple. She could see that there were more flowers by the lot. How many families were looking for a lost child? Chevy pulled on his leash but she held him back. She was the one on a mission this time.

The couple never turned to look at her or Chevy as they approached. Darn. She thought about letting him near enough to sniff their legs, as was his want when he met people. They might be afraid he would lift his, though, and that would spoil any chance of a friendly conversation. So she went to her back-up plan and just stopped beside them.

When they looked at her she saw that the woman's eyes were red and the man had a grim look on his face. She smiled faintly in acknowledgement and said. "What a terrible tragedy."

The woman turned back to the yard while the man nodded.

"I heard she was in her teens."

"Where did you hear that?" the woman asked, sharply.

"Uh... one of the neighbours," Elizabeth said, quickly. Obviously, they were from the group looking for a family member. "It's just a rumour."

When they didn't say anything more she asked in a quietly sympathetic voice. "Are you looking for someone?"

"That's none of your business," the man said abruptly. "What are you, a reporter?"

Elizabeth shook her head. "I'm sorry to bother you." She pulled on Chevy's leash and walked away. She would have to be careful who she approached from now on. There were families out there who were missing a loved one and it was rude of her to intrude.

After letting Chevy have his run, Elizabeth returned to the bed and breakfast. The sidewalk was empty. As she walked by a parked car, the window rolled down and the woman from earlier called to her.

"Excuse me."

Elizabeth walked over to the car. Whether they recognized her from their quick meeting, she didn't know nor did she say anything. "Yes?"

"Do you know of a good place to stay around here?"

Elizabeth smiled as she squatted down so she could talk with both of them. "I don't live here. I'm from Edmonton but I am staying in that bed and breakfast." She pointed to the building.

The woman turned to the man. "Do you want to be this close?"

Instead of replying to his wife he asked Elizabeth. "Do they have a vacancy?"

Elizabeth shrugged. "I really don't know. But you could ask. The owner's name is Beverly."

"Thank you," the woman said.

Elizabeth nodded and stood. She and Chevy headed to their room where she called Jared and left a message on his voicemail. She turned on the television, flipped through some channels and then left it on the news network.

Her cell phone rang. She scooped it up and said hello.

"I saw the news about the body being found in Whistler," her father said. "How close is it to where you are staying?"

Elizabeth cringed as she said. "Ah, it's right next door."

"What?" Phil yelled. "Next door?"

"But I have nothing to do with it," Elizabeth said quickly. No use telling him about Cynthia's request.

"That probably won't last for long," Phil said. "I know how you like to get involved in these things."

"The police are looking after it," Elizabeth said, soothingly. "There are lots of people who have come here looking for a family member and the police have all the technology to do the DNA testing. I can't compete with that."

"Good," Phil sounded relieved. "You stay out of it."

After Elizabeth hung up, she decided to phone her twin siblings, Terry and Sherry. If her father had heard about the body, so had they.

"You be careful," Sherry warned. "You've been lucky so far with your delving into other people's problems."

"Maybe you should think about taking some sort of self-defence course if you are going to continue to come up against killers," Terry said.

When she'd hung up she opened her laptop and began to transcribe some of her information from her recorder into her computer. Her cell rang again. She looked at the call display. Jared. She answered immediately, hoping for good news about his operation.

* * *

I'm so tired. Before coming here I never knew when the story would continue or how long the sessions would be but now that I'm at the retreat they seem to come almost as soon as I get to my room after class. There's just so much and it's coming so fast that sometimes I'm up all night.

It's almost as if they know that I have to have it done quickly to show Kat Mac. She wants to read the whole story before the retreat is over. I haven't told her that I'm still receiving the story. I've just told her that I'm editing it Chapter by Chapter.

I've asked Kat Mac about meeting the publisher on the last day and she said she'll put in a word for me with him. Oh, just the thought of being able to talk to a publisher gets me editing again.

I guess I shouldn't complain about receiving the story at night. At least it's better than during a lecture. The only reason I can think of as to why I don't hear from Mikk or Gwin then is because my mind is too busy with what I'm learning that they can't get through.

Gwin has told me about how she stole the wet clothes off a dead prisoner and put them on then found a blanket to wrap around her to keep warm. She found some scraps of food then headed to the cave. At first the inhabitants ignored her and wouldn't let her in but after a week, during which she huddled under a bush and came close to starving, they brought her out some food. A couple of days later they invited her in.

She spent the winter learning the gestures and language of the inhabitants and they in response learned some of her words so that their communication was a mixture of both. The men went out periodically to hunt for fresh meat. When the animal was brought back to the cave, the women did the butchering. Gwin was shown how to cut the meat into strips for drying and how to scrape the hides for tanning. She was given her own cooking utensils and a share of the food.

The evenings were spent in story telling. She listened to the stories of their lives and tried to tell them about the planet she came from. They could not grasp that she wasn't from their planet so one night she took them outside and pointed to the stars. Even when she told them that she had flown on a space ship from a planet near one of them they had no ability to understand. She finally gave up.

Whenever she was outside she watched the skies for a returning space ship. One had to come soon. She was sure the Leaders would want an investigation carried out as to why the experiment had failed. And, having already decided to use this planet as a penal colony, they would want to explore for a more suitable site. After all, they still had thousands of prisoners in the Orbital Prisons.

Three babies were born during the long, cold winter. Gwin watched in fascination as the first woman went through her labour. Finally, as the birth became imminent the mother-to-be was helped up from her bed by the attending women and held in the squatting position over a hide. She grunted as she strained to push the head and then the body of her newborn out. The quiet baby was caught by one of the attending women. Another grunt brought out the afterbirth.

While the mother relaxed in her bed the father took the infant and paraded around the cave showing the newborn to everyone. At last the baby was placed with the mother who held it until it began to fuss then brought it to her breast so it could eat.

Gwin asked to help in the next birth. Being there to bring a new life into their world gave Gwin a feeling of connection with them, and the planet, that had been missing.

Then one day the cave people told Gwin that they would be leaving soon.

* * *

"Where are you going?" Gwin asked in alarm. She had thought this was their permanent home.

"We have to meet the others," one explained. "Do you want to come with us?"

"How long will you be gone?"

"Until we decide to come back."

Gwin didn't know what to do. If she went with them she wouldn't be here when a space ship arrived. If she stayed, how would she survive without the food they provided?

"Will you teach me to hunt before you go?"

The inhabitants looked at her in surprise. "You want to stay?"

"Yes. I must wait for my people to return."

They looked at one another then shrugged. Gwin knew they were thinking she was touched in some way. She didn't try explaining further.

Over the next few days she was taught how to throw a spear and became adept at killing small animals and birds for her food. She went on walks into the forest to learn the poisonous and non-poisonous plants.

As Gwin watched the inhabitants organize their cooking utensils, their clothes, their tools, and their food for their trip she began to have serious doubts about her ability to survive alone, if she could sustain herself through her hunting. She also didn't know how long it would be until they returned because the inhabitants couldn't give her a time frame that she understood. She was very tempted to go with them and spent most of the final night thinking about it. The next morning, however, she said goodbye to them. They seemed as sad as she but she couldn't risk not being near the settlement when the ship arrived. She watched them walk down into the valley and over the far hill. None of them looked back.

Soon after her friends left Gwin went to her former home. She carried an axe for protection against wild animals

Gwin walked slowly down the streets between the partially finished slab buildings, remembering the hustle and bustle of their construction. All was silent now. The wood had weathered. Some of the buildings had been set on fire by the prisoners hoping for some warmth. There were no bodies, just skeletons, all their flesh having been eaten by wild animals or rotted away. She saw the cooking stoves that had been knocked over and the empty crates and boxes still scattered in the streets where they'd been dropped after the riot.

Gwin was surprised at her sudden rush of emotions. While she hadn't belonged there as a prisoner, she still felt an affinity for the place. Now that the warm weather had returned, the trees were back in leaf, the insects and colourful birds were flying again, and there were flowers blooming. Seeing all this new growth she began to think of this as her planet once more.

Gwin walked to the animal pens. Some of the fences had fallen down under the weight of the snow. She continued to where the fields had been plowed and seeded. There, she stood in surprise. Green shoots were growing in the soil. Even though the seeds had been under water during the rains and had frozen over the winter, they had sprouted in the warm weather. Gwin walked around the fields in wonder. There was going to be a crop of grain just as the scientists had hoped. And she was the only one to see it.

She also saw that the vegetables and tobacco were growing. She was glad for the vegetables but wasn't interested in the tobacco since it wouldn't feed her or the cave people. She wasn't even sure why it had been sent except maybe as a comfort for the prisoners.

Gwin looked at the rest of the area that had been marked for the seeding of grain. The grass was already high but if she was able to cut it and then dig up the soil, after the next cold weather she would be able to plant more seeds. Gwin stopped in her tracks. What was she thinking? A space ship would be here soon to pick her up and take her home. She didn't need to worry about planting more grain for food.

Then she had a sobering thought. What would happen to her if she went back? According to the law she'd still killed someone and was therefore, still a prisoner. She'd just be sent back to the Orbital Prisons to serve her sentence. And that she didn't want.

Gwin sat down beside the field in despair. There was no

way she could go back to her previous life, because it didn't exist any more. This was her life now and the cave people were her family. But she didn't know if she wanted to accept that knowledge. It was hard to think of not seeing Mikk again, of not marrying him as they had planned.

It was dusk when Gwin stood up again. She did not return to the cave that night. Instead she spent it in the dormitory she'd been assigned to, lying on the bed that had been hers. She stared at the stars overhead.

It was full daylight when Gwin rose from the bed. She hadn't slept much. It had taken hours for her to adjust to the idea that she was stuck here, alone. And to decide that if she was going to spend the rest of her life here, then she'd better start preparing more fields for grain.

Gwin found a scythe and over the summer cut the grass on the new field then worked the soil. She killed for her meat and gathered berries and roots. She found grain seeds that had somehow remained dry and moved them to the cave. She ground some into a flour between two rocks and mixed it with water to form a dough. She patted until it was flat and round and laid it on one of hot rocks surrounding her fire. When it was cooked she took it off and ate it. The taste was bland but it filled her hungry belly. To the next batch she added berries and the taste was better. She experimented with various plant products until she had a variety of ways to make the bread.

At night she stared at the stars wondering which one was her home planet.

She missed Mikk. She wished he would come and enjoy the planet with her. But, she realized, he was the only thing she missed. The artificial life in the artificial city where she had been born and raised in no way compared to the live plants and animals on this planet.

She was sitting in front of the cave grinding grain into flour when she happened to look up. Across the valley she could see the inhabitants walking down the hillside. She jumped up and rushed down into the valley to meet them. They were astonished and happy to see her. She knew that they hadn't expected her to survive. She hugged them all, glad that she had company again.

She walked with them to the cave. They were tired from the long day and just dumped their belongings on the floor. Gwin showed them the grain and told them about it growing at the village. She continued grinding and when she had enough for everyone she mixed it with water and berries to form the dough. She made the thin patties and cooked them on the rocks. She passed the patties around and when she saw the inhabitants didn't know what to do with them, she ate hers. They looked at the patty in their hands and because they were hungry they ate. The look of surprise on their faces made Gwin laugh. She knew they hadn't expected it to taste so good.

The people had returned just as she was harvesting the grain. A few days after their arrival she convinced them to come to the settlement and see the crop. They stared with open mouths at the half-finished buildings and walked along the streets in awe. No one spoke. She had gathered all the tools she could find and stored them in one of the warehouses. She led them into that building and explained the use of each tool demonstrating how the shovel dug the ground, the hoe chopped up the piece of ground, and the rake levelled it.

She picked up the scythe and took her friends to the fields. There she showed them the grain, half of which she'd already cut down. They asked about the tobacco so Gwin explained as best she could how it was used for smoking. She then began cutting the remainder of the crop. The men watched for a few minutes then went back to the barracks to get a scythe each. It wasn't long before they were sweeping it through the grain. The women quickly gathered up the stalks and piled them.

At the end of the day the shafts of grain lay in piles which were then tied by strips of hide. The piles were carried back to the cave. There the grain was stripped from the stalk by hand. Gwin explained that some of the grain had to be stored to use as seed the next year. The rest could be ground into flour. Over the week they dug up the vegetables and stored them near the back of the cave.

When the snows came again Gwin surmised that one of the planet's years had passed.

Chapter 9

Elizabeth was half listening to the television while working. Suddenly, the name Whistler caught her attention and she turned to watch. The two news anchors were talking about what the media was now calling Whistler's Murder. They took turns telling about the body found in Whistler and pictures behind them showed people lined up on the street looking at the lot.

"The police are still waiting to find out how long the body may have been there. But that lack of knowledge hasn't stopped families from across Canada and even from the United States from arriving in Whistler since the body was discovered. They are all hoping to find out if the young woman is their daughter or sister. We have interviews with three of the families."

The picture switched to an interviewer holding a microphone in front of a woman who was listening to the question the interviewer was asking.

"I last saw my fifteen-year-old daughter, Amelia, three years ago when my ex-husband picked her up for a two week camping trip. He never brought her back."

"Have you heard from her at all?"

The woman shook her head. "Nothing. I phoned all his relatives and friends but no one has seen him since that time either. I even called her friends to see if maybe he had dropped her off with one of them."

The name Sharlet Wesley showed up on the screen under the woman.

"Do you think he would have killed her?"

"I don't know what was going through his mind at the time," Sharlet said. "We were in the middle of a divorce and had both agreed to share custody."

"Did he like that idea?"

Sharlet shrugged. "He seemed okay with it at the time.

Now, I'm not so sure."

"There is the possibility that they may have had an accident."

Sharlet nodded. "I've thought of that also and I've been listening to newscasts and checking the Internet every day since then watching for any bodies or skeletons or wrecked cars that have been found anywhere in North America."

"Where were they going camping?"

"They started from Castlegar B.C. and were heading into the States, back up onto Vancouver island, and then home. They really didn't have a clear laid out route, were just going where their whim took them."

"Well, I'm not sure if I should hope that this body belongs to your daughter," the interviewer said.

"I'm not sure if I want it to be either." Sharlet turned away wiping her eyes.

These interviews must have been done during the day while Elizabeth was doing her research because so far she'd only seen the news vans the first day the body had been discovered.

The next person who came up on screen was a man. The interview was short.

"My daughter was a drug addict and prostitute," he said. "She disappeared just before the Olympic Games and I'm wondering if she came here to work and was murdered either during the Olympics or since then."

The third interview was with the couple Elizabeth had talked with a few hours ago on the street in front of the lot. Their granddaughter had come to Whistler last winter with some friends on a ski trip. She never showed up back at their apartment after going to a party.

The picture returned to the news room. "Finding this body under the demolished house is not a unique nor isolated event," the female anchor concluded. "Over the years bodies have turned up in the oddest places." She began running through a list of similar findings. "A mother's body was walled up in her bedroom by her hermit son for nine years. A young boy disappeared from his home and his skeleton was discovered under the house eighteen years later. A wife's body was unearthed from under a fishpond five years after her husband reported her missing."

Grizzly, grizzly, thought Elizabeth. She was about to shut the television off when the male anchor cut in.

"We have just received breaking word that starting tomorrow the police will be excavating the whole yard. They haven't stated if they are working on a tip but they did say they are looking for clues to the young woman's identity and are checking to see if there are any more bodies."

This is getting more and more interesting, Elizabeth thought. Do I want to get mixed up in it? She'd figured out who murdered a teacher in the city of Red Deer, Alberta, while working on a travel article about Highway 2A which ran south from Edmonton to Crossfield. Then there was the mystery of the bones found in a sceptic tank near Fort Macleod, Alberta. Last year had been Jared's mother's murder, plus the death of one of her neighbours. It seemed that no matter where she went to write her articles she became involved in some sort of untimely death. So far, she'd been lucky in that she'd managed to solve them. She would have more time to spend on this one since she was almost finished her research and her transcribing. She would have to think more about it, she decided as she turned off the television and went to bed.

* * *

The next morning Elizabeth heard a noise outside and went out onto the patio to look down on the yard next door. True to what the newscaster had said last night the police had a team working there. They had put up plastic tarps around the yard so no one could see them from the streets. She wondered how long it would be before helicopters with reporters would be hovering overhead taking pictures of the action.

The *Vancouver Sun* was sitting on the little table when Elizabeth and Sally entered the dining room. The headline read: Whistler's Murder Takes A New Twist. Elizabeth picked it up and carried to their table. She scanned the article which was accompanied by a picture of the house before it had been torn down.

"Anything new?" Sally asked.

Elizabeth shook her head. "Besides excavating the yard for more evidence the police in Vancouver are checking all the missing girls reports from that age group that have been sent to them from other parts of the country. Since the face is not recognizable and the clothes have basically disintegrated they are getting DNA samples from all the people who have shown up here and think they might be related. Getting the information back could take weeks."

No one else was down for breakfast so Elizabeth didn't know if that couple had booked a room here and she wasn't going to ask Beverly, who arrived with the breakfast plates.

"Where are Bonnie and Daryl this morning?" Elizabeth asked, as they ate.

"Probably working hard on their arguments for this morning's discussion."

"What position did you take?"

"I can't decide," Sally said, dismally. "Maybe I should skip the class today."

Elizabeth laughed. "You're not in high school. You won't be failed if you don't do the assignment. Maybe Kat Mac needs a moderator or a judge. You could volunteer for that."

"Except I wouldn't know what I was judging. I really think I am over my head here. It's not at all what I expected and I think I'm wasting Kat Mac's and my time, just like Daryl said."

"This is only the third day. Keep at it. You still might learn something that will help you."

"I'm so confused that I probably wouldn't recognize it anyway."

"Well, do you want to come with me today? We could do the Peak 2 Peak."

Sally took a deep breath, then let it out. "As much as I'd like to say yes, I'm going to put in my time." She stood. "And I'd better go."

* * *

Sally walked along the short path to the small parking lot in front of the bed and breakfast. She paused when she saw Bonnie sitting on a large rock in front of her vehicle.

"Do you mind if I walk with you today?" Bonnie asked, standing.

"No, not at all," Sally said, as Bonnie fell in step with her. "I didn't see you at breakfast."

"I wasn't hungry this morning."

They discussed the weather and then the class. As they turned onto Fitzsimmons Road South Sally saw that the man and his daughter were out in their yard bent over a flower bed in front of the house.

"Good morning," Sally called and raised a hand to wave to him.

They both straightened up and turned. The man smiled and returned the wave. His daughter, however, just stared at them. Was she having a bad day or was she normally that miserable looking? Sally wondered.

"Who's that?" Bonnie asked.

"I don't know his name but I talked with him yesterday about his beautiful yard."

The daughter took the man by his arm and began steering him towards the deck. He seemed caught off guard and stumbled a bit.

Bonnie looked at them. "That's funny," she said.

"What is?" Sally asked.

"He reminds me of someone."

"Who?"

Bonnie shrugged. "I don't know. There's just something about the way he was standing there." By that time they were past and Bonnie turned and took another look.

Sally swivelled in time to see the daughter dragging her father into the house. What was that about?

They walked in silence for a few moments then Bonnie turned to her and abruptly asked. "Would your friend help me find the person who murdered my cousin?"

"What? Oh. Um, I don't know." Sally was caught totally by surprise.

"Well, you did tell me that she had solved four murders and I was wondering if she would help me."

"You could ask her," Sally said cautiously. "But I do know that she is busy with her article. What about the police?"

"They're not interested. They ruled it an accident when it happened and they don't listen to me when I tell them I know she was deliberately killed."

There were a lot of questions that swirled in Sally's head and she suddenly knew what Elizabeth experienced when confronted with a possible murder.

"Could you help, then?"

"Me?" Sally asked flustered. "I know nothing about murder. I wouldn't have a clue how to find a killer." Well, that was a stupid way to put it.

"Surely, she's told you how she's done it."

"Yes," Sally nodded. "She did tell me about each mystery and what tipped her off to the murderer but that doesn't mean that I can do it."

They had reached the class room. "Can I at least explain it to you after lunch today?" Bonnie quickly asked, as they parted company.

"Sure." Sally walked slowly to her seat. What should she do now? She knew she couldn't help Bonnie. Maybe she could tell Elizabeth about it. But that didn't seem fair. After all, she knew how much Elizabeth was looking forward to just relaxing once her research was done.

"We have pictures of aliens from Roswell." Kat Mac began the lecture. "Many of the aliens in our movies look a lot like those pictures. Were the space aliens in the movies copies of them? Or were there drawing of space aliens for movies prior to 1947 and are those the ones used to depict the Roswell aliens as seen in magazines and on television?"

Kat Mac looked around the room. "What we are going to discuss today is, should stories about space aliens be classified as fantasy or science fiction?"

Sally saw that Daryl Cannon had a pile of papers and books laid out on his table. One of the books was titled *The Truth About The UFO Crash At Roswell* and another was *Alien Landing*. Wow, she thought. He's really into this. He must have gone to the library for the books. Once more she felt out of her league. What's wrong with me that I find it hard to concentrate on the lectures and really don't understand why we are doing these assignments?

She'd looked up Roswell on the Internet last night and had been dismayed to see that there were 1.4 million sites. And they weren't all about the aliens supposedly found there. Some were of the city itself, a television show titled "Roswell", a UFO museum, and much more. She'd browsed through a few of the sites on the aliens.

According to some of them the government and the air force were hiding the truth about the alien crash landing, while others pointed out that there were many contradictions to the stories and that some of the evidence was a hoax. Since she felt she didn't know enough about it to be able to take a stand, she'd decided to opt out of the discussion. When the time came to chose sides Bonnie and Kendra also refused to pick one.

Sally could feel the disgust emanate from the more serious students. But she'd begun to ignore their feelings. She'd paid her money and she would participate as much or as little as she wanted. Besides, this would give her a good chance to listen to both sides.

Daryl began. "I gathered all I could find on Roswell. According to the books written and the testimony given, the aliens at Roswell were real."

Sally sat back and listened as he talked about the evidence found and who had seen what that night and over the next few months. He must have been up all night working on this. The next person to talk was Kirk on the opposite side. The debate went back and forth and Sally soon began hoping that she wouldn't fall asleep.

She did look around and saw that one student had dozed off. So it just wasn't she who found it hard to get into.

At the end of the debate Kat Mac turned to Sally, Kendra, and Bonnie. "Do any of you want to add to what has been said today."

"Yes." After listening to both sides, Sally decided to have her say. "I looked up UFO on the Internet and there have been sightings dating back to the 1800s. In 1886, a director of the Zacatecas Observatory in Mexico took some photographs of objects he observed crossing the disc of the sun. These are supposed to be the oldest photographs of UFOs in the world. Also, in 1886 a bright, humming object appeared over a hut near Maracaibo, Venezuela. Afterwards, the people in the hut had what was thought to be radiation poisoning and nearby trees died. In 1897, there was an alleged UFO crash near Aurora, Texas and the supposed alien pilot was buried in the local cemetery.

"So for almost 130 years UFOs have been reported. It wasn't until Roswell that pictures of the alleged aliens were published. And, as stated by Reggie Shaw of the fantasy side, these were explained as being dummies used in a United States Air Force experiment. I don't believe that we can be the only planet in the universe that is occupied by thinking beings. I have no idea what form they take but I do believe that there are aliens. Therefore, I don't think their stories should be called fantasy writing."

"Well done," Kat Mac said. "Why didn't you take a side and state that during the debate?"

Sally felt herself blush and immediately thought about being back in school. How could she explain that she hadn't had the confidence in her thinking to do it until she had heard the other arguments. She shrugged. "I don't know."

Kat Mac looked at Kendra and Bonnie. Both of them shook their heads. "Okay, then we shall resume our regular lecture tomorrow."

After the class, Sally went up to Kendra. "It's been bothering me about what your Angel cards told you. When Bonnie mentioned children you got upset."

Kendra's eyes immediately filled with tears. "My sons."

"Did something happen to them?" Sally asked gently.

Kendra looked away and wiped her eyes. "My first husband got custody of them in our divorce. I get them every other weekend and this weekend is my turn. I really hate that I won't be seeing them and it will be another two weeks before I do. That's a whole month between visits with them. I'm so tempted to head back to Revelstoke so I can have my weekend with them."

"That's a tough decision," Sally said.

Kendra nodded and left the room.

"That was a smart take on the aliens," Reggie said, coming up to her. "It's a good thing you weren't on the other side of the debate."

Sally grinned. "Believe me, if I had stood up and tried to say that in front of everyone, that side would have lost points."

Reggie smiled and Sally felt her heart flutter. "Are you coming to the dining room for lunch?" she asked. She might was well be bold while she had him.

Reggie shook his head. "I have my meeting with Kat Mac this afternoon and I have to get my material in order."

Sally swallowed her disappointment and went to the dining room. She loaded her tray with a sandwich, soup, dessert, and an apple juice and went outside to eat. She looked but couldn't see Bonnie. Where was she? She had said she wanted to tell Sally about her cousin's death. Sally did see Michael Wolf sitting at one of the outdoor tables. He smiled at her and she walked over.

"How have your first three days been?" he asked.

"Not very good," Sally said, setting her tray down across from him. "I've found out that reading science fiction does not mean I know anything about the genre."

Michael laughed. "I totally understand. I was lost for the first week but then in the second week everything fell into place and I began to understand what science fiction really was about and how to write it."

"So I just have to get through two more days and then I'll see the light." Sally took a bite of her sandwich.

"Something like that," Michael grinned.

"What about your script writing? Are you finding that course's first week easier?"

"Not really. Again, I think it's going to take time for more of the information to be given before my mind can shuffle it into an order I can use."

"So what have you learned so far?" Sally took a drink.

"Well, I've been told not to send out my idea for a script. I have to wait until I have a script totally done before I start contacting anyone. And I have to format it, too."

"What's that?" She might as well learn what she could from him. It might help her make up her mind as to whether she wanted to try screen writing.

"That's putting in the time of day, the place, and whether the scene is taking place inside or outside. Then each character's name has to be capitalized when they say something and how they say it has to be noted. Then the scene has to be typed out. And there is much more to it."

"Phew, sounds like a lot of work."

"It is, so we were told to buy a software program that automatically does it for us to save us time."

"Ah, another time saver program. I'm waiting for when they develop software where you type in the story idea and it writes the book for you."

"You and me both," Michael laughed.

Sally was enjoying Michael's company and was a little disappointed when she saw Bonnie wave at her from the doorway. She excused herself and went over.

"Let's go inside," Bonnie said.

Chapter 10

Elizabeth headed back to where she'd left off the other day and continued on Highway 99 with her kilometres starting from Alpine Way.

"Soon you can see Green Lake to your right," she recorded, then laughed. "You pass Crazy Canuck Drive, which leads into one of the many new housing developments rapidly going up in the Whistler area." She thought of all the estates she'd seen along the highway on the way into Whistler. On impulse she turned onto Crazy Canuck Drive and looked at what she suspected were million dollar homes.

She returned to Highway 99 and recorded as she travelled. "The road is narrow and winding with an occasional passing lane and many hills. Keep alert."

She saw the sign for Wild Play Elements Park and turned left off the highway. It was a quick drive to the parking lot. She parked in the shade, rolled down the windows a bit for Chevy, then got out with her camera and recorder. Just as she reached the yard she saw a group was getting ready to go. She watched as they stepped into their harnesses and were shown how to tightened them. Each harness had two karabiners and a zip line pulley. Elizabeth followed them over to the training area. The guide demonstrated how to hook both the karabiners up to the coloured plastic cable and then unhook one at a time to move.

"Always have one attached at all times," she said.

Then she showed how to move the zip line pulley from the harness and attach it to the wire cable. "You can steer by twisting it a little each way," she said. "Keep your arms straight and your feet facing towards the padding at the other end."

Elizabeth looked at the blue padding with the feet painted on it. This looked like fun but again she knew she would feel more comfortable if Sally was with her. Plus, she suspected that Sally would be ticked off if she did it without her. She went to the building and asked about reservations and start times and picked up two waivers.

Back in the Tracker Chevy waited patiently on the passenger's seat. "You are so good," Elizabeth said, as she rubbed his ears.

Elizabeth recorded that she followed Green River for a ways then crossed the Soo River and Rutherford Creek. At one point she had to slow down to 40 km because of the ESS curves. Kilometre 24 from Alpine Way she turned right into the Nairn Falls Province Park. She parked and turned to Chevy.

"This is where you can get out, too," she said.

As if he understood her words he jumped into her lap.

"Just a minute," Elizabeth laughed. "Let me get organized."

There were no other vehicles in the lot so she let him explore a bit while she checked the tape in her recorder to make sure it wouldn't run out soon and changed the batteries in her camera. She would have to remember to recharge them when she got back to the bed and breakfast. Before leaving this morning she'd packed her and Chevy a lunch and put it in her backpack. She pulled her backpack on.

Chevy romped beside her as she walked a short distance through the trees to a metal fence.

"It feels good to be out of the vehicle, doesn't it?" she smiled at him.

At the fence she read that it was a 1.5 km hike from the parking lot to the falls and that she was to keep Chevy on a leash.

"We'd better get your leash then," she said and turned around.

Chevy stopped and watched her as she headed back. His ears and tail drooped.

"Come on," Elizabeth beckoned.

Instead of listening Chevy sat down.

Elizabeth grinned. "Okay, you wait there and I'll be right back." She ran to the Tracker, got his leash, and hurried back. He was still waiting when she returned.

She clamped it on his collar and he took off at a run. She had to run, too, in order not to jerk him back when he reached the end of the leash. Finally, a scent caught his attention and he stopped. Elizabeth pulled out her recorder and began recording the trail.

"It's a narrow, rugged trail over rocks and roots," she began. "It hugs the hillside to your right and has a drop off to the river on your left."

While it seemed to go up and down it did make a gradual descent most of the way. At the end of the trail she let Chevy off the leash and he scampered away. She climbed the huge silver-coloured rocks to a set of steps that led to a lookout platform where she could see the upper section of the falls. The water crashed between two rock walls creating foam on the river below. It snaked to her left where she could see the top of another cascade. She descended to a point where she could take pictures of the lower section which was wider and mightier than the first and sent a spray high into the air.

Elizabeth loved waterfalls and the sound of the thrashing water. She went back to the platform and settled on the steps. She took off her backpack and laid out the water bottles, Chevy's dishes, the sandwiches for her and the dog food for him. She opened a bottle and poured some water into his dish. He immediately lapped it up.

"Hiking is tough work, isn't it?" she said, as she topped up his dish again, then took a drink herself.

She filled up his other dish with dog food and opened a sandwich. Chevy looked at his dry food then at the sandwich in her hand. Elizabeth took a couple of bites hoping that he would get discouraged and eat his own, but he was more stubborn than she.

"Okay," she said, and tore off a piece. She set it on top of his food. He gobbled it down and looked expectantly at her again. Finally, she broke what was left of the sandwich into pieces and gave it to him. "It's a good thing I brought more." She took another one for herself.

As if to appease her, Chevy ate some of his food when he had finished the sandwich. After the meal Elizabeth leaned back and closed her eyes. This was what she liked most of all in life. Surrounded by bush, water flowing nearby, comfortably full. The only thing missing was a fire.

She felt herself relaxing. She was basically finished her research. There were just the adventures she was going to do with Sally. And, although they were for the article, she also wanted to do them for her own personal enjoyment.

It wasn't long before her tranquility was disturbed by voices. She sat up and hooked on Chevy's leash just as a couple with three children reached the bottom of the huge rocks. Elizabeth pulled on her backpack, smiled at the family, and began the walk back.

On the way she thought about the unknown young woman whose body had been found. She certainly had the time now to look into it for Cynthia. And she had to admit she liked the thrill of trying to piece together the bits of information she received. Plus, there was the fun in acting like Joan Kilbourn and Kinsey Millhone, her two favourite fictional detectives. The question again was did she want to or did she want to relax by the pool and spend some time sipping a drink at one of the outdoor tables in the Village, acting like a rich tourist?

The mystery pulled her as had all the ones in the past. How would a young woman end up buried in a basement? What had happened in her life to cause it to end that way? What sort of reason could make a person do something like that to someone else? She knew the police were asking the same questions and she felt a bit silly thinking that she would be able to assist them or even beat them to the answers.

By the time she'd gotten to her vehicle she'd decided to at least speak with Cynthia again.

* * *

Sally followed Bonnie into the atrium.

"Sorry, I'm late," Bonnie said, leading the way over to a corner area with two chairs and a small table. "I had some things to do."

Sally wanted to ask what they were but refrained. It was none of her business. She sat in the chair and put her pack on the table. Never having worked on a murder, or supposed murder, before she wasn't sure how to start? Did she ask to hear the story or make small talk first?

"My cousin died from a fall," Bonnie began, much to Sally's relief. "Apparently she hit her head and her death was ruled an accident."

"And you don't think it was?"

"I know it wasn't," Bonnie stated firmly.

"Why don't you tell me the story from the beginning?" Was that what Elizabeth would say? Sally wondered.

"Sylvia attended this retreat two years ago," Bonnie began. "Kat Mac was her instructor. There were fifteen students in her class. She liked the class and was learning a lot about science fiction writing. Then on the second last day of the retreat I got a phone call from my aunt telling me that Sylvia had fallen down the steps going to the Upper Village and had hit her head. She'd died immediately."

Well, that wasn't much to go on, Sally thought. Now what do I ask or say? "Why did she call you?"

"I'm like a second daughter to her. She wanted me to be with her when she identified the body."

"Did you two come here?" Should she be writing this down?

"No, Sylvia's body was sent to Vancouver."

"What about her father? Where was he?"

"My uncle left my aunt when Sylvia was eight. The first year he visited a few times then he married and started a new family. He never had anything to do with her or any of us after that."

Okay, that was good. "Um, why do you think Sylvia's death wasn't an accident?"

"Because, she'd already been to the Upper Village and wouldn't have visited it again."

"And that's the reason?" Sally blurted out, astonished. Even she knew that was ridiculous logic.

"You sound just like the police," Bonnie said bitterly.

Sally took a deep breath. She could tell that Bonnie really believed her cousin had been murdered, but so far she hadn't said anything that could be used as a clue as to how or why. Or maybe Sally just hadn't asked her the right question yet.

"So because she wouldn't have made a second trip to the Upper Village is why you think someone murdered her?" she asked, wondering if she was at least sounding like Elizabeth.

"Yes. It's just a gut feeling I have. She'd sent me a text that she had been there and once she sees something she usually doesn't go back unless she really likes it."

"And she didn't like the Upper Village?"

"Well, it's mainly for kids or families. There was nothing for her to do there."

"So, how are you planning to find out if she was murdered?"

"Tomorrow I'm going to let everyone in class know about Sylvia and see what kind of reaction I get."

"But they weren't here two years ago."

"I know, but Kat Mac was."

"Do you think she was involved?" Sally couldn't picture Kat Mac being a killer.

Bonnie shrugged. "She was here."

"Are you going to ask her directly about Sylvia?"

"Yes, if no one else gives me any information then I will go to her."

As Sally walked to the bed and breakfast she thought about calling Elizabeth and telling her, but decided not to disturb her while she was working. It could wait until she saw her later. She grinned. Wouldn't it be something if she had a mystery of her own to solve.

* * *

My mind is racing over what I received this afternoon from Gwin. It's a little scary.

* * *

Three more of the planet's years passed before the space

ship arrived. It was early spring and the inhabitants hadn't left yet. Gwin was planting grain seeds when she heard the noise overhead. She looked up in time to see it hover over the village then head to the meadow. She threw down her bag of seeds and ran to the edge of the trees by the meadow.

She watched as the door opened and guards stepped out. They surveyed the meadow then one of them spoke into his microphone. Soon a group of people exited the ship. None were in uniform. They could be scientists or from the Space Organization.

Then she drew in her breath. Mikk was one of them. Gwin watched him, her love overwhelming her. He'd come to find her. She had to hold herself back from running to him. She didn't know what the guards would do if they saw someone dash at them from the trees. They might shoot her with their guns before recognizing her. Besides she didn't want anyone else to see her. She'd become so used to the peace and quiet that she didn't want the hassle of all the questioning that would take place. She would wait for the opportunity to reveal herself to Mikk when no one else was around.

The guards led the way to the village, everyone stepping over the skeletons of the rioters as they went. Gwin followed silently. At each of the buildings the guards checked the inside first before the others went in to investigate. There was nothing for them to find except the bed frames and half rotted hammocks. Outside they looked at the crates and boxes still strewn along the streets. They inspected the stoves, the pits, and the areas of cut trees which new growth had begun to fill in. They lifted the few skeletons they found and carried them back to the space ship.

The group soon split up. Some wanted to take a closer look at the buildings, some wanted to wander around the area. Mikk found the path Gwin used to go to the fields and followed it. She hurried through the trees so she could be there when he arrived. She positioned herself by the nearest field and waited. Then she realized that she didn't know what she looked like. There were no mirrors and she only saw her reflection in puddles after a rain.

Her clothes had slowly worn out and now she spent her summers and winters wearing skins. She bathed and washed the skins regularly in the river but while she was getting the fields ready for planting she didn't worry much about cleanliness. She smoothed her hair down with her hands and tried to wipe the dirt off her face. There was only a small amount of water in a pail that she used for drinking. She quickly dipped her hands in the pail and rubbed her face. She dried it on her arm.

She stiffened when she heard Mikk's footprints. Suddenly she felt awkward. A long time had passed since she'd seen him and she'd changed from the woman he knew. What if he didn't recognize her? What if he hadn't come to look for her? After all, it had probably been reported that everyone should have died from starvation or the cold.

Mikk came out of the trees and his eyes scanned the black soil of the fields. They passed over her and then returned in shock. She smiled. He stared not believing what he was seeing.

"Gwin?" He asked faintly.

She nodded. "It's me."

"Gwin!" He ran to her and swept her into his arms.

She wrapped her arms around him. She'd dreamed of this day for four changes of seasons. And now it had finally happened. Mikk was here with her.

"How did you...? Where have you...? What did you...?" Mikk had so many questions to ask he couldn't form any of them. "I've missed you so much," he finally managed.

Gwin nuzzled her head in his shoulder. It felt so good to have his arms around her.

"Oh, Mikk," was all she could say.

He finally held her at arms length looking at her. "How have you managed to survive here? Are there others? What happened to the cold and the snow we heard about?"

Gwin held up her hand. She looked around to see if anyone else had followed the path. She didn't want to be found out. "First of all I've been growing the grain sent here and grinding it into flour and growing vegetables. And second of all, I've got friends who have been looking after me."

"Friends? What kind of friends?"

"Come with me and I'll show you."

She led him through the trees and meadows to the valley with the cave. On the way she told him about the frame-up that had led to her imprisonment and her life since the space ship had left. She explained about her discovery of the sprouting grain and vegetables and how she had taught her friends to seed and harvest both. As she talked she realized how proud she was of her accomplishments.

He listened in silence.

When she mentioned the inhabitants, she told him about their migration every spring. "They are still here because one of the women is about to give birth."

On the slope overlooking the valley and the cave, Gwin turned to Mikk. "You have to promise me not to tell anyone about these people."

"Why not?"

"Because I don't want their life disrupted. I've told them how I arrived here and they have seen the village but they have had a hard time understanding where I came from. If a bunch of scientists swarmed over them and began asking a lot of questions, I'm not sure how they would react."

"Okay, I promise."

"And don't mention me either."

"Why not? I'm sure the Leaders would be glad to hear that one person survived and even thrived here."

"I don't want to go through all the questioning that would occur. Plus, they would treat me as a prisoner again."

Gwin led Mikk to the cave. She left him at the entrance and stepped inside. She explained that the space ship had arrived and on it was a friend of hers. She said she had told him about how they had saved her from freezing and starving and how they had been her companions ever since. Because he was thankful to them he wanted to meet them. Then she left the cave so they could discuss the meeting without her.

"What did they say?" Mikk asked.

"They're talking it now. When they've made up their minds they'll let us know."

"How long will that be?" Mikk looked at his watch

Gwin shrugged. "Minutes and hours mean nothing to them. It is only the seasons that matter." As she said it she realized that she too had adopted the attitude of no time. The only deadlines now were to get the crop planted as soon as possible after the snow left and to get it harvested before the snow returned.

"I've told you about my life since coming here," Gwin said. "Tell me about yours."

"Other than spending most of my waking hours trying to find out what happened to you and working on my freezing experiment, there's nothing to tell."

Gwin didn't say anything. Now that the ship had finally come with Mikk on it her resolve not to go back was wavering. She still loved him, still thought about a life with him as her husband.

"What took so long for a space ship to come?" Gwin asked.

"It hasn't been a year since we learned about the disaster. It took that long for the Leaders to decide what to do."

"It's been less than a year?"

"Yes."

"If my figuring is right, it's been almost four years here."

"Four years?"

"Yes. There are four seasons. One of great warmth that would have been the exploration team and I first came here. One of cooler weather when the leaves fall off the trees. One of deeper cold when the snow comes and one when the snow disappears and the warm weather returns. I'm planting my fourth crop of grain."

Mikk looked at his watch again. Gwin could feel his impatience and knew that she should feel that impatience also. But she didn't and was happy with the thought. She liked not having the stress of doing things within a time frame.

Finally, one of the men stepped to the entrance and beckoned them. Gwin smiled at him. She'd thought that because of the days it had taken them to let her in the cave, they wouldn't make a decision so fast.

Gwin led Mikk into the cave. She introduced him to her friends including the children. Mikk nodded at each introduction. They just stared at him as they had done at her. They'd gotten used to her but to meet a male of her species was new to them.

Gwin tried to explain how they lived, how they hunted and dug plants and picked berries for food. Mikk looked around the cave and Gwin could see that he wasn't impressed. Seeing it through his eyes she could understand why. But seeing it from her eyes, she was still grateful for them taking her in and showing her how to live their life.

Most of their possessions had been packed for their journey. The woman, Lyla, who was giving birth lay on a robe of skins with the other women around her. Suddenly they raised her into the squatting position. The baby came silently into the world and was wrapped in a hide. As was the custom the father showed it to the rest of the tribe and then to Gwin and Mikk. The baby blinked innocently up at them. Gwin smiled happily at the newest child and congratulated the father.

"Why is the child so quiet?" Mikk asked.

"It takes about a year for the baby to learn to speak or to walk," Gwin explained. "Until then it is carried by the mother or the father."

"An unformed mind," Mikk said.

"What?" Gwin asked.

"Nothing," Mikk replied.

Gwin and Mikk left the cave.

* * *

Wow, does this mean what I think it does? Why did she stop? Is Mikk going to carry on? I wait expectantly but no aura, no story. I quickly email the chapter to Kat Mac without editing. This is so exciting. I phone her to make sure she got it. I want her to read it and call me back. She's a little disgruntled but I know she'll get over it when she has read this chapter.

Chapter 11

Elizabeth wondered where Sally was when she arrived at the bed and breakfast. Usually she was working in her room when Elizabeth got back. She dropped her camera and tape recorder on her bed and turn her computer on. She'd get some work done and then maybe the two of them could go out to one of the restaurants in the Village for supper.

She heard the door open and poked her head around the corner. Sally walked in, a lopsided grin on her face.

"What's happened?" Elizabeth asked, coming into the living room.

"You're not going to believe it," Sally said, setting her back pack on the couch.

"Try me."

"I've been asked to find out if Bonnie's cousin, Sylvia, was murdered two years ago."

"What?" Elizabeth stared in disbelief.

"Yup. Bonnie heard that you have worked on four murders and she thinks that because we are friends I can help her."

Elizabeth plopped into one of the chair. "So, tell me all about it."

Sally bit at her bottom lip. "There really isn't much to tell. Sylvia fell down some concrete steps by the Upper Village and died. Bonnie believes she was murdered but she doesn't know why or by whom."

"So what makes her believe she was murdered?" Elizabeth could feel her interest rising.

"Well, that's the catch. She says that Sylvia had already visited the Upper Village and said it was for kids, so there was no reason for her to go there again."

"That's it?" Elizabeth tried not to laugh.

Sally nodded. "That's what I said but she seems to think it's enough. I figured I'd ask you what you thought."

"I think she's a little weird," Elizabeth said, getting up. She could still get some transcribing done.

"Well, that could be true," Sally admitted, following Elizabeth into her room. "She does believe what her Angel cards tell her."

"That's those cards that Daryl got so mad about?"

Sally nodded.

"So what are they?"

Sally explained as best she could. "She'll give you a reading if you want," she concluded.

"Did you have one?"

Sally shook her head. "No. I'm content to wait and see what happens in my life. I don't have to know ahead of time."

Elizabeth opened her computer as Sally left the room. She was just about finished when there was a knock at the suite door.

"I'll get it," Sally called.

Elizabeth tried to get back to her work but at the same time listened to what was happening. Although she could hear the voices she couldn't quite make out what was being said. When Sally tapped on her door frame, she looked up.

"Bonnie is wondering if she could talk with you," Sally said.

Elizabeth grimaced. Damn, she just needed a little more time. She saved what she'd done and shut off the computer.

"Elizabeth, this is Bonnie," Sally introduced.

The women shook hands.

"I'm sorry to bother you," Bonnie apologized. "but I just need to talk with someone about this, someone who might be able to help me."

Elizabeth looked at Sally. This was her case, so to speak.

"It's okay," Sally said. "Bonnie and I already discussed it. I've been sitting here trying to think of questions to ask and people to talk to and I can't come up with anything. So I know that the person she is looking for isn't me."

"Sit down," Elizabeth said, taking the end of the couch after Bonnie had chosen a chair. "Sally has told me about your cousin but I really don't understand why you think she was murdered."

"I know it sounds silly but it's just a feeling I have,"

Bonnie said, setting her back pack on the floor beside her.

"Would you like a drink of juice or some coffee?" Sally asked.

"A glass of water would be fine," Bonnie said.

Sally brought back a glass of water for Bonnie, a Pepsi for Elizabeth and a juice for herself. She settled in the other chair.

"Okay," Elizabeth said. "Sally told me you and Sylvia were like sisters. Start from there." She would listen, give some pointers, and then tell her there was nothing she could do.

"My aunt, and my uncle until he left, helped raise me. I spent days at a time at their place when my parents were too drunk or high on drugs to remember they had a daughter to look after. My aunt asked for custody of me when I was about four and then a few years later my uncle left my aunt."

"How old were you and Sylvia when that happened?"

"Sylvia was eight and I was nine."

"Did you see your parents?"

"Occasionally. Every once in a while they would have a twinge of conscience and pick me up for a day of togetherness," Bonnie said, harshly. "Even my uncle only came back to see us for the first year then he married and started a new life."

Sounded like she had abandonment issues. "You and Sylvia grew up together. What happened after high school?" This really had nothing to do with Sylvia's death but at least it would sound like Elizabeth was taking an interest.

"Sylvia went through for a nurse, I became legal secretary. We shared an apartment until I married."

"Was Sylvia married?"

"Yes. She married a man named Ken Bush. He died in a small plane crash. After that she had a few serious relationships, but never took the leap again."

"Okay, fast forward to two years ago," Elizabeth said. Might was well get this over with.

"One day Sylvia told me she wanted to be a fantasy writer and had enrolled in the retreat here."

"You make it sound like that was a surprise."

"It was," Bonnie agreed. "She'd never mentioned it before

although I knew she like to read fantasy. Apparently, she'd completed a novel and was in the editing stage. She'd sent the first three chapters to the instructor, Kat Mac."

"The same person who is teaching you now?"

Bonnie nodded.

"So she came here to take the course," Elizabeth said. "Did she correspond with you at all?"

"She sent me text messages just about every day telling me what she was learning and how her editing was progressing. It seemed that Kat Mac liked it and was after her to hurry and finish it before the retreat ended so she could read it all."

"Did she tell you anything else about the retreat, like the people she'd met?"

"Yeah, did she have a person like Daryl in her class?" Sally asked, with a grin.

Bonnie smiled faintly then her face clouded. "She did say she'd met a guy in the class. They went out three times and then she said that he seemed to think they had a relationship while she thought they were just friends. 'I guess it's time I got out of this', was the last she'd text me about it."

"How close was this to when she died?" Love, or lack thereof, was often considered a good reason for murder.

Bonnie shook her head. "A couple days before, I think. She was always getting herself out of something like that. I'd quit paying attention."

"Did she give his name, describe him?"

"No name. He was in his forties with graying hair."

"Did she text you about anything else?" This was getting them no where. It was going to be difficult telling Bonnie that she didn't know how she could help her, that there just wasn't anything she could go on.

"Well, on the day she died, she did text me that she had great news and would tell me all about it when she got home."

"Did she hint what it was?"

"No, but I assumed it was about her novel. Maybe Kat Mac liked it enough to help her find an agent or a publisher."

"Do you know if there was a publisher who was to come on

the last Friday like is coming to our retreat?" Sally asked.

Elizabeth looked at her and smiled. She did know how to ask questions. And that was good because she knew about the retreat.

"No." Bonnie brightened. "But we could ask Kat Mac."

Sally nodded.

"Did you find her manuscript?" Elizabeth asked.

"I never thought to look for it. My aunt was given all her stuff from here. It may have been in there."

Elizabeth didn't know what else to ask. Nothing Bonnie had said pointed to murder. There wasn't a jealous husband, a divorce happening, and it was doubtful that a guy she'd just met would kill her, unless he was one of those serial killers. And that would be up to the police to know about.

"So tell me why you think it was murder instead of an accident."

"Ever since we were children Sylvia hated to see or do something twice. She wouldn't watch a movie she'd already seen, she wouldn't reread a book, she never wanted to go to a place she'd already visited. She always said, 'Been there, done that.'"

"Can you describe where she was found?"

"The police said that she tripped or slipped on the concrete steps leading into the Upper Village and fell down some of them, banging her head on the edge of one. She died instantly." Bonnie looked down at her hands. "I went there to see them. I really can't understand how she could fall on them. They are certainly wide enough and not steep."

"Yes," Elizabeth nodded. "I've been there."

"Why didn't you come last year?" Sally asked.

"Because Kat Mac didn't teach last year. She took a year off to work on a book and it's being published this year."

"Do you have a picture of Sylvia?" Elizabeth asked.

Bonnie reached into her pack and pulled out a small album. She turned to the back and showed Elizabeth a picture. Sally leaned over to look.

"Wow, you two do look alike," Sally said.

"Yes, people often mistook us for sisters."

"Do you have an extra one for us?" Elizabeth asked.

"Yes." Bonnie flipped through the album until she found one. "Here, this was taken a year before her death."

"Thank you." Elizabeth put it in her pack. She wasn't sure if she would need it but it wouldn't hurt to have it.

Bonnie pulled her box of Angel cards from her pack. "I don't know if Sally told you about these," she said, as she began to shuffle.

"Yes, she mentioned them," Elizabeth said. She looked at Sally who shrugged.

"So, she told you about Bridgette?" Bonnie turned over the card. "She's warning me about something and I'm sure it has to do with our class because there are thirteen students in it."

Bonnie selected the next card. "I never showed anyone else, but this card always follows." She laid down Adriana. "She tells me that she is leading me towards the answer to my prayers."

"So you feel because of these two cards that you will find an answer to what happened to Sylvia?" Elizabeth asked.

"Yes. And I think that it's too much of a coincidence that you just happen to be here. It's as if Adriana was pointing me in your direction."

Elizabeth didn't know what to say to that. She didn't know enough about the cards to believe in them or to ask any questions about their meanings.

"Are you really interested in taking the course or did you come specifically to find out what happened to Sylvia?" Sally asked.

"It was all because of Sylvia," Bonnie admitted. "I haven't done any assignments nor taken any notes. I've just been watching Kat Mac and wandering around listening to conversations."

"Have you learned anything?"

Bonnie shook her head. She looked at Elizabeth. "So, like I told Sally today, I'm going to mention Sylvia's death tomorrow."

"It's doubtful that any of the same students were here two years ago."

"Yes, but word will get around and maybe some one who is taking a different class now was here at the same time as Sylvia."

"Michael was," Sally said suddenly.

"Who?" Bonnie asked.

"A man named Michael Wolf was here two years ago taking Kat Mac's course. His novel is getting published and he's back now learning how to make it into a screen play."

"Where did you meet him?" Bonnie leaned forward excitedly. "When did you meet him?"

"I met him the first day," Sally said. "And now that I think of it, he does look like he could be the man Sylvia described."

"Can we talk with him tomorrow?" Bonnie asked. "Will you introduce me?"

"Sure, if I see him."

"Great." Bonnie rubbed her hands together. "At last I'm getting somewhere."

"Be careful," Elizabeth cautioned. "If a person has killed once, he or she will do it again."

* * *

I need to sleep. I was so embarrassed today. I fell asleep again in class. I don't know how long I was out but my classmate nudged me and woke me up. I hope Kat Mac didn't notice. But I can't sleep yet. Mikk is ready to tell his side of the visit to the planet. I have been waiting impatiently to hear it.

Mikk tells me how he couldn't get the idea of Gwin being dead out of his mind. It didn't seem right. If she hadn't been charged with murder and sent to a prisoner's colony possibly perishing there, they would be married by now. They would have gone to another planet for their honeymoon, then returned and settled down into married life. Possibly Gwin would be expecting their child. It just wasn't fair.

* * *

Since he had been on the team that designed the tools taken to the colony Mikk had put his name in to go on a rescue/info gathering flight to the colony. One day when he arrived at his office he found an envelope from the Space Organization. Inside was a note that a space ship would be leaving for the colony planet in a month and there was a place for him on it if he still wished to go. He immediately accepted.

He couldn't believe his luck at finding Gwin alive and at seeing a birth of one the inhabitants. When he'd learned that it took about a year for the baby to learn to speak or to walk he'd immediately recognized the child as the unformed mind that they needed for their experiment.

"Are there going to be any more births?" he asked Gwin on their way back to the village.

"Yes. Another one soon."

"Good." Mikk rubbed his hands together. "Are there any other people on the planet?"

"I haven't met any," Gwin replied. "But my friends leave in the spring for a large gathering of others."

He hesitated, then asked. "Will you come to the ship with me?" He could see her tense up and waited for her answer.

"I don't want to meet the people on the ship. I don't want the noise and the questions and the fact that they will still consider me a prisoner. They might even lock me up so that I can't go back to my friends."

Mikk didn't want to argue with her because he knew that what she said was probably true. "Will I see you tomorrow?"

"I'll meet you at the fields when the sun is high in the sky but only if you go there alone."

Mikk nodded. He put his arms around her. "I've missed you so very much. I can't wait until we have our life back." Gwin sunk her head into his shoulder. It felt so good to feel her again.

The next morning Mikk waited for her to appear. He knew that she would make sure he was alone first. When she was satisfied she stepped out into the open. Mikk smiled when he saw her. She ran to his waiting arms.

"Come for a walk with me," Gwin said, pulling on his arm. "I want you to see how beautiful it is here.

Mikk went willingly.

"How did your experiment work?" Gwin asked, as they

walked.

Mikk explained how it had been a partial success with the body thawing perfectly but the mind being lost. "Now I've combined forces with a group who were trying to separate the mind from the body. They managed to do that and sent the mind to another planet to occupy a mind there. Each time, though, the original mind proved too strong and fought the take over."

"So both experiments failed."

"Not really. In fact…" Mikk paused.

"What?" Gwin asked.

"We're trying it again."

"You are?"

"I sent a message to Bob about the inhabitants here."

"You promised." Gwin turned to him angrily.

He stopped, too. "I promised not to tell anyone on the space ship."

"So what are you going to do?"

Mikk put his hands on her shoulders. He hoped she would understand. "You know we need a place for our prisoners," he explained. "If we remove their minds and send the minds here to be placed in a baby's body then we can freeze the prisoner's body and keep it in storage until his or her prison sentence is up."

"What?" Gwin asked, horrified. She stepped away from him. "You're going to put the mind of a murderer from our planet into the body of a baby on this planet?"

"It's a perfect solution to our problem." He let his arms drop.

"But what about these people?"

"I can't see that it will make any difference to them. You said the baby doesn't talk until a year old. By then the learning of this life will have wiped out any memory of a past life."

"But these are basically peaceful people. There is seldom any controversy among them. You can't disrupt their lives just to make life easier on your planet."

"This won't disrupt their lives. They won't even know it's happening."

"Oh, Mikk," Gwin begged, almost in tears. "You don't

know them. You don't know how nice they are. They saved my life. You can't do this to them."

"It wasn't my decision," Mikk said. "Bob put it in front of the Leaders and they decided."

* * *

Then suddenly, Gwin takes over telling the story.

* * *

"Bob is sending a mind to enter the body of the baby about to be born." Mikk said, as he strode towards the valley.

Gwin hurried after him. She hadn't realized until now just how much his research meant to him. It came first in his life, ahead of any morality, any thought about consequences. It probably would have come ahead of her if she'd been around to find out.

"I forbid you to do it," she said.

"It's too late. Bob already has sent a signal to the cave. It will let him know when to send the mind."

Gwin couldn't describe her anger, her fear. What had she done to these people? "How will you know if it happened?" There always was the chance that it wouldn't work.

Mikk shrugged. "I'll be looking for a difference in the birth, something that has never happened before. And since I've only seen one birth, I'd like your help."

"You want me to help you destroy this group of people, my friends?"

Mikk sighed in exasperation. "This won't destroy them. All that will happen is that the mind of the baby will be taken over by the mind of the prisoner."

"That's all?" Gwin asked, with sarcasm. "And what happens as the child grows? Will it become like the prisoner, a murderer or a thief?"

"What do they have worth stealing?"

"It may not look like much to you but what they have means a lot to them."

They reached the cave and when the inhabitants saw that her friend had returned they invited him into the cave.

Mela was in labour. She had two previous children so her labour didn't last long. It had begun just before their noon meal and now she was in the squatting position. The baby's head appeared then it's body. When it was fully out and in the hands of one of the women it immediately began to cry. This startled everyone. They looked at the newborn boy then at each other. Never before had a baby cried at birth.

They gestured and talked. Was there something wrong with him? Was he deformed? Had the woman helper hurt him? She shook her head and was believed. After all, she'd helped with many births and each one of them had been normal. The little boy finally quit crying. The father lifted the naked baby and held it up so everyone could see that it looked like the rest of them. There were no missing limbs, no enlarged or shrunken head, no reason for the cry. He laid his son down, wrapped him in a hide and handed him to Mela. She took him and hugged him to her chest.

* * *

Mikk interrupts.

* * *

Mikk stood in awe remembering the scream of the prisoner when his mind had been separated from his body. The experiment had worked. The prisoner's mind was now in this little body and would be for the next four of this planet's years.

"The baby crying means the experiment was a success, doesn't it?" Gwin said bitterly. She left the cave and he followed her.

"What made him cry?" Gwin demanded when they were outside.

"Just as the mind is separated from the body the prisoners emit a scream. It must be carried over to when they enter the body which is right at the time of birth."

"So what are you going to do with this now?"

"We will signal the mind that it is to leave this body and return home."

"And when will this happen?"

"In four of your years. That's when I will return for the final time and watch to see if the young boy's body is discarded."

"Discarded? What do you mean, discarded?"

"The boy will die."

Gwin gasped. "You mean you're going to kill him when he is only four years old? How could you do that to him and his family, to all of us who will love him?"

"It is part of the experiment."

"I never thought you could be so cold. That your experiment would mean more to you than a people."

"They're not considered people by our standards."

"And so they can just be manipulated as you wish."

"We need to find a place for our prisoners."

"Find some place else where they can build a colony like the Leaders originally planned."

"It's not feasible anymore, now that this will work."

"And to think I thought I loved you," Gwin spat out then turned and walked away.

"Gwin, wait," he called. He ran over to her and put his hand on her arm. He turned her to face him. "I know it sounds harsh and cruel but it's no different than the takeover wars that have been fought for centuries by the planets. Every nation on every planet tries to enhance their circumstances and if it is at the expense of another race, so be it. That's life."

"But these people can't even fight back. They don't even know they have an enemy."

"We're not the enemy."

"What are you then, benefactors?"

"No. But we plan on coming back here periodically to see how the experiment is going. We'll be able to help these people, guide them to improving their lives."

"And how do you propose to do that?"

"We can show them how to make better tools, how to build

shelters, how to design something to make the transportation of their goods easier. After all, isn't that what you've been doing with your grain and vegetables?"

"They won't understand any of it."

"It will be introduced slowly over hundreds of years. And as they grasp more they will be taught more."

"How will you do that?"

"We're working on a special chip that can be put into certain minds. It will give the host an idea for some invention that will enhance their civilization. We won't do it often, just enough to advance the people into a society atmosphere. They will eventually gather into villages and work together."

"Just like our ancestors did?"

"Much the same way."

"So you'll ultimately turn them into us."

"Not us exactly. They will remain the same shape just have our minds."

"So once they know our technology they will wreck this planet as we did ours."

"Maybe not," Mikk said, softly. "Maybe we can program them so they won't make our mistakes."

Mikk left the next day. He was anxious to begin the process of choosing more subjects. If their experiment was a success then it would be tried on different groups in other part of the planet.

* * *

I sit back. I think it's finished at last. Then I reach for my cell phone and dial a number.

"Hello?"

"Hi, Mom. I have a question."

"Okay, sweetheart. Ask away."

"Did I cry when I was born."

"What a funny question. Why are you asking?"

"It's for my sci-fi retreat."

"Oh, then yes you did, loud and long. Just like you were angry at being born."

"Thanks Mom."

Wasn't it the 19th century Austrian composer Franz Schubert who said. "I don't make up my music, I remember it."

Chapter 12

Again, Bonnie walked with Sally to the retreat. They passed the yard with the flowers but no one was out.

"If you see this Michael Wolf point him out to me," Bonnie said, as they reached the parking lot."

Sally looked over the group out front, "I don't see him," she said. "In fact, I've only seen him twice so he might be spending his spare time working on his screen play."

"Maybe I'll go to the script writing room after class today and ask for him," Bonnie said.

Before the lecture began Kat Mac announced that Kendra had dropped out of the class. "That should put to rest the worry about thirteen students," she said, looking meaningfully at Bonnie.

The first part of the morning those students who had completed the assignment read their versions of the Armageddon ending. When it was Sally's turn she hesitated, then decided to take the leap. After all, she had come here to find out if she could write science fiction. The reaction to her version would give her a good idea.

The reading went better than she expected. There were a few positive comments, then it was Lisa's turn.

During break most of the class went to the atrium for a snack.

"How did your meeting go with Kat Mac?" Sally asked Reggie, as they each got a coffee.

"Better than I though. She gave me a few pointers about how to keep my story on track and not to put in too much extra stuff that will confuse the reader." He took a sip. "Are you booked to see her?"

Sally shook her head. "I haven't got enough done to really know where the story is going."

"Well, you should at least chat with her. You could get some questions asked."

Sally nodded as they walked over to the regular group at

the couches. They arrived in time to hear Daryl sarcastically ask Bonnie. "What did your cards tell you today?"

"That someone in my class doesn't like me and resents me being here," Bonnie said calmly.

"Maybe you should heed them and get out of this class. After all, you really aren't getting anything out of it and you certainly aren't contributing to it."

Instead of answering Bonnie asked. "Did you know that a woman from Kat Mac's class was murdered here two years ago?"

Sally watched the shock on everyone's face at this announcement. Daryl even started in surprise, then regained his composure. "What has that to do with Angel cards or taking this course?"

"Well, the Angel cards are warning me to be careful."

"And my reading was so true," Lisa said. "The cards know what is going to happen."

"I don't believe this." Daryl threw his hand in the air. "I really can't understand how any of you were allowed into the class." He walked to the coffee machine.

"I never heard that someone was murdered here two years ago," Kirk said. "What happened?"

"She fell down some steps and died from her injuries."

"So, it was an accident," Lisa said.

"That's what the police said," Bonnie answered. "But I know differently."

Before anyone could ask how she knew, Kat Mac came up to them. "It's time for class," she said.

"Hey, Kat Mac," Daryl called. "I have a question for you."

"Sure," Kat Mac smiled. "What can I help you with?"

He smirked at Bonnie. "Well, Bonnie here has been warned by her Angel cards to be on guard because something bad is going to happen," he explained. "And she also said that a woman from your class was murdered two years ago."

Sally saw Kat Mac's face tighten for just a moment and then relax. She wondered if any one else had noticed the quick change.

"She wasn't murdered," Kat Mac corrected. "She died from

an accident."

"No, she didn't," Bonnie said emphatically.

"How do you know that?" Daryl asked. "Did your cards tell you?"

"She was my cousin and I just know."

"Your cousin?" Lisa gasped.

Sally was watching the reaction to this statement. Again, some appeared shocked, but others varied from mildly interested to looking as if they weren't quite sure if they should believe it. Kat Mac seemed uneasy as she walked towards the classroom.

"And I've asked Sally and her detective friend to help me prove it," Bonnie said.

Everyone looked at her and Sally wished that Bonnie had kept quiet about that. If there was a murderer at the retreat, they had just been warned.

"How many students were in the class Kat Mac?" Daryl asked.

Kat Mac turned and looked at him. "I don't remember but I doubt that it was thirteen, if that's what you want to know."

As they gathered up their books and packs, Bonnie leaned towards Sally. "Maybe now something will happen to help us," she whispered.

Sally nodded although she couldn't think what it might be, other than the supposed murderer trying to kill them.

Kat Mac's talk for the rest of the morning was about world building, creating cultures, and coming up with names in fantasy writing. Sally actually found it worth listening to.

* * *

I was different from most of the students in high school. I didn't play any sports, didn't have the physique and coordination that was required. I didn't attend many social functions. Instead I belonged to the photography club and I played in the band. I was shy and had trouble expressing myself verbally so I spent much of my time writing on my computer. I was called a geek, a nerd, and was easy prey for bullies.

Although I'm trying to participate in the discussions and assignments, I'm sure that Daryl thinks I'm the nerd of this class. But, I wonder, now that I am an adult am I still classified as a nerd? Does the word nerd have a best before date? Are you a nerd in school and then something else as an adult or does the term follow you throughout your life? Are there senior nerds with gray hair and canes? I shake my head and think about the class.

It's certainly a mixture of writers and wannabes. Maybe, as Daryl keeps saying, the applicants should have been screened better. Maybe, they should offer different classes, one for beginners, one for those who have something written, and one for those who have something published. At least then the more experienced or serious ones would not be held back by the beginners.

But, it seems that if they are willing to pay the money they are accepted. I know that ticks off Daryl as well as some of the other students but from my point of view everyone should be given a chance to learn if writing science fiction or fantasy is really what they want to do, and how better to find out than to take a class like this.

Take Sally Matthews for instance. She admitted not knowing much about the genre except that she likes to read it. She continually downplays her S/F writing and experience but she does have some good ideas. Her revision of the ending for Armageddon was so totally different that it took me by surprise and I could tell that Kat Mac was caught off guard also. Afterwards, I heard her tell Sally that she would like to see some of her other works and that she still had an opening one afternoon if Sally wanted to discuss her writing. Sally replied that she didn't really think she had something worth discussing, yet.

I wonder what type of relationship Sally has with her friend Elizabeth. I would like to ask her out for a drink some evening but I don't want to intrude. I could, however, suggest that some of us students get together. So far, once lunch is over everyone has headed in their own direction, me especially since I know that I must receive the rest of my story. I'm sure Sally would think a drink a good idea since she seems to get along with many of us

Then I could ask her out....

* * *

Elizabeth took Chevy behind the bed and breakfast and climbed the hill to reach the trail system.

She started out on White Gold Traverse with Chevy on his leash. The restriction didn't hamper his exploring and his darting from tree to tree. Elizabeth came to a sign and the Dinah Moe Humm Trail. On her map she saw that it would cross Centennial and when it did she swung onto it. This trail paralleled White Gold Traverse back the way she'd come. When it eventually intersected with it she returned to the bed and breakfast on the traverse.

She didn't want to go to her room so Elizabeth decided to walk around the neighbourhood. She walked to Fitzsimmons Road South and followed it, then turned onto Toni Sailer Lane. Some of the houses and yards were impressive while others were quite normal. On her way back to the bed and breakfast she saw Cynthia in her yard. Before she could decide if she should she go and talk with her, Cynthia looked up and raised her hand. Elizabeth waved back and sauntered up the driveway.

"Come around to the back," Cynthia said. "I'll get us some juice and we can talk."

By this time Chevy was tired and ready to rest. When Elizabeth sat at the patio table Chevy laid down under her chair and quickly went to sleep. While she waited she looked around. There wasn't much of a yard, mainly the patio and a small grassy area.

"How long have you lived here?" Elizabeth asked, when Cynthia came back with the pitcher of juice and two glasses.

"About twenty years. I came here to teach school for a year and ended up staying." Cynthia poured them each a glass.

"It is a beautiful place to live."

"So, do you want to work for me?" Cynthia asked abruptly, as she sat in her chair.

Elizabeth had been expecting this. "As I've said, I'm not a professional private investigator."

"Do you want to hear what I would pay you?"

This time Elizabeth shook her head. "I really can't do it for you. I don't have a licence and besides, the police are looking into it."

"Please, think about it," Cynthia said. "It's very important to me and to a lot of other people, especially the girl's child."

"What child?" Oh, oh. She shouldn't ask that.

"The one she put up for adoption."

"How do you know so much?" Elizabeth took a sip of her juice.

"I talked with her."

Elizabeth recognized the feeling of intrigue that she'd had at the beginning of the other mysteries. She wanted to know more even though she wasn't going to work for Cynthia. "Where did she come from?"

Cynthia smiled. "I'll only tell you more if you take the case."

"But, I'm not a private investigator." Elizabeth tried to keep the exasperation out of her voice. "I haven't had any training and I don't have a licence. I can't take your money and I can't legally "take any cases", as you put it."

"I'll give you cash and that way no one will know."

Elizabeth shook her head and stood. As much as she hated to turn down this mystery she said. "If I took money I would have to make it a priority and my writing comes first right now."

Cynthia sat back in her chair. "Okay," she said. She seemed to be contemplating what to say next. "If I tell you the story, will you think it over?"

Elizabeth knew she would because she was already curious as to why the woman wanted the information. She sat back down.

"Just over two years ago there was a knock on my door. When I opened it a young woman was standing on the step. She was nervous and apologized for bothering me but said she needed to ask me some questions. What kind of questions, I asked. She hesitated then turned and looked at the house across the road. 'About that house,' she answered. I asked her what about the house and she said she needed to know everything about who owned it and who looked after renting it out."

Cynthia reached for her glass and drank half of it. Elizabeth wondered if she was actually thirsty or thinking of how much more to tell her.

"I told her that I didn't know who the owners were but as far as I knew they lived in Vancouver," Cynthia continued. "And I didn't know who looked after the renting of it."

"What did she do when you told her that?" Elizabeth asked. She looked under her chair. Chevy was still fast asleep.

"She started to cry."

"Cry?" Elizabeth hadn't expected that answer.

"Yes," Cynthia nodded. "I didn't know what to do so I invited her in. She said her name was Penny but it took me a while to get the story out of her. Apparently she'd lived in that house for a week the year before. She'd been pregnant and had come here to have her baby and give it up for adoption."

"What?" Elizabeth had a hard time following Cynthia.

"Let me try to clarify it for you. From what she told me, Penny was seventeen when she got pregnant. She'd gone to a clinic in Vancouver and one of the nurses there had told her that she could make some money by putting the child up for adoption. Since her parents didn't want her to have the child and had told her they wouldn't help her raise it, she agreed. When she was close to her due date she came to Whistler with the nurse and stayed in the house across the street. She went into the hospital to have the baby and a woman showed up right after the birth to pick up the child."

"So why did she come back here?"

"She told me she had inherited some money and she wanted to find the son she had given up. She'd been to the clinic to see the nurse who had been her first contact but the woman no longer worked there. So, she came here to see if she could find out anything from us neighbours."

"And you think her story was true?" Elizabeth asked.

"Well, she was driving a new car and her clothes were pretty fancy."

"So what happened to her? Did she find her son?"

"That I don't know. She came back to see me the next day

and we talked a bit about her life. We made a date to meet the next morning for breakfast but she never showed up."

"And that's why you think the body may be hers?" This was getting very vague, verging on the make believe.

"Yes," Cynthia nodded.

Elizabeth didn't want to come right out and say that she thought Cynthia's reasoning was a bit off. "Just because she forgot about a breakfast date doesn't mean that she was murdered."

"I don't think she forgot. She was the one who asked me to meet her."

"Okay, so where was she staying?" Elizabeth asked. "What happened to her car? If she hadn't checked out of wherever she was staying and her car had been left in the parking lot then someone would have gotten suspicious."

"I don't know. There was nothing on the news or in the paper about someone not returning to their room and no car was ever found abandoned, at least not that I heard about."

"So who do you think killed Penny?" Elizabeth wasn't sure if she should encourage Cynthia's thinking.

"I don't know but someone did."

"The only problem with that is that we don't know if the dead girl is Penny."

"I have a feeling it is," Cynthia said sombrely.

"Did you tell the police?"

"I did but because I don't have anything solid to give them as evidence, I don't think they believed me."

"Do you know if there were other girls who came to stay in that house?"

"There could have been. Like some of the houses around here that place was rented out to many different people especially during the skiing season."

"So, no one lived there on a permanent basis for any length of time?"

Cynthia shook her head.

"Why wouldn't you tell me this in front of Alison?"

"I don't trust her."

"You don't? Why?"

"Because she and her husband look an awful lot like a couple who lived on Fitzsimmons Road North for a few years."

"I don't understand," Elizabeth said.

"A few years ago a couple who look like Alison and Rick lived in a house on Fitzsimmons Road North. About two years ago they sold their house and then three months ago they rented the place next door."

"And you figure they moved away and then came back?"

"Yes."

"What if they just lived somewhere else in Whistler?"

"They could have, except Alison told me they had moved from Kamloops."

"How do they act?"

"What do you mean?"

"Well, are they hiding the fact that they lived here before or has it just never come up?"

"It's never really come up. I haven't had the guts to say anything and they haven't volunteered any information about themselves except that they didn't really care for Kamloops and they have three children."

"And you think their moving back here has something to do with the young woman?"

"It seems funny to me that they leave and then return a couple of years later."

"Maybe after they left they realized how much they like it here and decided to come back," Elizabeth pointed out. "Other people have moved back to places they have left."

"Or," Cynthia said. "maybe they killed Penny and left. Then they heard the house was being demolished and they came back to see what happens."

"You'd think they would get as far away from here as possible."

"Well, like they say on the crime shows, the killer sometimes likes to come back to the scene of the crime."

"Were they known as Alison and Rick when they lived here before?"

"I've been trying to remember if their names are the same

but I can't."

"Did you ever meet them?"

"No. I just saw them around the neighbourhood and town."

"Then you don't know if they changed their."

"No, but if they are murderers, they probably did."

"Did you see them at the house across the road?"

Cynthia shook her head. "I don't remember that either. But if I did it probably wouldn't have stood out in my mind."

"Do they know that you recognize them?"

"I don't think so. When they first introduced themselves to me I thought they looked familiar. But it was a few days before I realized who they were. Then when Penny's body was found I pieced it together. Alison used to have mousy brown hair and dressed in regular clothes and Rick was about twenty pounds heavier. Now her hair is streaked reddish/blonde and she goes to the spa every week and you can tell their clothes are high end. She has a Mercedes and he drives a new BMW convertible. They dine out just about every night."

"Do you have anything else to go on, something they may have said that would point to them being involved in her death?" She would need more than Cynthia's piecing it together.

Cynthia shook her head. "That's it, but I know I'm right that they lived here before." She scrutinized Elizabeth. "So are you going to take the case?"

Elizabeth gave up trying to tell her she wasn't a real private detective. It seemed that she had that fixed in her mind. "I'll see what I can do," she said. "But don't expect me to do anything faster than the police."

"Oh, thank you," Cynthia said excitedly. "How much do I owe you?"

"Nothing right now."

Cynthia looked disappointed. "Don't you have a flat daily rate plus expenses?"

It dawned on Elizabeth that Cynthia liked the idea of the mystery and of hiring a private detective to solve it. "If I find out who killed this young woman, whether it's Penny or not, you have to donate one thousand dollars to the local SPCA."

"Our nearest SPCA is in Squamish."

Elizabeth nodded. "That will do. And if the police beat me to it, you will donate five hundred dollars to the SPCA for the time I spent on it."

That seemed to mollify Cynthia. "Do you have a contract for me to sign?" she asked.

"No," Elizabeth said seriously, although she had the urge to laugh. "I use a handshake, as in what used to be called a gentleman's agreement."

"You do? Isn't that a bit old fashioned?"

"It is but I still believe in taking people's word."

"Okay." Cynthia held out her hand. "We now have an agreement."

"We do." Elizabeth solemnly shook her hand.

"So what are you going to do first?"

"I'll probably speak with Alison and Rick and then maybe go to the police and ask what they've learned." She didn't think they would tell her anything but it seemed to be what Cynthia wanted to hear.

"Good." She rubbed her hands together. "And you will report back to me every day?"

Elizabeth stifled a groan. This was getting out of hand. "I will report when I have something to tell you." She leaned forward conspiratorially. "I don't think it would be a good idea for Alison and Rick to see us together too much. It might tip them off."

"You're right," Cynthia nodded. "I hadn't thought of that."

Elizabeth stood. "Let's go, Chevy," she said, looking under the chair.

Chevy woke at the sound of his name. He stood and stretched.

"I'll talk to you when I know something," she said to Cynthia.

Elizabeth grinned as she crossed the road to the bed and breakfast. Wait until Sally heard about this.

* * *

I thought I was finished, that I had written the end. I had even taken the last chapters on a disk over to Kat Mac, making sure no one saw me as she requested. She said there is a rule about instructors and students visiting each other. But tonight Gwin gives me one last account.

* * *

Over the four years until Mikk's return, Gwin watched the boy, who had been named Trog. His parents and fellow inhabitants, after their initial shock, adjusted to the birth and accepted him. Although he was growing normally, playing games with the other children, and learning the language and ways of his people, there was something different. He seemed more aggressive and more brutal than the other children. But that may only have been because she knew about his birth.

Other babies were born. None of them cried. Gwin decided that Mikk and his fellow scientists must be waiting to see if the discarding was a success before trying again with these people.

She was tempted to say something to the boy's parents, to warn them that he might not grow into an adult. But how could she explain it in a way they'd understand? How could she say that their lives were now controlled by the Leaders and scientists on a far away planet? They wouldn't even know what she was talking about.

She wondered, too, that if she hadn't been part of these people, if she still lived on her former planet, would she have given them any thought at all? Would she see it Mikk's way, that it was more important to sentence a prisoner than to protect a primitive people?

The children were playing in the remaining snow, making balls and throwing them at each other. Gwin was sitting outside enjoying a warm spring morning and watching them when she saw the space ship. She immediately looked around for a place to hide. She wanted to leave, to head into the trees and not return until it left. She couldn't bear to watch the boy die. But she knew she would be needed by the family. All the inhabitants were needed when one of them died.

It was just before their midday meal when Mikk walked along the path. She went up to him. They didn't embraced. Gwin's love had died. She surmised that Mikk's had, also.

"You don't have to do this," Gwin said, without even saying his name first.

"Yes, I do."

"But what about us and our feelings for the child?" Gwin asked, tears in her eyes. "We've watched him grow for the past four years. We've taught him, played with him. Don't we matter?"

"I'm sorry," Mikk said. "But this is our experiment and we must carry it through."

Gwin watched helplessly as Mikk went to the cave where he was again welcomed. The children quit their playing and headed inside for their meal. Gwin slowly followed them in. The meal of boiled meat and vegetables and flat bread was almost over when Trog began choking on a piece of meat. His hands clawed at his throat. He turned to his father who quickly put his finger down Trog's throat and dislodged the food.

Gwin watched Mikk expression as he stared at the boy. She felt excited, relieved. The plan had failed. She saw Trog look over at Mikk. He seemed to sneer as if he knew what had happened.

Mikk stomped out of the cave, Gwin following.

"It didn't work." She couldn't help gloating. "Are you going to leave them alone now?"

Mikk shook his head. "We thought that might happen," he said.

"That he wouldn't die?"

"No, that he wouldn't want to die. That he would fight not to go back."

"You think that's what happened? The prisoner refused to go back home."

"Yes, so we have a contingency plan."

Gwin felt her stomach knot. She wasn't sure if she wanted to hear this.

"We're going to send Enforcers." Mikk said, his attitude restored.

"Enforcers? What are they?"

"They will be the ones who are sent here to make sure that when a sentence is over the body dies so that the mind goes back."

"Will they be put into babies, also?"

"Yes, they will grow up like everyone else."

Gwin hesitated before asking the question. "Why do you want the minds back? Why not let the person here just grow up and die naturally?"

"We have been discussing that possibility but the prisoner's families and the Society for the Rights of Prisoners don't want them to die on another planet. They want everyone to come home to die."

"So you will be sending more minds," Gwin said, defeated.

"Yes."

"How many?"

"Before leaving last time, we scouted this planet. There are thousands of people living on it. Some are in groups the size of this, some in larger ones. We plan on sending all the murderers and tobacco dealers first, then we will be sentencing the lesser criminals here, too."

He started down the path to the former colony and the waiting space ship. Then he turned and looked back at her. "I got married last month and the Leaders have decided to call this planet Earth."

Over the next few years more babies cried at birth. Gwin watched them grow. She knew that they were being raised by good parents and taught the ways of the people but she wondered how much of their criminal past they would remember when they were older. She was glad she wouldn't be here to see it. She carefully watched the ones who didn't cry at birth. They were the natural ones, the ones who really belonged here. She hoped they thrived over the thousands of years that lay ahead and didn't let the invaders win.

* * *

It dawns on me. Am I an Enforcer? Was this story a way of

telling me that I am to end the lives of those who don't wish to return to Terrene once their sentences are over. Is that why there are killers, murderers? Are they just doing their job?

I go on the Internet and look up murderers. There are so many different types, serial killers, mass murderers, sadistic, power driven, sex driven, youth. Are some given multiple assignments, like serial and mass murderers? And some just one assignment like those who only take one life? Am I to be a killer? Will I be told what type of killer I am to be? Will I be kind, doing the deed fast so that the victim doesn't suffer? Will I be a sadistic murderer, wanting to see the pain and suffering, or maybe the type of murderer who likes the feeling of power, the control of seeing the fear in their eyes, wanting them to beg? Am I supposed to get some sort of satisfaction from the way I murder? Is it some sort of reward to me for something good I did on my home planet?

Then I wonder if the way they are killed here has something to do with what their crimes were on their planet. The worse their death here the worse their crimes there? Is this the last part of their sentence, to suffer in their death here as a lesson so that they don't repeat their crimes once they go back?

Chapter 13

"Oh, that's really sad if it is Penny," Sally said, when Elizabeth had told her the story. "Getting pregnant, giving up your baby for adoption, and then being murdered."

"Yes, but as the newscasters are pointing out, there are many, many other missing girls that she could be and more sad stories from families."

Sally nodded. "Plus, it sounds like your client watches a lot of crime shows and reads a lot of mystery novels. She seems to like the idea of hiring an investigator. You have to be careful that a lot of this isn't made up."

"Yes, it does sound quite involved but she doesn't have any real evidence."

"If this scenario is true about who the dead girl is then the owners may have been involved. Did Cynthia know who they are?"

"She said she didn't and so far, I haven't heard it mentioned on the news. I imagine the police know."

"Are you going to ask the police that when you talk to them?" Sally asked with a grin.

"We both know that I'm not going to ask them anything," Elizabeth said.

"Oh, but Cynthia will want to hear what you learned from them."

"If she does then I will tell her that I am doing some checking on my own. I'll say that I need the exact address of the place Rick and Alison lived in on Fitzsimmons Road North so that I can go to the town hall and see if they have indeed changed their names. That will keep her busy for a while. And if I delay things long enough, the police will figure it out before I have to tell her anything." Elizabeth changed the subject. "So did Bonnie tell everyone about her cousin?"

"She did. It seemed to catch Kat Mac off guard but I'm not sure if it was because Bonnie used the word murder instead of accident. Or it might have been that she didn't expect anyone to know about it."

"What did the other students say?"

"Some were surprised, others acted bored with it. The news certainly didn't put a damper on the lecture today."

"Did she talk with that Michael Wolf?"

"She was going to go upstairs to the screen writing room after class and see if he was there. I haven't seen her since so I don't know if she did get to speak with him."

* * *

It's evening. Kat Mac has invited me over to her place to discuss my manuscript. I take along a DVD with the whole story including the last chapter. I hand it to her.

"What is this?"

"It's the manuscript with the final chapter."

"Final Chapter? I thought you had given me everything."

"This just finishes the story."

She takes the DVD eagerly from my hands and puts it in her computer. I can almost follow the words as she reads it.

Kat Mac looks at me when she is finished. "Yes, that's a better conclusion." *She grins.* "After reading your work I am wondering if I cried at birth."

I nod. "As soon as Gwin had finished telling me I had to phone my mother to ask her that."

"What do you mean that Gwin told you this?"

I hesitate. Do I tell her that two voices revealed this story to me, that I believe it to be true? No, I don't think that's wise. Because, while this is credible to me, to her it's just fiction. "I guess I just got so wound up in the story that the characters seem real to me."

"Ah, the sign of a natural born writer." *Kat Mac nodded.* "You are lucky. Most writers struggle from word to word with the plot and the story."

She held up the DVD. "What a great idea that the babies who cried at birth here on Earth are murderers from another planet. And the people who are murdered here are at the end of their criminal sentence and are sent back home. I think the best is that you make it look like the people here on Earth who are murderers are the Enforcers. You have a great imagination."

I blush and feel like a fraud. For it wasn't my writing. I was just the instrument through which Mikk and Gwin told their story.

"It still needs more editing. There are other angles you could add, some you could take away."

I open my mouth, then close it. What can I say? I edited it as I was going but not to change anything. I was just correcting my mistakes and trying to remember what I may have missed. I did take out a few things that I thought wouldn't change the story. But I kept them in a separate file in case what I was told later was related to something I had removed.

"What did you have in mind?" I ask.

"Well, this does make it look like it's an explanation of how our ancestors, the cave people, went from hunter gathers to growing their own grain and vegetables about 10,000 years ago. But I don't think many people know about that change in our history so that has to be embellished a little more."

Kat Mac's eyes have a far away look to them. It seems as if she's talking to herself instead of to me.

"And," she continues. "Mikk states that chips will be put in some minds to teach the people here to improve their circumstances to make it look like this was the way that people developed the great ideas that have gotten us to the techno age where we are now. I think that needs to be changed to the minds of the prisoners are much more advanced than the cave peoples so that they would naturally have the ideas on how to improve their lives."

Again, I pretend to think that over.

"Do you have more copies?" She suddenly asks me.

"Yes."

"Are they safe?

"Yes, I have it on my laptop in my room, then a backup DVD, and the DVD I brought you."

"Just the three?"

"I think that's enough. If I lose my computer or if it's stolen I still have the DVDs."

I'm on cloud nine, as they say, when I leave Kat Mac's place. She really does like my story. She's going to talk with the publisher about it, pitch it to him before next Friday. This is so much better than I expected. I don't feel like going to my room. I have to walk a bit and enjoy this feeling. It's already dark, though. I've never been one to be out after dark but I just can't sit. I begin walking down the street going over the story and my conversation with Kat Mac. It's still surreal that it happened so fast.

But I also have a question. We all die. Are those who die of natural causes the authentic inhabitants of this planet and those who are killed in accidents or murdered the ones from Terrene?

Then I notice footsteps behind me. My heart jumps in fear. Is it someone out enjoying the evening like me or is someone following me? Then I think, how stupid. Why would anyone follow me? But they steadily keep coming, seem to be catching up to me. Is the person in a hurry?

I want to turn and look to see who it is but I'm afraid to. Why didn't I go straight to my room? Should I run to one of the houses and bang on the door? I feel my cell phone in my pocket. I could dial 911 and plead for help.

A stupid thought enters my mind. Is my sentence up? Have I refused to die so am about to be murdered? Is he or she an Enforcer from Terrene who's job it is to send me back home? Was that why I was told this story? To let me know that I can run but I can't hide?

* * *

After walking Chevy, Elizabeth joined Sally in the dining room for breakfast. They were the only ones there although the table next to theirs had the remains of food on two plates.

"We always seem to miss the breakfast crowd," Elizabeth said.

"Well, I don't mind not being in the same room with Daryl," Sally said. "But I wonder where Bonnie is."

"Yes, I was looking forward to hearing how her meeting with Michael Wolf went."

"Do you want me to call you after I see her this morning?" Sally asked with a grin. "Or are you going to be busy tracking down the killer of the young woman for your client?"

Elizabeth made a face. "I don't have a client. But I will probably go talk with Alison and Rick."

Their conversation stopped as Beverly brought in their breakfast of omelette, fruit bowl, and biscuits.

"This looks so good," Elizabeth said, eyeing her plate. "Do you have a hard time coming up with something different every morning?"

Beverly shook her head. "No, I have a number of menus that I've made up and I go through them and pick out the ones that I think my guests will like."

"Any idea of what to ask Alison and Rick?" Sally asked, after Beverly left the room.

"No. I have to be careful that I don't say anything that will point to the fact that I know they've lived here before."

"If they actually have." Sally ate a strawberry.

Elizabeth nodded. She cut into her omelette and ate a bite. "Um, is this delicious."

"What day are we going to see your grandmother this weekend?" Sally asked, trying her own.

"Whatever one works for you. Do you have any homework to catch up on or want to work on your novel?"

Sally shook her head. "No. I could use some time away from lectures and writing."

"Are things starting to make more sense, like that Michael said it would?"

"Actually, yes they are. Plus, now Kat Mac is getting more into what to include, and not include, in science fiction. Her talk today is about how some modern inventions were predicted in past science fiction novels and short stories and how to take inventions of modern science and project them, or their offshoots, into the future."

"Sounds heavy," Elizabeth said. "So, let's set Sunday as the day to go to Vancouver. I'll call Grandma and let her know we'll be there sometime late morning. That will give us time to visit Granville Island also."

"Good." Sally looked at her watch and stood. "I'd better go. See you later."

Elizabeth remained at the table enjoying another glass of juice. By the time Beverly returned to clean the table Elizabeth had formulated some questions to ask her.

"How long have you had this bed and breakfast?" she asked as an opener.

"Oh, years," Beverly answered, gathering up the dirty plates.

"So you would know many of the people who have lived in the area in the past."

"Are you working on the death of the young woman?" Beverly asked, setting the plates back on the table.

Boy, how did she answer that question? "Not really working on it," Elizabeth said crossing her fingers behind her back. "I'm just a little curious."

"And you want to ask me some questions," Beverly smiled.

"Do you mind?"

"Not yet, but that might change depending on what you ask." She sat in the chair Sally had exited.

"What do you know about the people who owned the house next door?"

"Not much. They bought it about ten years ago and then have mostly rented it out."

"Did they ever live there?"

"No."

"Not even during skiing season?" Wasn't coming to Whistler for the winter the reason most people owned a place here?

Beverly shook her head.

"How long did the tenants stay?"

"Not long. I think it was rented out mainly to the skiing crowd in the winter and the occasional tourist in the summer."

"Did you ever meet any of the tenants?"

Beverly shook her head. "I would sometimes see the renters

but seldom ever talked to them. Running a bed and breakfast means that I spend a lot of time inside cleaning rooms, baking, and doing laundry."

"Did a young woman come to you about two years ago asking about the owners of the house?"

Beverly thought a moment. "If she did, I don't remember."

"Do you remember any pregnant girls being there?"

"There may have been, but like I said, I didn't have much time to notice what was going on next door."

* * *

Sally watched for Bonnie on her walk to the retreat. She wasn't in the group talking outside the building and she wasn't in her seat when the class started. Where was she? Had Michael Wolf given her some information about her cousin and was she now checking into it? But surely she would have contacted us if she'd learned anything. After all, Elizabeth was the one who solved these things and Bonnie had stated she wanted help from her.

Sally decided that speculation on her part would get her nowhere. Bonnie may just be ill and staying in her room until she felt better. But even as she thought it she knew that Bonnie wouldn't miss this morning. She'd been so excited yesterday about getting word out about her cousin's murder, as she called it, that she wouldn't have taken the chance that someone might have something to tell her today.

"Give it a rest," Sally admonished herself. "There's nothing you can do right now." She tried to take her mind off Bonnie by concentrating on Kat Mac's lecture.

"A lot of what is modern inventions could have started out as Science Fiction gadgets. Take for instance the Joymaker from the 1965 novel Age of the Pussyfoot was a transponder that connected you to a central computer in your city. This computer was shared by everyone else in the city. Early in life this Joymaker began to decide what each person wanted to do or watch on television or where they wanted to eat based on their interests, their likes and dislikes, etc. It was supposed to take away the guess work about which party to go to, where to shop, whether you should be friends with a certain person. There was no going on impulse, everything was figured out for you so that your day ran smoothly."

Kat Mac paused and looked around the room. "Can anyone guess today's application of this fictional tool?"

"It sounds kind of like a wireless personal digital assistant," Daryl said.

"Good," Kat Mac nodded with a smile. "Anyone else?"

"Well, Google eventually wants to have everyone's information in their data base so that could be the forerunner of Google's plan," Lisa said.

"Very good. I'm glad you picked up on that," Kat Mac said. "Does anyone else have an idea?"

The rest of the class was silent. Sally found herself watching the door willing it to open and Bonnie to enter, apologizing for her lateness. That didn't happen.

"Then there was The Game Players of Titan written by Philip K. Dick in 1963. A car in that book had an auto-mech that wouldn't let the driver drive it if he was drunk. Also, the car talked to the driver. Both of these features are now offered in many of today's vehicles."

Sally was getting more and more worried as the morning progressed. Where was Bonnie?

"Did you know there is a word for modern science imitating science fiction stories?" Kat Mac asked. "It's called Technovelgy." She wrote it on the blackboard breaking it into its components Tech novel gy.

Sally smiled while the others in the class laughed at the new word. She wrote it down in her notes wondering if it was actually a word accepted by the publishers of today's dictionaries.

"The informal definition for Technovelgy is: the creative ideas and inventions of science fiction writers," Kat Mac continued. "So one of the things a science fiction writer has to do is take modern inventions and tweak them to fit in your future world. Or better still come up with new inventions in your novel that could someday be used in real life."

During the break Sally looked for Michael Wolf in and

outside the building. When she didn't see him she got herself a cup of coffee and went over to where Lisa and Kirk were talking with Russ Peters and Reggie Shaw. Daryl walked up to her and asked. "So where's Ms Angel cards? Did she finally quit the class?"

"I don't know where Bonnie is," Sally said. "And I'm a little worried. Has anyone seen her since yesterday afternoon?"

The four others in the group shook their heads.

"I wouldn't worry about her," Daryl said, scornfully. "She has her cards to protect her."

"Why don't you knock it off with the cards?" Kirk asked.

Sally didn't wait to hear Daryl's reply. She headed to the stairs and climbed them to the second floor. She walked down the hallway looking for the sign for the screenwriters class. When she found it on one of the open doors she paused then walked into the room. There were three people sitting at tables typing on their computers. One of them was Michael.

"Excuse me, Michael," Sally said quietly, as she sat down beside him. She hoped she wasn't interrupting him in the middle of a great idea.

He looked up from his work and smiled. "Hi," he said.

"I haven't seen you for a while," Sally said.

"Yeah, I've been working on my script."

"Could we talk for a few minutes?"

"This sounds serious," Michael said. He hit save and turned to her. "What's the problem?"

"Did a woman named Bonnie speak with you yesterday?"

"Yes," Michael said. "She told me about her cousin Sylvia being murdered and she wanted to know if I had been in the same class with her two years ago."

"And had you?"

Michael nodded. "It took me a while to remember but then she described her red hair and I did. But I didn't recall anything about a murder. As far as I knew Sylvia death had been accidental."

"What else did Bonnie want to know?"

"If Sylvia liked the class and if she had talked with Kat Mac about her manuscript."

"And what did you answer?"

Michael looked at her quizzically. "Why are you asking me these questions?"

Sally hesitated. How much should she tell this man? If he knew Sylvia two years ago there was a chance he may have had something to do with her death, assuming, that is, that Bonnie was right. "Bonnie didn't show up at class this morning. I'm trying to find out where she might be."

"Well, the questions you are asking suggest there is more to it than that."

Oops. Was she that obvious? Now what did she say? How would Elizabeth handle this?

"Well," Sally said slowly, her mind racing through all the answers she could think of. He knew that Bonnie thought her cousin had been killed so would it be safe to say that she was worried about Bonnie's sudden disappearance because of that? "It's just that her Angel cards warned her that something bad might happen."

"What?" Michael asked, his eyebrows furrowing.

Oh geeze, she was sounding like an idiot. She should have thought this out better before racing up here acting like an incompetent detective.

Sally took a deep breath. "I'm just worried about Bonnie and I wanted to know if you had seen her yesterday."

"You know." Michael cocked his head to one side. "I could almost get the feeling that you think something has happened to her and that I might have had something to do with it."

"Oh, no," Sally protested quickly. "That's not it at all."

"Then maybe you should tell me what it is about."

"Okay," Sally sighed. What did she have to lose? She couldn't say anything worse than she had already.

Michael seemed to listen attentively as she explained Bonnie's suspicions about her cousin's death and that now she hadn't showed up for class.

"Did you check her room?" Michael asked.

Sally shook her head. "I'm going to after class but I wanted to talk with you before you left."

"So she could be sick and you are on a wild goose chase."

The room began to fill with students back from their break. Sally grimaced sheepishly. "Yes," she conceded.

"Well, why don't you find out before you ask any more questions?"

Sally knew when she was being dismissed and she thankfully left. She never wanted to go through that again. How did Elizabeth ask her questions so smoothly and get the answers so effortlessly?

Sally hurried to her class. She was no further ahead than before the break except she knew that Michael and Sylvia had been in the same class. Big deal. By now Elizabeth probably would have had most of it figured out.

Chapter 14

Elizabeth wondered how best to approach Alison and Rick. She couldn't outright ask them what their real names were and if they had lived here over two years ago. She couldn't even think of a reason to go knocking on their door.

With Chevy on his leash Elizabeth went to her vehicle and took out his ball. Immediately Chevy began jumping and whining. He loved his ball and would spend a whole day chasing it and bringing it back for her to throw again if she let him. She looked up and down the street. No cars were coming.

She threw the ball across the road and when Chevy headed after it, she let the leash slip out of her hand. She raced after him before he could find the ball and bring it back. It took him a while to locate the ball in the shrubbery and when he did, Elizabeth picked them both up and went to the front door. She rang the bell.

Alison opened the door.

"I'm sorry," Elizabeth said quickly. "I accidentally threw Chevy's ball too far and he got away from me and ran into your yard. I'm afraid he dug up some of your dirt trying to find it."

"That's okay." Alison smiled at Chevy and rubbed his head.

Elizabeth felt a bit ashamed. She had lied to this woman who was now petting her dog.

"Would you like to come in for a drink?" Alison asked.

Elizabeth pretended to hesitate not wanting to make it look like this was exactly what she had wanted in the first place. "Okay," she said, and stepped into the foyer. She removed her shoes and told Chevy to stay by the door.

"Oh, he can come in," Alison said. "I like dogs."

Elizabeth felt the shame return. How could someone who liked dogs be a killer? There had to be another explanation. But how was she going to find out what it was?

"Would you like a glass of wine or a cup of coffee?" Alison asked.

Wine this early? "Actually neither, thank you. I don't drink coffee and I'm not that fond of wine."

Rick entered the room. "I thought I heard voices," he said, with a smile.

"Elizabeth came to apologize because her dog dug in our dirt looking for his ball," Alison explained. She turned back to Elizabeth. "Well, we have juice or pop or water."

"I'll have a pop," Elizabeth said.

Alison headed to the kitchen and Rick followed leaving Elizabeth and Chevy standing in the living room. Why did he leave also? Were they having a quick discussion, deciding what to say to her? Don't be silly, she chided herself. Why would they think she was here for any other reason but on a friendly visit?

Alison returned with a glass of ginger ale and a cup of coffee. She handed the glass to Elizabeth then indicated for her to sit on the couch. Chevy laid at her feet. Alison sat down across from her on a chair. There was an awkward moment of silence.

Now what did she do? Elizabeth wondered. Jump right in and begin to ask questions? Make small talk? And where was Rick? Listening at the door or had he gone somewhere?

"How is your article coming?" Alison asked.

"Very good," Elizabeth replied, taking a sip of her drink. "I've been to most of the tourist attractions on my list. But it's the out-of-the-way places that I really like to find. Do you know of any hidden gems that only the locals go to?"

"If I told you that then they wouldn't be a hidden gems, would they?" Alison smiled. "They would be quickly overrun with tourists."

"You have a point there," Elizabeth acknowledged. Well, there went that conversation. "It must be so romantic living in Whistler," she gushed. She had to try something. "You must love being here."

"It's no different than living any other place," Alison shrugged. "And sometimes it can be very aggravating in the winter. Too many people so that the streets are crowded, the restaurants are crowded, the road in and out is crowded. And if we get a heavy snow fall...."

Did she hear right? Did Alison just admit that they had lived here before? "Didn't you tell me that you've only been here a few months?"

"Yes, this time. We moved away a couple of years ago but we missed living here so much we decided to come back this spring."

Okay, they weren't hiding that but what about their name changes? If they were in a witness protection plan it wasn't working very well since Cynthia had recognized them.

"Did you live in this house before?"

"Oh, no," Alison laughed. "we lived on Fitzsimmons Road North."

So, Cynthia had been right. But did that mean that they had something to do with the young woman's death? It was a stretch considering Alison wasn't hiding anything.

"Do you and Rick ski much here?"

Alison's face lit up. "Skiing is the main reason we are here. This winter our children are coming to spend Christmas with us and to ski."

Elizabeth didn't know what to do next. Alison sure didn't sound like a woman who would be involved in killing someone.

"How well do you know Cynthia?"

Alison shook her head. "We nod to each other and say 'Hi' occasionally. That day you met her was the first time she's been over here and I've never been in her house."

Rick entered the room, a light jacket slung over his arm.

Alison looked at him, then stood. "I'm sorry to cut this short, but we've got things to do."

"Right," Elizabeth said, standing and heading to the door. "It was nice talking with you and thanks for the drink."

Just before Alison closed the door Elizabeth heard Rick say. "Why was she asking all those questions?"

* * *

Sally had lunch with the usual class group but her mind

wasn't on the conversation about what everyone was going to do for the weekend. She didn't even feel like spending some time talking with Reggie. As soon she had finished her sandwich she hurried to the bed and breakfast.

Bonnie's car was still there. She went directly to Bonnie's room on the second floor. She knocked on the door. No answer. She tried louder in case Bonnie was asleep. Still no response. Sally tried the knob. It was locked. She looked around, then went to find Beverly, who was watering the flowers beside the pool.

"Hi Beverly," Sally said, getting right to the point. "I'm looking for Bonnie. Have you seen her?"

Beverly thought a few moments, then shook her head. "Not since last night."

"So she didn't come down for breakfast this morning?" Sally felt her stomach tighten.

"No." She looked at Sally quizzically. "Is something wrong?"

Was there? She really didn't know for sure. "She didn't come to class and I just tried her room. There was no answer." Sally took a deep breath. "I think she is missing."

"Missing? Why do you think that?"

Why indeed? There was the warning of the Angel cards but this time Sally kept her mouth shut about them. There was Bonnie's belief that her cousin had been murdered, but if that was true, what were the odds of the murderer being here again this year. She stopped. Did she believe that Bonnie was dead, had been murdered? No, of course not.

"Can we check her room?"

"That would be invading her privacy," Beverly said. "And we have no reason to. She may have gone home to Vancouver for a day or two."

"Her car is still here."

"Maybe her husband came up and she spent the night with him at a hotel."

Bonnie had said that she and her husband were going through a divorce. But he could have come to Whistler to talk with her and they could have spent the night together. It wasn't as if she and Bonnie were such good friends that Bonnie would feel the need to tell her about it.

"Wouldn't she have told you?" Sally asked.

Beverly shook her head. "You'll be surprised how many people take off for a few days of hiking or exploring north to Lillooet or Gold Bridge without telling me. They figure they've paid for their room so they don't owe me an itinerary of their plans."

Sally went to her own room. There were probably many good reasons for Bonnie to have left the bed and breakfast. However, she found she couldn't concentrate on her assignment so to take her mind off it she went down to the pool and began to swim. Although the pool was small Sally swam laps until Elizabeth appeared in her bathing suit.

Sally climbed out and they went over to the lounge chairs. As Sally dried herself off she told Elizabeth about Bonnie.

"So you think she may be with her husband?" Elizabeth asked, stretching out on the chair to get a little sun.

"Well, Beverly suggested it," Sally said. "I don't know what to think really. She didn't mention anything last night and I'm sure she would have wanted to be in class today in case someone had news for her about her cousin."

"Yes," Elizabeth nodded. "She's quite wound up about proving that Sylvia was murdered. I think it would take something very serious to make her leave. Did you talk with that Michael?"

"Yes. He was a little suspicious about why I was asking about her and I really made a fool of myself trying to explain about the Angel cards and their warning."

"Did he remember Sylvia?"

"Yes, he did and he did tell Bonnie that, but after that he clammed up with me."

Elizabeth shrugged and grinned. "Some people are like that in this business."

"But he acted like I was accusing him of having something to do with her disappearance."

"Don't take it personally. Maybe he has something to hide and he was scared you would worm it out of him."

"Like that would happen with the way I ask questions." Elizabeth laughed.

"We could go try her room again," Sally said. "She may be a heavy sleeper and didn't hear me knocking."

"Okay," Elizabeth said standing.

Carrying their towels they entered the bed and breakfast and headed up to Bonnie's room. Sally knocked. They waited but no one answered. Sally knocked again, louder. Suddenly, the door across the hall was yanked open and Daryl stood in the doorway.

"What are you doing?" he demanded. "I'm trying to work in here."

"We're looking for Bonnie," Sally said. "Have you seen her?"

"No, and it was such a pleasant day at class without her talking about her Angel cards."

"Did you see her at all between class yesterday and now?" Elizabeth asked.

"What are you, the police?" Daryl asked.

"No, we're just friends who are concerned," Sally said.

"Well, be concerned somewhere else. I don't have time for distractions." Daryl stepped back in his room and shut the door.

"You were right about him being serious about his writing," Elizabeth said.

* * *

When Bonnie didn't show up for breakfast the next morning, Sally really began to worry. "Have you seen Bonnie this morning?" she asked Beverly when she delivered their plates.

"No." Beverly shook her head. "But I'm not going into her room, either," she added forestalling Sally's next question.

"How long are you going to wait?" Sally asked her.

"Our policy is to give our guests three days and if they haven't returned or we haven't heard from them we let the police know."

"And then what?"

"Well, if the police decide to set up a search, they usually check the room first for any clues as to where they might have gone."

"So no one is going to even start looking for her until Sunday," Elizabeth said.

"That's right."

Two more guests had entered the dining room and Beverly left to make their breakfast.

"Something must have happened to her," Sally said to Elizabeth, as they ate their crepes and strawberries covered in whipped cream.

"I agree, but what?" Elizabeth said, taking a large bite of crepe.

Sally shrugged. "I don't know, but with her claiming her cousin was murdered and now disappearing herself, it scares me."

"If something happened to her because of her spreading the word about Sylvia, then that would suggest that the murderer, if there is one, is still here."

"So what we have to do is find out who she and Sylvia both met while here," Sally said.

Elizabeth grinned. "You're beginning to sound like a detective."

Sally smiled. "I totally understand how you get drawn into the puzzle. Once you start asking questions, you really want to find the answers to them."

"Maybe you will find out something at the retreat. She might have called Kat Mac and let her know where she is."

"You're right," Sally said. "I think I'm just making too much of her missing a day."

Elizabeth stood. "I've got some work to do so I'll see you later."

On the way to the retreat Sally saw the gardener in front of his house. He was cleaning the water in the pond. She looked but didn't see his daughter.

"Morning," she said, realizing that she didn't know his name.

"Hi," he smiled. "Last day of the week for you. What do you think of the retreat now?"

Sally thought about what she had learned this past week. Some of it had been helpful but a lot of it had been over her head.

"I know more about the genre than when I first came. I've learned when the first science fiction story was written and about the men and women writers whose stories have made it so popular."

"Would you recommend me taking it?"

Sally hesitated. "That really depends on what you want to learn. If it's the history of science fiction and fantasy and who the best writers were, then yes. We are only now getting into what should be in the story, which is what I really came to learn. I don't know how much information we are going to receive and I'm not sure what's on for next week."

"Didn't you receive an outline for the course?"

"A partial one. Kat Mac, our instructor didn't want us coming in with any preconceived ideas about what she was going to teach. She wanted our minds clear and open."

"A good idea," he nodded.

Sally waved goodbye and headed to the retreat. The visit with him had taken her thoughts off Bonnie for a short time but within a couple of steps her mind was going over everything she knew about the woman.

Once at the parking lot Sally scanned the crowd for Bonnie. She didn't see her. She went up to Lisa and Kirk.

"Have you seen Bonnie this morning?" she asked.

Both shook their heads.

"She wasn't here yesterday, either," Lisa said. "Do you think something has happened to her, like her cards predicted?"

"I don't know," Sally said. "Maybe she will show up in class."

Surely by now someone would have heard something from her. Maybe Kat Mac knew something. After all, if Bonnie had dropped out of the retreat, she would have told their instructor, wouldn't she?

Bonnie hadn't appeared by the start of the class and Kat Mac didn't say anything about her leaving the class. Maybe she thought it was no one's business. Sally decided she would ask at the break.

Part way through the lecture there is a knock at the classroom door. Kat Mac opened it and Sally could see a police officer standing there before Kat Mac quickly stepped into the hallway and closed the door behind her. Sally's breath caught. What did he want? Did it have something to do with Bonnie? Surely not. She looked around the room and could see that several others had seen the officer also. They waited, staring at the door until it opened.

Kat Mac entered. She walked slowly to the front of the class. It was a few moments before she could speak.

"I'm afraid that Bonnie was killed in an accident last night," she said.

Sally gasped and the rest of the classroom buzzed with reaction.

"The cards were right," Lisa said.

"What kind of accident?" Kirk asked.

"Where?" Daryl asked.

Sally couldn't speak. She was suddenly very cold. Bonnie had been so certain her cousin had been murdered and now she herself was dead. This couldn't be right.

Kat Mac held up her hands. When it was quiet she said. "The police aren't sure exactly what happened. Someone found her lying in the street and called the police. It looks like she may have been run over. They've sent her body to Vancouver for an autopsy."

There was silence in the class as everyone digested what they had just heard. After a couple of false starts, Kat Mac called an early break. They all went outside. Some lit their cigarettes and wandered away. Daryl, Henry, and Luke stood in a group. Near them Lisa, Kirk, Russ, and Reggie were huddled in a circle. Sally joined them.

"Do you think her death had anything to do with her cousin's?" Kirk asked Sally. "After all, it seemed she was here to find out who had killed her cousin."

Before Sally could answer Daryl stepped over and said. "Her cousin's death was an accident."

"How do you know?" Lisa asked.

"Because I looked it up on the Internet," Daryl said. "She fell down some steps and died of head injuries."

"So why did Bonnie think she was murdered?" Russ asked.

"Because she wanted to disrupt the class and hide the fact that she wasn't doing any work." Daryl turned back to Luke and Henry and they walked away.

Sally wasn't going to say anything about what she knew. Bonnie's reasoning had seemed too far fetched and Sally didn't want to have to explain it.

At the end of the break they filed silently back into the class room. Kat Mac was waiting.

"I think we'll cut short today's lecture and resume on Monday when we are more able to concentrate. Have a good weekend."

As Sally stood she heard Daryl mutter. "Again we're losing valuable teaching time because of a dabbler."

She gathered up her material and hurried to the bed and breakfast hoping Elizabeth was there. She had to tell her what happened. This was just too frightening.

Chapter 15

Elizabeth spent most of the morning working on her article. She and Sally still had to do the Peak 2 Peak Gondola and the Wildplay Elements Park so she could take her pictures and write about the experience of being on each of them.

Finally, when her back got tired and stretching her muscles didn't help, she saved her work on the computer and shut it off. She went out on the balcony to do some stretches and look down at the yard next door. Work was progressing slowly and it didn't seem that they were finding much. Nothing had been mentioned in the papers or on the news.

She went back in and picked up Chevy's leash. Time to go for a walk. On their way out Elizabeth saw a police car parked in front of the bed and breakfast. How long had the police been here? Had they come about the young woman found next door or had Beverly called them about the missing Bonnie? Oh, how she wanted to go find Beverly and ask, but for once her good sense won out over her curiosity. She would find out after the police left.

However, her normal hour long walk was shortened to twenty minutes and when she returned the car was gone.

"Elizabeth," a voice called. "Elizabeth Oliver."

Elizabeth looked to see Cynthia waving at her. "Come here, I have to talk with you."

Elizabeth put a smile on her face and crossed the street with Chevy.

"I saw Alison and Rick go out shopping," Cynthia said, as she guided Elizabeth around to the back of her house. "They won't see us together."

There was a pitcher of ice water and two glasses on the table. "We may not have much time so tell me all that you've learned," Cynthia said, pouring them each a glass.

"There isn't much to tell," Elizabeth said. "Alison admitted that she and Rick have lived here before."

"She did?" Cynthia asked surprised. "Why would she do

that?"

"Probably because it's true and easily checked if a person wanted to."

"So she figured that she would throw you off their tracks if they admitted that openly," Cynthia said, nodding. "Very clever."

Elizabeth wondered how many mystery books Cynthia read and how many crime shows and movies she watched a week. There were certainly a lot of them out there.

"Did you go to the police?" Cynthia asked.

"No, not yet. I'm waiting for them to finish the excavation of the yard. I've been doing regular surveillance on them from my balcony. It's going pretty slow." She thought throwing out some police terminology would keep Cynthia happy.

"Excellent," Cynthia beamed. "I knew I could count on you to help me. When this is over you can use my name as a reference for your future clients."

"Thank you," Elizabeth said, straight faced. She looked at her watch and stood. "I've got to go and do my afternoon check on their progress."

As she crossed back to the bed and breakfast Elizabeth wondered about the police car. She hadn't mentioned it to Cynthia and it was obvious that Cynthia hadn't seen it. Which was good. Less questions to answer.

She climbed the stairs to their suite and found Sally pacing back and forth in their living room.

"Where have you been?" Sally demanded.

"I took Chevy out, then talked with Cynthia." Elizabeth stared at her friend. Her face was pale and her hands were shaking. "Why? What's wrong?"

"Bonnie was killed last night," Sally said, her voice suddenly subdued.

Elizabeth stared at her. "Bonnie's dead?" A shiver ran down her back. "What happened?"

"The police came to the retreat today and said that she had been found lying in the middle of a street. They think she may have been run over."

"Let's go out on the balcony and you can tell me

everything." Elizabeth went and got them each a cooler. She handed a bottle to Sally and sat in the chair opposite her.

"There isn't much to tell," Sally began, taking a sip then setting her bottle down on the small table. "Bonnie didn't show again this morning and I had decided I was going to ask Kat Mac if Bonnie had quit the class when someone knocked at the door. Kat Mac answered it and I could see a police officer. She stepped out and when she returned she said that Bonnie had been found lying on a street last night and that the police thought she may have been run over."

"So that's why they were here this morning," Elizabeth mused.

"Who were here?"

"When I went to take Chevy for our walk there was a police car in the parking lot. They must have come to talk with Beverly and to look through Bonnie's room."

"Should we go to the police with what we know?" Sally asked.

"I don't know," Elizabeth said thoughtfully. "Do you think that they will buy into the fact that Bonnie's suspicions are based on the notion that Sylvia wouldn't have gone to the Upper Village twice."

"That really is a silly reason, when you think about it," Sally admitted. "But she sure was adamant about it."

"And it seems too much of a coincidence that Sylvia died here and when Bonnie came here because she thinks Sylvia was murdered, she dies also."

"I wonder if she ever asked Kat Mac about Sylvia," Sally said. "Do you think we should speak with Kat Mac? She seemed quite shocked by the news this morning. She couldn't continue with her lecture."

"Why don't we wait and see what's on the news tonight. But we could see if the police told Beverly anything."

They headed down to the kitchen where they found Beverly sitting at the table, a cup of coffee gripped in her hands. Her eyes were red as she looked up when they knocked on the open door.

"May we come in?" Elizabeth asked.

Beverly nodded her head. She looked down at her cup again.

"We heard about Bonnie," Elizabeth said gently, as she and Sally sat down.

"Yes, the police were here today to tell me and to search her room."

"Were they looking for anything specific?" Elizabeth asked.

"I don't know. I was in such shock that I just gave them the key and told them the room number."

That's too bad, Elizabeth thought. "What's going to happen with her things?"

"I phoned her aunt and she will be here tomorrow to pack them up."

"Oh, the poor woman," Sally exclaimed.

"Yes, she seemed quite broke up. She kept saying, 'not Bonnie, too.'"

Elizabeth glanced at Sally and shook her head. Best not to say anything about Sylvia. Let Bonnie's aunt tell Beverly if she wished to.

"Is there anything we can do?"

Beverly shook her head. "I've told the other guests so they won't be surprised if they hear it on the news. Especially since some of them are here because of the body found next door."

"Oh, yes, that would be tough to take when you are waiting to hear if it was your relative who was murdered," Sally agreed.

Beverly looked at Sally. "You were right to be worried about her."

"I sure didn't expect this, though," Sally said.

"Who would?" Elizabeth said, quietly. "Do you know what time Bonnie's aunt is coming tomorrow?"

"She said she would be here around noon. Why?"

"I just thought we could help her if she wants. I don't imagine it will be very pleasant for her."

"You could ask her. I'll be there, also."

"It might be good for her to meet some people who had gotten to know Bonnie a bit while she was here," Elizabeth said

Beverly nodded.

"Did the police say where Bonnie was found?" Elizabeth asked.

"Yes, just off Nancy Greene Way on Fitzsimmons Road South."

"That close?" Sally asked, shocked. "Was she on her way here from the retreat?"

"They don't know what she was doing," Beverly said.

Sally's stomach rumbled. "I guess I didn't eat enough crepes for breakfast," Sally smiled. "We'd better go."

"Let's go into the village and have supper," Elizabeth said, on their way to their room. "Then we'll come back and listen to the news."

They grabbed their money wallets and went to the Tracker, Chevy following.

"If she was coming here from the retreat last night, where was she all day yesterday? Elizabeth asked as she drove.

"Well, we know she wasn't in class, but that doesn't mean she wasn't in the building. There are a number of students staying at the retreat. She could have visited with any of them."

"Did she know someone that well to stay with them the all day? That would have meant they would have missed class, too."

"She was the only one missing from our class, but I don't know about other ones."

"If Michael is staying there she could have spent the time with him."

"Except I talked with Michael yesterday."

"Right," Elizabeth nodded. She pulled into the free parking lot and they walked across to the village. Elizabeth took Sally along the brick inlaid Village Stroll showing her all the hotels, shops, and restaurants.

"This is so romantic," Sally said. "I can imagine myself here in the winter, skiing down the snow covered mountains during the day, walking along this lighted walkway at night, and sitting in front of a fire in one of the hotel fireplaces."

"It would be fun to do it at least once," Elizabeth said.

They had their supper at Earls sitting at one of the outdoor tables overlooking part of the Village Stroll. After they ate Elizabeth took Sally to the Upper Village. They walked across the wooden bridge over the creek and then under the roadway bridge. They stopped at the concrete steps where Sylvia had died.

"These certainly don't look dangerous," Sally said.

"No," Elizabeth agreed. "The individual steps are deep and they aren't steep." She walked up the first four steps to the landing, then the next seven steps to another landing. "I don't see how Sylvia could have lost her balance on these stairs."

Sally ran past Elizabeth. "They are easy," she said, as she reached the top. "Plus, they have the railings in the centre to hold onto if necessary."

"They sure don't look like the scene of a murder, do they?" Elizabeth said.

"But I can't see someone accidentally falling on these either," Sally said.

They went back to their suite and turned on the television. The news station was from Vancouver and they had to listen to all the accidents and robberies in that city before the anchor person turned to what had happened in the rest of the province. Whistler's Murder was the first up and pictures of the vacant lot next door were shown.

"Police are still trying to identify the body of the young woman found in the demolished house in Whistler. Many people have come forward with dental records and descriptions of birth marks but so far none of them has been a match."

Bonnie's picture was shown next on the screen.

"In an unrelated matter the body of a woman in her thirties was found on a street in Whistler sometime early this morning. Police have identified her as Bonnie Stone from Vancouver. She was attending a writer's retreat in Whistler when the tragedy occurred. The police believe she may have been the victim of a hit and run driver. And in a tragic coincidence, Bonnie's cousin, Sylvia, had attended the same retreat two years ago and had died from an accidental fall."

Elizabeth shivered as she looked at Sally. Suddenly, solving murders wasn't the fun it used to be. For the first time she realized it wasn't a game. People she knew were being killed, people who had asked for her help.

"Do you think we may be in danger?" Sally asked.

"I don't know," Elizabeth replied. "It depends on if Bonnie mentioned us to whomever killed her."

"She did tell everyone at the retreat that we were helping her find her cousin's murderer," Sally said.

"She did? Why would she do that?"

"I don't know but maybe we should be careful." Sally was quiet a moment. "But if it was a hit and run, then it had nothing to do with her search."

"Or maybe that was how the person decided to kill her. That way it wouldn't look like actual premeditated murder. The police would be looking for a hit and run driver not a murderer."

"So where does that leave us? Should we go to the police?"

Before Elizabeth could answer that there was a knock at the door. Chevy jumped up from where he was sleeping on the floor and rushed to the door barking. Sally turned off the television while Elizabeth scooped Chevy up and shushed him as she opened the door. Two RCMP officers, a man and a woman stood in the door way. Chevy squirmed in her arms wanting to get down. She held him fast.

"I am Constable Black and this is Constable Pierce," the man introduced them. "We are looking for Sally Matthews."

Sally came up beside Elizabeth. "I'm Sally Matthews."

"We would like to ask you some questions about Bonnie Stone. May we come in?"

Elizabeth held the door wider to let them enter. When the door was closed she set Chevy down. He immediately headed to give the officers' legs a sniff. Sally pointed to the living room and the officers sat in the chairs while Elizabeth and Sally settled on the couch. Elizabeth wasn't sure if she should stay but they didn't ask her to leave. Plus, she wanted to be there to support Sally if she needed it.

"Ms. Matthews, I'm assuming you have heard the news about Ms. Stone," Constable Black began.

Sally nodded.

Chevy had finished his inspection and jumped up between Sally and Elizabeth. He turned around twice then laid down.

"We understand that you were in the same science fiction/fantasy class as Ms. Stone," Black said.

Again Sally nodded. Elizabeth reached over and squeezed her hand.

"We are interviewing all the students in the class," Constable Pierce said, smiling at Sally. "We're not singling you out for any reason."

"Was there anything unusual about Ms. Stone's attendance at the retreat?" Constable Black asked.

Sally glanced at Elizabeth who nodded. Might was well tell them everything. After what they had learned today, neither felt very safe.

Sally began with the first class and the introduction, telling them that Bonnie had felt uncomfortable with thirteen students in the class. She progressed to the Angel cards, Bonnie's assertion at the retreat that her cousin Sylvia had been murdered, and then her disappearance.

"Who all were there when Bonnie mentioned her cousin's death?" Black asked.

Sally thought back. "Lisa, Daryl, Kirk, Reggie, our instructress, and a few more hanging around."

"Did she tell you why she thought her cousin had been murdered?"

Sally looked at Elizabeth. Elizabeth smiled. She knew this was going to sound weird.

"She said that Sylvia didn't like to repeat anything, like going to a movie twice and that she had already been to the Upper Village, so she wouldn't have gone there again."

"Did any of them react oddly to what she'd said?"

"Not that I noticed. I think most of them thought she was a bit flaky because of her Angel cards and her being superstitious about the number thirteen."

"Tell us about those Angel cards," Constable Pierce said.

Sally explained how Bonnie had done readings for the other students and how every time she did her own, one special card came up.

"What card was that?"

"Bridgette. I think her message was that Bonnie should be cautious."

"Cautious about what?"

"I'm not really sure. Bonnie thought it had something to do with the class or the retreat."

"She selected you to tell all this to," Black said. "Why is that?

"I think it's because she heard that Elizabeth had solved some murders and she was wondering if she would help her."

Black gave a loud sigh. "Oh, so you're an amateur sleuth. Trying to put the police out of work, are you?"

"I've never actively sought out a murder to solve it," Elizabeth said, quietly. "They just seem to happen when I'm around."

"Well, we'd appreciate it if you stayed away from this."

"Are you saying Bonnie was murdered?" Elizabeth asked, fear gripping her stomach. Where did that leave them? Did the killer know that Bonnie had been talking to them? Would the killer try to get to them?

"I'm not saying anything," Black said, standing. "I'm just warning you not to get in the way of our investigation. We do know how to do our jobs."

"Do you think we should be careful?" Sally asked, as they walked to the door. "Is there someone out there who might try to kill us, too?"

"You have nothing to worry about. No one wants to harm either of you."

Elizabeth closed the door behind the constables and locked it. She turned to Sally. "What do you think?"

"In spite of what he said, I think Bonnie was murdered. It's just too much of a coincidence that the two cousins die in the same town attending the same retreat."

"The question is, what are we going to do?"

"Well, he did warn you to stay away from the investigation," Sally grinned. "Your prowess as a detective must have scared him."

"That's not what I meant," Elizabeth smiled. "Maybe we should go home. After all, if she was killed by someone, that person might think she told us something."

"But I can't remember anything she said that sounded like a clue," Sally said. "And if she was killed because she thought her cousin was murdered then everyone in our class will be a target."

Elizabeth went and got them each a cooler and they sat down again. "Let's go over what we know," she said, twisting off the cap of her bottle.

"We know that Bonnie thought Sylvia had been murdered," Sally said, taking a sip.

"We know that Bonnie believed that her Angel card, Bridgette, was warning her about something," Elizabeth said.

"We know that there were some irritated students, like Daryl, who thought she shouldn't be in the class."

"But would he have killed her because of that?" Elizabeth asked.

Sally shrugged. "I'm just looking at everyone who had something against her."

"Okay, who else thought like Daryl?"

"At least two other men in the class, Luke Johnson and Henry Freisen. Two men, Kirk West and Russ Peters were in with us women. The rest went their own way."

"Who were they?"

"Bill Young, Luis Vivieris, and Bruce Wong. Another man, Reggie Shaw has begun hanging around with us lately."

"You like this Reggie?"

"What makes you say that?" Sally reddened.

"That red face for one thing, but your voice changed when you said his name."

"I'll admit that I think he's cute and we have talked a bit."

"I'm glad to hear that but to get back to our think tank, it sounds like Daryl has a following."

"I guess. Those guys seemed to be as angry as he was about us not taking this class seriously."

"What about Kat Mac? Did she say anything about how

much effort the students are supposed to put into their work?"

Sally shook her head. "No, she just gives her lectures and gives us assignments. The doing of the assignments is up to us. There is no exam or certificate at the end so we only get out of it what we want to."

"Kat Mac taught the class that Sylvia took."

"Yes, so she is something Bonnie and Sylvia have in common."

"What do you know about Kat Mac?"

"Not much, really. She's passionate about science fiction and fantasy. I think she's a writer although I don't know what she has written."

"We could look her up on the Internet," Elizabeth said. "What about Michael Wolf. He took the same course as Sylvia, and Bonnie had asked him about her."

"Yes, he's another common thread between them. I wonder how many other students take one course like Michael did and then come back the next year or year after for the one of the other courses offered."

"There may be someone else who knew Sylvia and heard about Bonnie asking questions. We'd have to ask the organizer of the retreat and I doubt that she would let us look at her list of attendees."

Sally flopped back in her chair. "There's so much and yet nothing, really."

Elizabeth grinned. "I know, it's hard figuring things out, but usually something happens that puts everything in order."

"Well, I hope that happens before the killer thinks to come after us."

Elizabeth sobered. "I know you paid a lot of money to attend the retreat but I'm wondering if maybe we should go home and leave this to the police?"

"One part of me wants to, but the other tells me to stay and try to find out what happened to Bonnie. After all, she did ask us to help her."

"Okay, we'll talk with her aunt tomorrow and go to Vancouver on Sunday to see Grandma. Maybe by then the police will have found out more. But we have to protect ourselves; we don't go anywhere alone."

Sally laughed. "Famous last words in all the mystery and horror movies. But, alas someone always thinks they have a good reason to go somewhere alone or is lured by the killer and of course they get murdered."

"After all these years you'd think they'd come up with something new."

"If we do decide to go home what are you going to say to your client? You don't want to leave her hanging, do you."

"Speaking of Cynthia, I was talking with her today."

Sally leaned forward as Elizabeth filled her in on their conversation.

"So when was the last time you did your surveillance," Sally chuckled. "and what if she wants to see your surveillance tapes?"

"I'll think of something, I hope." Elizabeth said, yawning. "But right now, I'm off to bed. It's been a long day."

"Yes, me too," Sally said. "I'm glad it's the weekend."

Chapter 16

Saturday morning Elizabeth and Sally both walked Chevy then headed to the dining room. There was only one table open. Elizabeth recognized some of the people who were here because of the young woman being found next door. None of them looked up when she and Sally walked by. Obviously their thoughts were centred around this part of their lives.

Sally nudged Elizabeth and nodded her head towards the corner. At the table was Daryl. An empty plate sat to one side and he had his head buried in a book. Elizabeth couldn't make out the title.

Beverly came into the room with plates piled high with hash browns, sausage, scrambled eggs, and toast. She set them at one of the occupied tables then left the room. The atmosphere was hushed. No one spoke, the only sound was the clinking of cutlery on plates.

While they waited Elizabeth went and picked up the newspapers. The *Whistler Question* had come out on Thursday, the day before Bonnie's body had been discovered. The *Vancouver Sun* had nothing on the front page. It's surprising how loudly a newspaper crinkles in a quiet room, Elizabeth thought as she tried to open the pages as softly as possible. She finally found a small write-up on page six. "The police are now calling Bonnie's death suspicious," she whispered to Sally.

They ate their meal in silence, not wanting to disturb any of the other patrons. Daryl got up and left the room when they were almost finished. No one else made a move to leave. It was almost like, where else would they go? Sitting here was probably better than sitting in their rooms or standing at the lot next door or visiting the police station looking for news. They knew the police would come to them.

Elizabeth and Sally went up to their suite. "I wonder why Daryl is still here," Sally said. "He lives in Victoria, close enough for him to go home for the weekend."

"Do you know how many were planning on leaving Whistler for the weekend?" Elizabeth asked.

"The subject did come up during the week because some were discussing whether we should get together for a drink Saturday night," Sally said. "But those who live close like Russ Peters and Luis Vivieris were going home to Vancouver while Bill Young was headed to Pemberton. The others like Kirk West from Hope, Lisa Zhang from Chilliwack, Bruce Wong from Trail, and Reggie Shaw from Hinton were all staying here this weekend but they wanted to explore the area. Henry Freisen is from Kamloops and Luke Johnson is from Lillooet but they are part of Daryl's group so I don't know their plans."

"Wow, how do you remember where they each live?"

"It's easy. I wrote it all down during introductions the first day and I've been reminding myself all week whenever I talk with them."

"While we're waiting for Bonnie's aunt to come let's look Kat Mac up on the Internet," Elizabeth said, heading into her bedroom and turning on her computer.

There were many sites offering Kat Mac's books for sale. They looked at a few of those then clicked on one which was a write-up about Kat Mac that had been published in a newspaper.

Katherine MacKenzie was born in Fort St. John B.C. in 1956 and now lives in Vancouver B.C. Her first publication was a short story about a teenage girl in school who discovers that she is a lesbian and how her family and friends react. She openly admits that it is based on her own experience. Katherine is internationally known for her contribution to the science fiction world and for furthering the idea that women can write about the fantastic as well as men. She received a Bachelor of Arts at UBC and a journalism diploma from Langara College. Katherine currently teaches at Langara College, puts on workshops, and is a regular instructor at The Whistler SF/Fantasy Retreat.

Kat Mac, the name she writes under, has written four science fiction novels, one of which, The Cornerstone, won the Aurora, Canada's science fiction and fantasy award. She has also had hundreds of short stories published but she is most famous for her Inside Out World Trilogy. However, since the publication of the final book seven years ago not much has been heard from Kat Mac in the writing world. Over the years some reviewers have said she has taken a hiatus from writing while other, harsher critics said she was washed up, that she used up the best of her creative powers in the trilogy and can't come up with another idea. However, Kat Mac has a new book coming out and insider word is that it is equal to, or better than, her trilogy. We will soon see who is right.

"Someone said that she had taken last year off from the retreat to finish writing her book," Sally said. "Looks like it paid off."

Elizabeth's cell phone rang. She glanced at the call display and was tempted to ignore it. Sally looked at her.

"Dad," Elizabeth said. "Probably about Bonnie."

"I'll leave you two alone," Sally said, heading to the living room.

"Hello, Dad," Elizabeth said.

"What's happening in that place?" Phil demanded. "A murder spree?"

"No, Dad," Elizabeth said patiently. "The deaths aren't related."

"I don't care. Did you know that woman?"

"Uh, Sally did and she introduced us," Elizabeth said, hoping to deflect some of the responsibility. "They were both at the same retreat."

"And I suppose you're knee deep in solving the murder," Phil said.

Geeze, what did she say? She couldn't very well lie to her father. "Not really." Ankle deep maybe.

"Well, I want you to come home right now."

"I can't leave Sally here. She still has a week left at the retreat."

"Oh, damn!" Elizabeth could picture him pacing in his living room. "Will you at least listen to reason and stay away from the case?"

Elizabeth knew she couldn't do that. She was already

caught up in it and so was Sally. "Uh, Sally kind of promised we would do some checking for the woman's aunt." She knew they would be doing that once they met her so she was off by a just couple of hours.

"What? Have you converted Sally into a detective, too?"

"No. We just want to help the woman deal with her loss."

"Can't you just send a condolence card like everyone else?" Phil sounded exasperated.

"Dad. It's a little more complicated than that."

Phil sighed loudly. "I might as well be talking to a stick. I suppose you won't stop until you've tracked down the murderer like before."

"I'll be careful."

"You'd better be."

Again, Elizabeth knew she should call Sherry and Terry and explain what was happening. Then she phoned Jared. The phone was answered by Paul, the man he had called .Dad up until a year ago. Paul told her that Jared's recuperation from the operation wasn't going as well as expected and he was still in the hospital. She sent her love and as she hung up, wished that she was there with him.

* * *

While making ham sandwiches for lunch, Elizabeth told Sally that her dad had heard about Bonnie's death now being considered murder.

"Boy, was he ticked off when I told him we were checking into some things about her death."

"You told him we were being careful, didn't you?"

"Oh, yeah. But that didn't make him feel any better. He wanted us to come home. And Terry and Sherry were both ready to come here and drag us back until I said that you had paid a lot of money to attend this retreat and didn't want to leave."

After cleaning up the kitchen, Sally and Elizabeth went to Bonnie's room. The door was open and a woman in her early sixties was sitting on the bed. Sally knocked on the door frame. The woman looked up. Her eyes were red.

"Hi. I'm Sally Matthews. I'm attending the same retreat as Bonnie is …ah, was. And this is my friend Elizabeth Oliver. We're both staying here."

The woman attempted a smile but it didn't quite come off.

"We've come to help you if you wish," Sally said. They waited.

The woman sighed. "I thought I could do this and told Beverly so when she offered but now that I'm in here I can't seem to get at it."

Elizabeth and Sally stepped into the room. "We'll do it," Sally said gently. She went over to the woman while Elizabeth went to the closet and retrieved Bonnie's suitcases.

"I'm sorry. My name is Madeline Crowe," she said, as she moved out of their way to a chair. "You said you were taking the course with her?"

Sally nodded. "Yes." She tried to think of something else to say, something about Bonnie. "We seemed to think the same way about the class."

"And what was that?"

"That we were both lost most of the time. And we weren't the only ones. There was a group of us who were wondering what we were doing there."

"Do you know why Bonnie was taking the course?" Elizabeth asked, as she lifted some t-shirts from Bonnie's dresser drawer. "I mean, why she came here?"

Madeline was quiet.

"She wasn't really interested in science fiction," Sally prompted. Neither one of them wanted to bring up Sylvia's name. "She didn't do any of the assignments."

"No, she wasn't interested in writing," Madeline admitted. "That was Sylvia, my daughter's, dream."

This was the perfect opening. "Yes, Bonnie told us about Sylvia being here two years ago," Sally said.

"Then she must have told you that she died here, also." Madeline's voice shook and tears ran down her cheeks.

Sally felt like putting her arm around Madeline but held back. She didn't know her that well. And some people liked their space, even in grief.

"Yes she did," Elizabeth said, jumping in. "She also told us that she thought Sylvia had been murdered and that she had come here to try and prove it."

"Yes, I know," Madeline said softly. "I couldn't talk her out of it even though the police said Sylvia's death was accidental."

"Did she tell you why she thought Sylvia had been murdered?" Sally asked. She found she was holding her breath as she waited.

"Something about Sylvia not going to that place twice unless there was a good reason. Did she tell you the same?"

"Yes," Sally nodded. "We really weren't sure what to make of it." She didn't want to say that they had thought it was a strange reason.

"Well, she was right that Sylvia didn't like to return to a place she'd already been to but I never thought she was as stubborn about it as Bonnie implied."

"So you think Bonnie's reasoning was wrong?" Elizabeth asked.

"I think she was looking for a way to explain Sylvia's death other than a freak accident."

"Do you know why she would want to do that?" Sally asked.

"I know she had a hard time dealing with Sylvia's death. After what she had gone through as a child, she couldn't believe that her sister, as she and Sylvia called each other, could be taken that easily from her."

"Bonnie did tell us about her parents and how you and Sylvia's father took her in."

Madeline got a far away look in her eyes as if reliving the past. "Yes, she had parents from hell. Starting when she was a baby they would leave her with anyone who would baby sit and go out drinking or to drug parties. I finally told them to bring her over to our house and we would look after her. Sometimes they would leave her with us for a week before sobering up enough to remember her. Finally, I couldn't take any more and I went to the court and asked for custody. They never even fought it."

"How old was she at the time?"

"She was four. Luckily, I don't think she remembered much about it."

"Was she the reason you and your husband split up?" Elizabeth asked.

"Good heavens, no! He loved both girls."

Not enough to stay in the family or to even keep in contact, Sally thought remembering how Bonnie had said they hadn't heard from him once he remarried.

"Do you mind me asking why you two split up?" Sally asked.

"Why are you asking all these questions?" Madeline asked, straightening up. "I've told the police everything I know."

Sally looked at Elizabeth, who nodded. She took a deep breath. "Elizabeth has been involved in solving some murders in the past and when Bonnie found that out she asked Elizabeth to help her find out who had killed Sylvia."

"And you agreed?" Madeline turned to Elizabeth.

"Well, not really," Elizabeth answered.

Sally took over. "She had explained the story to us one evening and the next day she told our class members about Sylvia being in Kat Mac's class two years ago and that she had died. She also talked with a man who had been at the same retreat as Sylvia. We never saw her after that. The next we heard was that she was dead."

"Do you think her death and Sylvia's are related?"

"We don't know but the more we can learn about their lives the better our chances are of finding out."

"Why don't you leave it for the police?"

"Because they think that Sylvia's death was an accident and right now we don't," Elizabeth explained. "So we will be looking for a connection between the two while they won't. And we won't know what that connection will be until we stumble across it, so we just keep asking questions until we receive that one answer."

"Okay," Madeline sighed. "The reason my husband and I

split up was that I had had an affair with a co-worker and when he found out about it he left. We divorced and I married my lover, but it didn't last very long."

A typical story, Sally thought.

Elizabeth had finished packing everything into the suitcases. She sat beside the cases on the bed and looked at Madeline. "Did you see Sylvia's manuscript, the one that she came here with.?"

"No," Madeline smiled for the first time. "She was very secretive about it. She kept telling me that I could read it when it was a best seller."

"Did you come and pack her things?" Sally asked.

Madeline shook her head. "She'd been staying at the retreat so someone there did it and sent the suitcases to me. I put them in her room and I still haven't gone through them."

"Could you look through her things when you get back and find it for us."

Madeline nodded.

"What have the police told you about Bonnie's death?" Elizabeth asked.

Madeline shivered. "They think she was walking down the street when she was hit by a vehicle."

"That would have been just off Nancy Greene Way on Fitzsimmons Road South," Sally said. "Quite close to the retreat."

"Did the police say anything else?"

"They said her Angel cards were strewn around her."

"As in having been knocked out of her pack in the accident?"

Madeline shook her head. "No, as in it looked like someone had thrown them down on top of her."

"So someone ran over her then stopped, got out, and threw her cards at her. That would suggest that she had left the cards somewhere and this person found them or the person dug them out of her pack."

"It does imply that this was deliberate, doesn't it."

"Yes," Elizabeth said. "Now let's try a different track. Maybe her death had nothing to do with the retreat. Bonnie said she and her husband were splitting up. What do you know about that?"

"Oh, Gerald was terrible to her. Going out with his friends and not coming home for days, drinking while at work and getting fired from his jobs, laying around the house and not lifting a finger to help with the housework. She had a steady job and was paying all the bills. Then after work she would have to cook their meals, and clean the house on her days off. She is so much better off without him."

"Would he be the type to get mad enough about the split to kill her?"

Madeline's eyes widened. She put her hand to her throat. "I never thought about that." She shook her head. "I don't think so, he was usually too drunk to care about anything."

"But he was losing his meal ticket, the person who was supporting him."

"Still, I can't see him doing it, not because he wouldn't have gotten mad but because he didn't have the mental ability to plan something like this nor the physical energy to execute it."

"Did Bonnie have a life insurance policy?" Elizabeth asked.

Sally was watching and listening to Elizabeth. She now understood how she worked when she was trying to figure out who had committed a murder. Her mind seemed to be going in many different directions. The questions she asked proved it. She didn't settle for just one possible theory, she wanted to explore as many as she could think of.

"She did at work."

"And I'm assuming Gerald was the beneficiary."

"I believe so." Madeline nodded.

"Do you think he would kill her over that?"

"Oh, I don't think so. It was only for about twenty-five thousand dollars."

"Well, if you are out of work and your wife is calling it quits probably leaving you on the streets, twenty-five thousand is a lot of money."

"Oh, my god."

This time Sally put her arm around Madeline as she rocked

back and forth.

* * *

"Let's go into the Village," Elizabeth said, after they had eaten supper. "I could use a strong drink and lots of people around."

"Okay, I'll phone for a cab," Sally said.

Elizabeth and Sally wandered along the Village Stroll and stopped at one of the outdoor patios. They found an empty table and sat down. When the waitress came over Elizabeth ordered a Caesar while Sally asked for a rye and water, neat.

Sally was taking a sip when she noticed the man from the flower yard coming across the Village Stroll. She rose and waved to him. "Hi," she called.

It took a moment for him to recognize her, then he smiled and nodded back.

"Would you like to join my friend and me?"

"Thank you, I would."

Sally noticed that he staggered a little as he walked towards their table. Had he already had a few drinks? When they were seated, she said. "I'm Sally Matthews and this is Elizabeth Oliver."

"My name is John Peterson." He shook both their hands.

"Is your daughter joining you?"

"No, I called a cab and snuck out. I do that sometimes just to get away on my own."

Elizabeth looked quizzically at Sally.

"John has the prettiest yard in Whistler," Sally explained their relationship. "I walk by it on my way to the retreat."

The waitress came over. "I'll have a cup of coffee," John said. "I'm not much of a drinking man."

So that didn't explain his unsteadiness. "The first day we met you said you left your job and moved here," Sally said. "How long have you lived here?"

"Six, no seven years. And I hate it."

"You do?" Sally asked, surprised. "This is Whistler. Most people would do anything to live here."

John shook his head. "Not me. I liked it better in Sparwood where we lived before."

"Then why did you move?" Elizabeth asked.

John seemed to think that over. "My wife died and I was very lonely. I had a few girlfriends but nothing serious. Then I won the lottery." He stopped, remembering.

"Did you buy the ticket here in Whistler?" Elizabeth asked.

"No, in Sparwood. My picture was on the front page of the paper and women began to throw themselves at me. My daughter, Wendy, moved in. To protect me, she said. She wanted me to quit my job and move somewhere else to get away from all the charities, friends, and relatives who wanted money. She loves to ski so insisted we buy here."

He played with his cup a few moments. "Now she tries to run my life, not letting me go anywhere without her. She's even talked about selling my car."

Poor man, Sally thought. It sounded like he needed someone to talk to. "Why would she want to sell your car?"

"About three years ago my doctor prescribed some pills for my high blood pressure. She's worried that something might happen while I'm driving."

"You should be okay as long as you take the pills," Sally said.

"Well, I have no choice about that. She makes sure that I take them every morning. Sometimes she also gives me vitamin pills. I think she gives me too many of those because I don't feel well after taking them and I can't always remember things."

"What type of vitamins are they?" Elizabeth asked.

"I don't know," John answered. "She keeps them somewhere in her bedroom."

"You said you see a lot of people who attend the retreat every year," Sally said, changing the subject

John nodded. "The ones who stay in the bed and breakfasts along Ambassador Crescent."

Oh. Madeline had said that Sylvia had stayed in a room at the retreat itself. Well there went that idea.

"Why do you ask?" John said.

"Oh, there was a woman who was here two years ago and I was just wondering if you might have met her. But she stayed at the retreat so I doubt it."

They were quiet then suddenly John asked. "Have you seen her?"

"Who?" Sally was caught by surprise.

"My daughter. I haven't seen her in a long time."

Sally and Elizabeth stared at each other. Oh, oh, Sally thought. Hadn't he just said he had snuck out to get away from her?

"Dad!"

John winced and his shoulders slumped. "Oh, oh. There's my daughter, the Warden."

"Who?" Elizabeth asked.

John sighed. "My daughter, Wendy.'

His daughter hurried over to the table. "What are you doing here?"

Sally wasn't sure what to make of what was happening. John seemed afraid of Wendy and yet he had just wondered where she was. Was there something wrong with his mind?

"Just having a coffee with these nice women," John said. "Would you join us?"

"No, we're going home."

"But…"

Wendy put her hand under his arm and pulled on him. He clambered to his feet. Wendy led him away without a word to Sally or Elizabeth.

"Wow, what was that all about?" Elizabeth said.

"I don't know but I've seen her treat him like that before. He sure isn't a happy man."

"No, he doesn't appear to be."

They watched as Wendy led him over to a bench and made him sit down. Then she came back to their table. "Please stay away from my father," she said, putting some money on the table to pay for his coffee. "He's an old man with the beginnings of dementia. The meds he's on make him think that younger women are always falling in love with him. Then when he makes advances and finds out they don't share his feelings he gets very angry at them and at me. It would be so much easier on me if you just left him alone. He said you were attending the retreat so you are only going to be here another few days."

"That was strange," Sally said, as she watched Wendy walk over to John and help him up by his arm. "From ignoring us to politely asking us to leave him alone."

Elizabeth shrugged. "Maybe she has to be firm with him and that doesn't include being nice to the women he meets."

"Well, those meds could also explain why he was confused about where his daughter was." Sally became thoughtful. "You know, the first day I met him he seemed so nice, so easy going, so alert. Then the next time Wendy basically dragged him into the house when she saw us."

"Us?"

"Bonnie was with me."

"Maybe his daughter was afraid you would find out about his money or that you wouldn't be able to resist his advances and want to marry him."

"Oh, very funny." Sally said

"It has been known to happen.

"I think his daughter is scared that everyone he meets will be after some of his lottery winnings. Maybe it's not him she'd protecting as much as it is his money. So why did you ask if he had bought the lottery ticket here?"

"I was told that someone had bought a winning ticket from a store here in town. I thought I might be able to talk with the winner and get an idea of what life is like after the win."

"Judging by John and his daughter, for some people it might not be all that great."

Chapter 17

Both of them walked Chevy again then Elizabeth turned on the television to listen to the news while Sally had a bath. The news anchor was speaking about the body found in the demolished house in Whistler.

"Our reporter, Les Hargrave, did an interview with yet another mother, Jessica Smallwood, who is in the resort town awaiting word about the identity of the young woman."

The picture cut away to a hotel room where two people sat facing each other in chairs.

Elizabeth sat down to listen.

"I understand your daughter was pregnant and left home to give the baby up for adoption," Les Hargrave began. "Could you give our listeners an idea of what happened."

"My daughter was seventeen when she got pregnant. She went to an abortion clinic but was told it was too late, she was too far along. She was then told by someone at the clinic that she could get money for her baby if she offered it for adoption."

"And what was your response to this?"

"Her father and I had already insisted on the abortion so we were definitely in favour of the adoption. She didn't need a child to look after at that age and we figured she could use the money for her education."

"And what happened?"

"When she was almost due the nurse from the clinic came to the house and picked her up."

"Did you know where she was going?"

"No."

"Weren't you the least bit afraid or concerned about her welfare?" Les Hargrave's voice sounded shocked. "There are some pretty strange people out there."

"She'd been assured by the nurse that she would been safe."

"And that was what you went on?"

"Plus, they gave her some money up front," Jessica said.

"So where did they take her?"

"They brought her here to Whistler. She spent the week before the birth and a few days afterwards at a place here."

"Did you know that at the time?"

"No, she told me when she returned home."

Elizabeth leaned forward in her seat. Was this what Cynthia had been talking about?

"Did she meet the adoptive parents?"

"No. The nurse was in the room with the doctor and when the baby was born she took him out of the room. My daughter never saw him."

"You say 'him'. Does that mean the baby was a boy?"

"Yes, she was told that much."

"How much was she paid for her child?"

"She was paid three thousand dollars up front and five thousand dollars after the baby was born."

"So she sold her child for eight thousand dollars."

Jessica bristled at that statement. "She was giving him a better life."

"And what did she do with the money?"

"Well, she went through it pretty fast, spending it on clothes and going out with friends."

"She didn't keep any for her education?"

Jessica smiled. "She was a teenager who suddenly had a lot of money."

"So she spent it on frivolous things?"

"Not all were frivolous. She bought us a new wide screen television."

"Well, that was nice of her."

Jessica nodded. "She was a very kind daughter."

"So if she showed up at home again, why are you here?"

Jessica's eyes teared and her voice became shaky. "Because she came back to Whistler to find her son and never returned home the second time."

"Why did she want her son back?"

"A year after she gave him up for adoption she inherited a

large sum of money from my mother. She decided she had enough money to be a stay-at-home mom to her son."

"But why the change of heart? She basically sold him and now she wanted him back because she had some money?"

Elizabeth was surprised at how harsh some of the questions were. And yet the woman answered them.

"I think she grew up a lot in that year and she realized that she had given up a part of her. She was thinking of trying to get him back even before the inheritance."

"And how did you and your husband feel about losing a grandson?"

"We knew it was best for her and for the baby."

"And how did you feel about her looking for him?"

"We tried to talk her out of it but she became adamant that she wanted him back because she could give him a better life than even his adoptive parents could."

"Did she know who they were?"

"No, but she came here hoping maybe someone else did, that maybe they were from here."

"Do you mind telling us your daughter's name? Maybe someone will recognize it."

"Penny. Penny Elena Smallwood.

Elizabeth gasped. Penny was the name of the girl Cynthia had talked about. She wondered if Cynthia was watching the program.

"So Penny came back to Whistler to find out something about her son. Do you know if she did?"

"No, I never heard from her again."

"Now this money that she inherited, does she have access to it?"

"She received a lump sum at the time and is given an allowance every month. She will receive the bulk of it when she turns twenty-one."

"Has she been using her allowance since you last saw her?"

"No."

"You reported Penny missing a month after she left, is that right?"

"Yes, the police have been looking for her since then. They are the ones who contacted me to come here."

"I guess the question is, did she make out a will before leaving?"

"We've never looked for one but I doubt it. She was eighteen and something like that wasn't a priority."

"So if this body proves to be her, who will inherit the money?"

Jessica shrugged. "Me, I guess."

"What about her son?"

"He would have to be found first."

Elizabeth was surprised at the woman's lack of emotion. Maybe she had cried all her tears out, or maybe she was clinging to the hope that it wasn't her daughter and so wasn't getting worked up about it.

Sally came into the room wrapped in a housecoat and drying her hair. "Anything interesting on the news?"

"Just something that proves my client was telling the truth," Elizabeth said and proceeded to tell her about the interview.

"Are you going to talk with Cynthia?"

"Yes, I was thinking about going over and seeing her."

"Alone?" Sally raised her eyebrows.

"It's just across the street."

"And Bonnie was killed just a few of blocks from here. Let me get some clothes on and I'll go with you."

Elizabeth felt a little stupid waiting for Sally but she knew it was the best thing to do. The killer could be lurking outside right now. It felt strange thinking that. She had never thought about a murderer as wanting to kill her. They always went after the other person. And she had never felt this threatened while working on the other murders. She laughed nervously. Maybe she was getting paranoid. Maybe the killer was long gone with no thought about her or Sally.

They left Chevy in the room and walked cautiously across the yard to the road. The bushes made a good hiding place. When they reached the street they looked both ways, then laughing at their fears, ran to the other side. Elizabeth knocked on Cynthia's door.

"Come in," Cynthia said, leading them into the living room. "I was just watching the news."

"So you saw the interview with Penny's mother?" Elizabeth asked.

"Yes. The police were here earlier this evening asking me about Penny. Apparently, they now believe my story." She indicated for them to sit down.

Elizabeth took a moment to introduce Sally then asked. "What did the police say?"

"Jessica had been told about the body but couldn't identify it the way it was. She gave her sample for DNA testing like everyone else then came here. When she told her story, the police here realized that it matched with mine so they came to find out what more I knew. Of course I had nothing new to add." Cynthia leaned forward conspiratorially. "I didn't tell them that I had hired you. I know that the police don't like private investigators working their territory."

"Thank you," Elizabeth said, catching Sally's smirk out of the corner of her eye. "It will save me a lot of hassle." Especially since the police had already warned her to stay away from Bonnie's investigation.

"I knew it." Cynthia sat back, a satisfied smile on her face. "So what are you going to do now?"

The question caught Elizabeth off guard. She thought the fact that Penny's mother was here would have been enough for Cynthia.

"Well," Elizabeth started talking off the top of her head. "the police packed up their things in the yard and I didn't see that they had found anything more. I will try to find Jessica and talk with her but I doubt that I can learn more than what she already stated. She doesn't even know if it is Penny so I will still be talking with other family members to try and eliminate other possible girls."

"How many other families have you talked with?"

This was tricky. How to make it sound like she was working hard without really lying.

"There are two couples staying at the bed and breakfast and one mother who is staying elsewhere. I'm not really privy to how many people are actually in Whistler, only the police would know that. I can only watch for those who come to see where the body was found."

"And some of them have already been ruled out because of dental or other records," Sally said.

"Are you helping Elizabeth?" Cynthia asked.

"Oh, no. She's in this all by herself," Sally grinned.

"But we'd better go," Elizabeth said standing. "It's late and we are headed to Vancouver tomorrow."

"Something to do with the case?" Cynthia asked, following them to the door. "We never discussed travel expenses."

"That's all right. This is pro bono."

Cynthia nodded. "Thank you. So what do you expect to learn there about Penny?"

"I really can't discuss that with you right now. It is a delicate matter and if doesn't work out I might be accusing the wrong person."

"But you will let me know as soon as you find out something, as per our agreement?"

"Yes, I will report back to you everything I learn."

Elizabeth and Sally hurried across the road. When they were out of earshot, Sally said. "Where did you learn all those phrases like privy to, pro bono, and delicate matter?"

"Hey, I read books and watch television, too."

* * *

It was just after eleven o'clock Sunday morning when Elizabeth and Sally arrived in Vancouver. They followed the highway to Taylor Way, crossed over the Lions Gate Bridge, drove through downtown and turned right onto Burrard Street. After crossing the Burrard Bridge, Elizabeth turned left onto 1st Avenue. She followed it as it curved and ended at Fisherman's Wharf. Elizabeth found a place to park. Just as she shut off the vehicle her cell phone rang.

She dug it out of her bag. "Hello?"

"Hi, this is Madeline. I went through Sylvia's things from the retreat and I didn't find a manuscript either on paper or on DVD."

"What about in her room? She may have left a copy at home."

"I thought of that too and didn't find anything there either."

"Okay, thank you for letting us know."

They climbed out of the vehicle and Elizabeth told Sally about the conversation as they walked to Mariner's Walk. When they reached her grandmother's condo they went through the gate.

Elizabeth led the way down the steps to the brick laid patio with a table and chairs. There were large pots with numerous flowers and bushes on the patio and to their right was a brick wall covered in hanging ivy. They went down three more steps to the red door. Beside them on the left were patio doors leading into the dining room.

Elizabeth rang the bell. In a couple of moments it was answered by a tall, slender woman dressed in black shorts and a blue sleeveless blouse. Her mostly gray hair was curly and cut short.

"Elizabeth," she smiled and grabbed her in a hug. "it's so great to see you."

"Grandma." Elizabeth wrapped her arms around her grandmother.

"Sally," the woman said, pulling Sally towards her.

"Evelyn," Sally smiled, hugging back.

Chevy was jumping at her legs so Evelyn leaned down and patted him on the head. "Yes, I didn't forget you," she said. She straightened. "Come in. I've got a lunch ready for us."

Elizabeth and Sally entered the dining room Chevy at their heels. "Elizabeth will show you to the patio while I get the lunch," Evelyn said.

"Can we help?" Elizabeth asked.

"No, I've got most of the things out there. I just have to bring the devilled eggs and salads."

Elizabeth led Sally down the hall to the living room and out through sliding door to the front patio. Sally had met Evelyn in Edmonton when she'd come to visit but had never been to her place. Elizabeth waited for the reaction.

"Oh, this is so beautiful," Sally said, standing in the doorway. The patio was about four metres by four metres and overlooked a lagoon. Another door to the left opened into a bedroom. There was a row of flower boxes around the edge of the other two sides. Out on the lagoon a mother duck and six ducklings swam. The lagoon was surrounded on three sides by other patios and across it was the Island Park Walk with people strolling along it. On the other side of the park walk were the masts of sail boats docked in the marina.

"Yes," Elizabeth agreed, sitting at the bistro table. "I love coming here. I just don't get to do it as much as I would like."

The mother duck and duckling swam over to the patio. "Quack, quack," the mama said.

"Just ignore her," Evelyn said, coming out with a plate full of eggs and a bowl of green salad. "She's already had her lunch. I throw her bread crusts every day and so do most of the other residents here."

They watched the constant parade of people on the walk as they ate their lunch. Evelyn had even bought Chevy some home made dog treats which he chewed on with gusto.

"Before we get onto other topics," Evelyn said, as they munched on grapes and pear slices for dessert. "I want to discuss my plans for next summer. We haven't had a family get together since your mother died and I think it's about time we did."

"Yes," Elizabeth agreed. "I haven't seen most of the family since Mom's funeral. What do you have in mind?"

"Well, you know that your cousin Tabitha has been taking dance lessons for years," Evelyn began.

Elizabeth nodded. Tabitha was thirteen, the youngest daughter of her mother's youngest brother. He'd married while in his late thirties and had had two children after he turned forty.

"Her dance school is going to Disneyland next summer and I thought all of us should go there to watch her and to spend some time together."

"Oh, that sounds wonderful," Elizabeth said. "Count me in." Then she had a thought. "If Dad's coming what will I do with Chevy?"

"I'll look after him," Sally offered.

"But you'll be working."

"I can take some holidays. Chevy and I can go to my cousin's farm for a few days. I'm sure he would love to roll in some cow pies for a change."

"Just as long as you clean him up before you bring him back," Elizabeth laughed.

"Good," Evelyn said. "Now, because it's my idea I'm paying for everyone's hotel room, they just have to get there on their own."

"You don't have to do that," Elizabeth exclaimed. "I can pay my way."

"It's not a question of anyone being able to afford it. It's something I want to do for my family."

"Then, it's okay with me." Elizabeth had learned long ago not to argue with her grandmother.

"So, now that that's settled give me the low down on what's going on in Whistler," Evelyn said, taking a sip of water. "I've been watching the news about the bodies found there."

"What makes you think I would know anything about them?" Elizabeth asked, giving Sally a wink.

"Oh, come on, quit fooling with me. I know that whenever there's a suspicious death where you are you get involved, whether you want to or not."

Elizabeth laughed. "Well, this time it's not me, it's Sally who had the murder dropped in her lap."

Evelyn looked at Sally. "Go ahead, tell me," she said, and listened intently as Sally explained about Bonnie and her quest to find Sylvia's murderer and then dying herself.

"Are you going to see her husband while you are here?" Evelyn asked.

"Yes," Elizabeth said, digging a piece of paper out of her pocket. "Madeline gave us their address. We were hoping you could tell us where it is."

"Don't you have a GPS?"

"No, I haven't invested in one yet." Elizabeth had thought about getting one but decided she would stick to maps for now. Sometimes she got lost driving from one place to another and found a lovely setting that she hadn't known about. Plus, a GPS usually needs an address and waterfalls and lakes don't always have that.

"You should with your writing. Maybe I'll get you one for Christmas. Now what is the address?"

Elizabeth read it off.

"I believe that's on the corner of Cypress Street and 6th Ave. It's very close by."

"Oh, great. I hated the idea of having to drive very far."

"Go back along 1st Ave, cross Burrard Street and the next corner is Cypress. Turn left on it and go to 6th Avenue. You could walk from here if you want."

After lunch Elizabeth and Sally offered to help clean up.

"No," Evelyn said. "Go see the husband while I put things away and then we can go to Granville Island when you get back. I'll keep Chevy here."

To save time Elizabeth and Sally drove to Bonnie's apartment building. On the corner was a huge three storey place. It almost looked like it could have been a rooming house or a regular house with many additions, but on closer look it appeared to have been built like that. And there were two separate buildings. The outside of both was a combination of stucco and yellow siding. Elizabeth and Sally climbed the steps to the landing and knocked on the Stones' door.

The door opened but the smile on the man's face was quickly replaced with a look of confusion. He was dressed in a gray shirt and jeans. His brown hair was short and combed to the side. He was shaven and smelled of after shave. Not the picture Elizabeth had expected after what Bonnie's aunt had said. She waited for Sally to speak, since she was the one who had been in class with Bonnie.

"Hello, I'm Sally Matthews," Sally said, stepping forward. "I was at the retreat with Bonnie and I've come to offer my condolences."

The man looked from her to Elizabeth. "I'm Elizabeth Oliver. Both of us were staying at the same bed and breakfast as Bonnie and I met her there."

"I'm Gerald. Thank you for coming." He made no move to invite them in.

"Have you decided when the funeral is?" Elizabeth asked. She really wanted to ask about their marriage and whether he had killed her but that would give him an opportunity to shut the door in their faces.

"No."

"If I give you my cell phone number would you call us and let us know?" If they kept talking and sounded like they really did care maybe he would feel guilty and let them in.

"Okay."

Elizabeth rummaged through her small purse and Sally did the same. "I guess we don't have a pen and paper," Elizabeth said, glad that Sally seemed to understand what she was doing. "Do you have some?"

Gerald hesitated. "Come in," he said, grudgingly.

Elizabeth looked at Sally and they both smiled as they followed him into the apartment. They entered immediately into the living room which looked like it had been hastily cleaned. There was a pile of papers stacked beside the couch, a bunch of pizza boxes partially hidden under the coffee table, and a vacuum in the corner.

Elizabeth wondered if Gerald was expecting someone. That could have been why he had been reluctant to let them in.

Gerald found a paper and pen in a drawer of a desk in the corner and brought them over to Elizabeth. She began to slowly write.

"Bonnie was looking into the death of her cousin while she was in Whistler," Sally said. "Did you know she was going to do that when she left?"

Gerald looked surprised. "No, why would she be doing that?"

"Because she thought Sylvia had been murdered. Didn't the

police ask you about it?"

"No, probably because it wasn't true. Sylvia died two years ago in an accident."

"Don't you think it's strange that Bonnie was killed in the same town as Sylvia was."

"I guess, but why are you asking me?"

Sally shrugged and looked at Elizabeth, who handed the paper back to Gerald. "We were just wondering if she had phoned you about what she may have found out."

"Bonnie wasn't talking much to me before she left and she never called me while she was gone."

"She did say that the two of you were getting a divorce," Elizabeth said, jumping into the opening he had given them.

"What's it to you?" Gerald asked.

"Did you visit Whistler in the past few days?"

Gerald snorted. "No, I never went to Whistler and I've already told the police that. Now if you will excuse me, I have things to do." He led them to the door and opened it. Unable to think of anything else to ask, they left and went back to Elizabeth's grandmother's.

"Did you learn anything?" Evelyn asked.

"Just that he hadn't been to Whistler to see Bonnie," Elizabeth said.

"Then are you ready to go to Granville Island?"

"Yes," Sally said. "I've heard so much about Granville Island, I want to make sure I see it while I am here."

The three women went out onto Mariner's Walk and turned onto Island Park Walk. They wove their way through the joggers, bicyclists, walkers, parents with strollers, and couples walking hand in hand. When they reached Anderson Street, which ran under Granville Bridge, they turned onto it and entered the island. Evelyn showed them the artistic section along Cartwright and Johnston streets and they ended up at the Public Market. There they wandered up and down the aisles looking at all the fresh fruit and vegetables, the meat counters, the baked goods, and the food outlets. Elizabeth and Sally purchased some blueberries and raspberries and some buns and cheese to take back to Whistler with them. Then they looked through the shops along Duranleau Street before arriving back at Anderson.

At the condo Elizabeth and Sally said goodbye to Evelyn and headed to Whistler.

"Are you going to class tomorrow?" Elizabeth asked on the way.

"I've been wondering what to do. So far I haven't heard that the course has been cancelled."

"Your poor teacher. Two years and two deaths. She must be taking it hard."

"Speaking of Kat Mac, it's strange that there's no trace of Sylvia's manuscript. Her mother made it sound as if she had been working on it for awhile."

"So maybe there wasn't a manuscript," Elizabeth said.

"What do you mean?" Sally asked.

"Well, Bonnie registered in the course without having a manuscript and without any desire to learn about science fiction writing. Maybe Sylvia did the same."

"Why would she do that?" Sally asked. "It cost a lot of money to take it. And according to both Bonnie and Madeline, she seemed excited about coming here. Bonnie said she kept texting her about how much Kat Mac liked it."

"I wonder if Bonnie talked with Kat Mac. She said she would if no one else came forward with something."

"I'll ask Kat Mac if she had and also ask her about Sylvia's manuscript. If she saw it she might know where it is. And if she never saw it then what was Sylvia really doing in Whistler?"

Chapter 18

"What are you going to do today?" Sally asked Elizabeth, as they ate breakfast.

"Work on my article, maybe read by the pool."

"I don't like you being alone."

"I won't be alone. Chevy will be with me. He may be small but his bark can be intimidating when he's protecting me."

The fear that had made them agree that they should stick together had diminished somewhat over the weekend but they still felt the need to be cautious.

"I'll drive you to class and then come back here."

Sally directed Elizabeth to Fitzsimmons Street South and showed her John's yard.

Elizabeth slowed to take a good look.

"Lovely," she said.

"I don't see John," Sally said. "But there's Wendy." She waved but Wendy just stared at her. "I hope John's okay."

"Why have you taken such an interest in him?"

"I like him. He seems like a nice guy. It's too bad he has to put up with his daughter."

Elizabeth glanced at Sally. Ever since they were teenagers Sally had liked older men, even having a crush on Elizabeth's father, and she usually dated men up to fifteen years older than she.

"You don't know the whole story. Maybe he's lucky he has a daughter to look after him."

"True," Sally agreed.

No one from their class was waiting in front of the building. Sally wondered if she was the only one who was going to show up. She couldn't remember if there had been any assignment she was supposed to have done. It didn't matter. When she reached the class room everyone was in their seats. Kat Mac was at her desk. Sally headed to her spot and took out her things.

There was a pall over the class as everyone waited for Kat Mac to begin. Kat Mac stood and looked at them.

"I have checked with admissions and unfortunately there will be no refunds if you decide to withdraw from the class. So I'm going to ask you if you wish me to continue with the lectures and assignments or do you wish to leave?"

The class was silent. No one wanted to take the initiative. Finally Daryl spoke up. "We all know that Bonnie wasn't interested in this class. She had come here to find the phantom killer of her cousin. So I think there is no good reason for us to stop the class because of her."

"What do the rest of you think?" Kat Mac asked.

"I agree with Daryl," Luke Johnson said.

"Me, too." Henry Freisen said.

Slowly the rest of the class nodded their assent.

"Thank you," Kat Mac said. "Today I would like to continue with how to incorporate science fiction and fantasy with other genres such as mystery or romance."

During the break Sally looked for Michael Wolf again. She hadn't talked with him since before Bonnie's body had been found. Maybe he had something to offer that would help them. Before she could ask her questions, though, Michael asked her how the class was surviving after the death.

"We decided to finish out the week."

"Ah, yes. Because Bonnie wouldn't have wanted everyone to forfeit their money on her account."

"I doubt that anyone thought that. We have some students who are quite passionate about getting everything they can from this course."

"And the others?"

Sally grimaced. "Many are like me, here on a scouting trip to see what writing science fiction is all about. More like a tentative step into the genre."

"What do you think of Kat Mac as an instructor?" Michael asked

"I think she knows her subject, but at least for me, she doesn't seem to know how to teach it."

Michael nodded. "Does she have any favourite students?"

"There are a couple that seem to hang around with her more

than the rest of us."

"You have to watch her. Rumour has it that she steals ideas from her students."

"She does?" This was important. "Then how come she's allowed to teach?"

"Well, it's just a rumour and nothing has been proved since she hasn't had anything published for years. Many students like her, giving her top marks on the evaluation papers that are passed out at the end of the retreat. Plus, she has helped some get published. Me included."

"How did Kat Mac treat Sylvia during your course?"

"Do you want to tell me why you are asking about Sylvia again?"

Sally hesitated then explained everything to Michael. "Elizabeth and I are not sure what we are looking for but we feel we have to carry on what Bonnie asked us to do. So will you help us?"

"Okay," Michael agreed. "But I don't remember Sylvia being treated any different from any other student."

"Did she discuss her manuscript with you?" Maybe he knew where it was.

Michael shook his head. "I asked her once and she said she was working on one but didn't want to talk about it until she had it just right. Why do you ask?"

"Her aunt can't find it anywhere. Do you think she gave it to Kat Mac or to a publisher who was here?"

"I really don't know."

Sally tried a different subject. "When Bonnie talked with you last week did she ask you anything about a man Sylvia had met?"

"Yes and she sure caught me off guard when she asked if Sylvia and I had dated."

"And did you?"

"No," Michael looked shocked. "I barely knew her."

"What did Bonnie do when you said that?"

"She looked disappointed, then asked me if I was sure. I said of course I was sure."

"Was there anyone who didn't get along with Sylvia, someone who may have had an argument with her?"

"Not that I recall," Michael said thoughtfully. Then he stopped. "Bonnie did say something odd the day before she died."

"What was that?" Sally asked eagerly.

"We were talking and she suddenly brightened and said something like, 'Now I remember.'"

"Now I remember," Sally repeated. "Do you know what she remembered? Did it have something to do with Sylvia?"

"I don't know. She just smiled and said goodbye."

Sally had trouble concentrating on the lecture. Her mind kept going over the conversation with Michael, especially the last part. What was it that Bonnie had remembered? Did the memory have something to do with her death?

At the end of class Sally waited until everyone had left the room then went up to Kat Mac.

"May I speak with you?" she asked, leaning against the table across from her desk.

"Sure." Kat Mac put down her pen and looked up.

"First, I'd like to congratulate you on your upcoming book. I read about it on the Internet."

"Thank you. I'm pleased with it."

"I've been talking with Michael Wolf who was part of your class two years ago. He said you were instrumental in getting his book published."

Kat Mac shook her head. "I can't take credit for that. He had a good idea and the publisher was receptive to it. It's that old publishing mantra: right day, right idea, right publisher. And speaking of manuscripts, have you thought about discussing your work with me. I still have Thursday afternoon open."

So much had happened since she arrived at the retreat that Sally hadn't thought about her manuscript. She could understand how Elizabeth got wrapped up in a mystery and had to fight to do her research.

"I'm really not ready for that yet," Sally said. "but I would like to ask you if Bonnie talked to you about her cousin, Sylvia, last week?"

"And why would you like to ask me that?" Kat Mac cocked her head to one side.

Geeze, what was with everyone? Why couldn't they just answer her questions so she could get on with finding out about what happened to Bonnie and Sylvia? Where were the blabbers, the ones who readily answered and even gave more information than asked for?

"Bonnie thought her cousin had been murdered and had asked my friend and me to help her prove it."

"Why would she ask you that?"

Sally sighed inwardly. Should she tell her or just leave? She hated to be telling so many people what she and Elizabeth were doing and especially not Kat Mac with what she had learned about her this morning. But there was nothing else she could do. It didn't look like Kat Mac was going to volunteer anything.

So for the second time that day Sally explained about her and Elizabeth's quest.

"And what do you want to know from me?" Kat Mac asked at the end of Sally's speech.

"What did Bonnie speak with you about last week?"

"She wanted to know what I could tell her about Sylvia. Honestly, I can't remember much about her. I've had lots of students over the years plus it's been two years since Sylvia was here."

"But wouldn't her death stick out in your mind."

"Oh, yes, the death does but the person doesn't."

"Did Sylvia take much part in class, had she booked a time to discuss her manuscript with you?"

"I really don't recall."

"Sylvia's aunt hasn't been able to find Sylvia's manuscript and we were wondering if maybe Sylvia gave it to you."

Kat Mac shrugged. "If she had I would have returned it with her things."

Sally was stymied. What more could she say? Should she mention the rumour that Michael had told her about? She decided not to. It was just hearsay but she would tell Elizabeth about it.

* * *

Elizabeth took Chevy and went down to the pool. She stretched out on the lounge chair and closed her eyes. Her article was complete except for the few attractions she had to visit this week. And for those all she had to do was give a few words about what the reader could expect and take pictures.

For the first time her work was done before the mystery was cleared up. She liked that. It took the pressure off. She lazed a while longer then, telling Chevy to stay under the chair where he had crawled, she dove into the pool. A few laps and she climbed out. Sally should be back from class soon, hopefully with some news.

She and Chevy went to their room where she stepped into the shower. When she was dressed she checked the clock. Where was Sally? Surely she would have talked to Michael and Kat Mac by now. Maybe she should have gone with her. Maybe they should have made arrangements for her to pick Sally up.

Elizabeth put Chevy on his leash and went out to the street. She looked both ways expecting to see Sally coming towards her. Instead she saw a woman on the sidewalk staring at the lot. She was crying.

Even though her investigation had become a bit of a joke between her and Sally since Cynthia had hired her, there were still questions that ran through her mind. Now, one of them was, could the young girl who died here be a relative of this woman's? Elizabeth thought of the couple she had accosted last week just after the body had been found. They had been shaken by her questions. While she still felt the pull of the mystery, she wasn't in favour of intruding on anyone's grief again.

She waited a few more minutes. Chevy looked up at her impatiently. He was ready to go for the walk he had thought they were heading on. Elizabeth wondered if should she go over and talk with the woman. She looked for Sally again then, her curiosity getting the better of her, sauntered over to where the woman stood.

"Are you one of the relatives waiting for news?" Elizabeth

asked quietly.

The woman looked at her.

"It's really sad," Elizabeth said, beginning to feel stupid. Obviously this woman wanted to be left alone.

The woman wiped at her eyes with a tissue.

"Are you okay?" Elizabeth asked.

"I think the young woman found here was the mother of my grandchild."

"I'm sorry," Elizabeth said. Instead of asking more questions, she decided to let it alone. Now was not the time. She turned to leave. Chevy hurried ahead.

"She and my son were dating."

Elizabeth stopped causing Chevy to hit the end of his leash. He glared back at her. Elizabeth wasn't sure if the woman was talking to her or just out loud. Should she say something or leave?

"I'm Polly MacNeil."

"Elizabeth Oliver." Elizabeth held out her hand. Polly's shake was fast. Elizabeth took a deep breath and ask the question that was on her mind. "Who was she?"

"Her name was Leslie Brown." Polly's eyes got a far away look to them. "It's a typical teenage story. She was sixteen, my son was seventeen and she got pregnant. My son wasn't ready to be a father so he broke up with her. Leslie took off and neither her parents nor my husband and I have heard from her since."

"What makes you think the young girl is Leslie?" Elizabeth wondered if this had something to do with the adoption group that had involved Penny.

"Her parents reported her missing and now every time there is a body found they are notified. They are on a trip to Europe so the police contacted me as the backup person."

Polly paused. She took out a fresh tissue from her purse and dabbed her eyes. "Three months ago my son was killed." Her voice caught. "He was our only child." The tears began to flow again and Elizabeth wondered if she had been crying for Leslie or for her son or for her grandchild.

Chevy dug his claws into the ground as he pulled on his leash. Elizabeth wanted to hear more from this woman who seemed to need to talk and tugged back. He looked up at her with disgust and went over to the fire hydrant to lift his leg.

Polly blew her nose. "Since we are never going to have any more grandchildren now, we are hoping to find Leslie and learn where our grandchild is."

"So really you are hoping the girl is not Leslie."

"Yes. We have hired a detective to locate her but so far he hasn't been able to find anything about her. It's like she's vanished."

"When did she leave?"

"Eleven months ago. She was six months along at the time so the baby would be eight months old."

Chevy gave a little yip. Polly looked down at him as if seeing him for the first time.

"What type of dog is he?"

"He's a cross between a cocker spaniel and a poodle. He's called a cockapoo."

"Cute."

"I'm staying in the bed and breakfast next door," Elizabeth said, pointing. "If you need a place to stay while you are here, I think there's an empty room."

"Thank you," Polly said. "I'm not sure of my plans yet."

Elizabeth felt guilty leaving Polly standing staring at the empty lot, but there was nothing more she could do.

She walked Chevy along the way she had driven Sally that morning. She smiled with relief when she saw Sally coming around the corner. Sally waved and hurried up to her.

"So how did it go this morning?" Elizabeth asked. "Did you learn anything new?"

"Yes," Sally said, excitedly. "Michael never saw Sylvia's manuscript but he did tell me about a rumour that Kat Mac has stolen ideas from her students."

"What?"

"Yes. And the reason she's still teaching is because it has never been proven and most students give her high marks at the end of the classes."

"But didn't you tell me that she had helped Michael get his

manuscript published?"

"Yes, so that kind of negates the rumour, doesn't it?"

"Did you talk with Kat Mac?"

"Yes. She said that she didn't see Sylvia's manuscript. I didn't ask her about the rumour."

"So we have Sylvia telling Bonnie how much Kat Mac liked her manuscript and Kat Mac saying she never saw it."

"Right. Which one is lying."

"Well, since both Sylvia and Bonnie are dead we will have a hard time figuring that out."

"Madeline said that Sylvia told her she would get to read it when it was a best seller."

"Making it sound like there is a manuscript."

Polly McNeil was gone when they reached the bed and breakfast and they went up to their suite.

"I don't know what to make of all this," Sally said, flopping on the couch. "And I'm getting tired of thinking about it."

"I know what you mean," Elizabeth agreed. "Do you want to do something different this afternoon?"

"Sure, what do you have in mind?"

"Well, I still have to do the Peak 2 Peak Gondola."

Sally grinned. "I could go for that."

Elizabeth looked at her watch. "We've got to go now. I was told that I should head up before three o'clock in order to see the whole thing before it closes down. As it is we won't be able to do any of the hikes."

Elizabeth quickly took a ginger pill for her motion sickness and grabbed her tape recorder and camera. Since animals were not allowed on the gondolas, Elizabeth left Chevy with Beverly. They drove to the free parking and hurried across the road. They stopped at the ski lift and watched as some mountain bikers loaded their bikes onto a bike lift then ran to the seat ahead and hopped on. Bikers were zipping down the hill, dismounting, and getting in line again.

"That looks like fun," Elizabeth said.

They went over to the Whistler gondola building and bought their tickets. Elizabeth could feel the butterflies in her stomach at the thought of going up in the gondola. She hated that she had the combination of motion sickness and fear of heights. The ginger pills took care of the motion sickness but there was nothing to combat her heights issue except staying firmly on the ground. She smiled grimly at the joke she had read about the woman with a fear of heights who liked staying on good old terra firma--the more firma, the less terra.

Luckily the line was short and she didn't have to spend too much time thinking about the ride. She climbed on the gondola quickly not giving herself time to back out. Sally and two other people followed her. They sat down. The door closed and the gondola moved ahead. Suddenly they were outside and rising.

Elizabeth gasped at the fear that stabbed her stomach. She fought the urge to close her eyes. Instead, she took out her camera to take pictures. However, the plexiglass was too scratched to get a good shot. She searched for a spot that was clear.

"Good luck with that," the young man said.

"How come this glass is so marked up?" Elizabeth asked.

"When there are lots of mountain bikers or if they are having a meet, the bikers are allowed to go up in the gondolas."

"They can get their bikes in these?" Sally asked.

"If they work at it they can get three bikes and bikers in at one time. They hold the front wheel up or prop them against the windows."

Part way up they reached a station where the gondola stopped and the doors opened. That was short, Elizabeth thought as she and Sally prepared to get off.

"No, stay on," the young man said. "This is where they let the bikers off for their downhill trip."

Elizabeth made a mental note to put that in her article as she and Sally sat back down. The gondola took them ever higher up the mountainside and she looked out the marred glass in awe at the mountains all around and the sight of the town of Whistler getting smaller and smaller. Her fear was still there but as usual once she got up and going the adventure overrode her anxiety.

Eventually they reached the Roundhouse at the top of Whistler Mountain where they disembarked. They toured through the Roundhouse, a huge log building with shops and a restaurant inside. Elizabeth took pictures of the building and the mountains around.

They walked across the grass and Elizabeth took pictures of the large Inukshuk that looked out over a valley. They walked past the Inukshuk to see the valley better.

"This is so beautiful," Sally breathed.

"Is that a rat?" A woman shrieked behind them.

They turned in time to see a giant black rat sitting on the Inukshuk. Suddenly two men laughed and went up to it. One of them held it up so that everyone could see that it was just a stuffed rat. He carried it over to one of the tables and the other man took pictures of it with the mountains behind.

Elizabeth and Sally smiled at each other, then went to the Peak 2 Peak station. Elizabeth recorded all the World Records on the Peak 2 Peak such as: it is the world's longest unsupported (free) span for a lift of this kind; it is the world's highest lift of its kind; and it is the world's longest continuous lift system.

"Look, we will be travelling at 7.5 metres per second," Sally said, reading the sign. "It's 4.4 km across and will take us eleven minutes to the other side."

Good, just what I want to be thinking about as I'm hundreds of metres above the ground, Elizabeth thought.

They entered the station where there were two lines. One was to get on the red cabin which came every few minutes and the other was for the glass bottomed silver cabin which arrived every fifteen minutes. Elizabeth and Sally opted to wait for the silver cabin. They climbed on with six other people, two of them the men with the rat, and headed across the valley to Blackcomb Mountain.

The bottom wasn't totally glass. There was a square of glass surrounded by a barrier that came up to their waists. They could look over the edge of the barrier and see the ground below but couldn't stand on the glass.

Elizabeth took her pictures of the mountains, the other cabins going by, the towers holding the cables, and the river in the valley below. Looking out one side of the cabin she saw Whistler in the distance, looking the other way was mountains. She noted that there are about sixty black bears in the peak to peak area so hikers should be aware of them.

The two men snapped pictures of the rat on the glass bottom, sitting on the seat, and hanging from the ceiling.

"Where are you from?" Elizabeth asked.

"Switzerland," one of the men replied with a thick accent.

"This was given us by our friends," the other explained. "They want us to put him in the pictures we are sending back home."

This story reminded Elizabeth of the garden gnome prank where gnomes are 'liberated' from their dull lives and returned to the wild. Some pranksters would take the stolen gnome on holidays and send pictures back of it at famous attractions. Sometimes the gnome was returned to his spot in the garden with no one admitting to being the liberators or the thieves depending on a person's point of view.

Elizabeth and Sally had a juice and pop at the restaurant on Blackcomb Mountain then climbed aboard a red cabin for their return trip to Whistler Mountain.

They were the only ones on the gondola heading back down to Whistler.

"Look at the doors," Sally said. "They don't look very secure."

Elizabeth checked the door. The rubber on the edge where they joined barely met and the doors themselves didn't quite reach the floor.

"You know this would make a perfect way to commit murder," Sally said.

"What do you mean?" Elizabeth asked.

"Well, someone could push open the doors and shove someone out. No one would know because they don't seem to keep track of how many people get on each gondola."

"I doubt that the doors will open if you push them," Elizabeth said. "Too many people would accidentally fall out."

"Why don't you try them?" Sally grinned.

"No way," Elizabeth responded. "What if it does open and I fall out? What if it stops the ride?"

Sally sobered. "Yes, I'm sure there is security on the doors so they don't open but it would be a great way to dispose of someone in a mystery novel."

"That would probably work better on a ski lift especially if you are one of the last skiers."

"I forgot to tell you that Michael said that on the day Bonnie talked with him she said she remembered something but she didn't say what it was."

"I wonder if it had anything to do with Sylvia or if she just remembered where her car keys were," Elizabeth mused

"That's what's been going through my mind, too."

"What do you think of this Michael?"

"What do you mean?" Sally asked.

"I'm just wondering how much we can trust him?"

"He seems nice. I can't think of why he would lie to us."

"Well, Sylvia said she had a manuscript but Kat Mac didn't see it. Michael claims he didn't either and then he tells you of the rumour about Kat Mac. Of course our first thought is that Kat Mac may have stolen Sylvia's manuscript and found a publisher for it."

"Is that a good reason to kill someone, though?" Sally asked.

"Well, if you were one of the top of science fiction writers and then had nothing published for seven years it might be for you."

"So she killed Sylvia for the manuscript that is now so eagerly anticipated by the sci-fi world. But why would Kat Mac have killed Bonnie? All she was doing was asking questions."

Elizabeth thought that through. "Maybe that something Bonnie remembered was something that Sylvia had sent in a text to her about Kat Mac. Maybe Bonnie thought she had proof that Kat Mac had killed her cousin two years ago and stole her manuscript. She may have told Kat Mac what she knew and was killed because of that."

"Or she could have tried blackmailing her," Sally said. "After all, it sounded like Kat Mac was going to make a lot of money from this newest book of hers."

"You're right. I never thought of that."

"So Kat Mac killed her to save herself money."

"I have a question," Elizabeth said. "Who sent us down that path?"

Sally thought a moment. "Michael," Sally said.

"Right. And he was in Sylvia's class and he is also getting a book published."

Sally's mouth gaped. "So, he could have killed Sylvia for her idea."

Elizabeth nodded. "Maybe, for a few minutes, his desire to get published overrode everything else in his life."

"Plus, Bonnie did say that Sylvia had met an older man who could fit Michael's description."

"And to top it off Bonnie talked with Michael on the last day of her life," Elizabeth said.

"Now what do we do?" Sally asked exasperated. "We have no real proof that points to either of them."

Chapter 19

"Thank you for looking after Chevy, Beverly," Elizabeth said, when they got back to the bed and breakfast. Chevy jumped at Elizabeth's leg and she picked him up. He licked her face.

"Oh, he was so good, I'd do it again," Beverly laughed, patting him on the head. "He followed me everywhere and he has such expression in his eyes."

"Yes, he's quite the dog," Elizabeth agreed.

"Did you enjoy your ride?"

"The town and valley are a beautiful sight looking down from the gondola," Elizabeth said.

"You should see it during the winter when everything is covered with snow and the ski is a bright, bright blue."

After Elizabeth and Sally took Chevy for a walk they climbed the stairs to their suite. "What do you want to do for supper?" Elizabeth asked, as she put the key in the lock.

"I don't know. We should have bought something when we were in the village and brought it back with us."

"It would have been nice if you had thought of that before," Elizabeth laughed and pushed the door open. She stopped short when she saw a white envelope laying on the floor. Their names were scrawled on it in block letters. She looked at Sally who was staring at the envelope. They walked around it and closed the door. Chevy went over to his water dish and had a drink.

"What do we do?" Sally asked quietly.

"I'll go ask Beverly if anyone came to see us while we were gone."

"I'm sure she would have told us."

"Maybe she forgot. I'll be right back." Elizabeth hurried down the stairs hoping that, in deed, Beverly had just forgotten to mention a visitor. She found Beverly cleaning the dining room.

"Hey, Beverly, I was expecting someone to drop off a package this afternoon and I was wondering if she showed up."

Beverly shook her head. "I didn't see anyone, but I could

have been cleaning a room. Did you check by the front door? Sometime people leave things there."

"Thank you." Elizabeth headed up the stairs and into the suite.

The envelope was still on the floor.

"Beverly didn't see anyone," she said.

"Should we call the police?" Sally asked. She had sat on the couch but was watching the envelope as if expecting it to move.

"I'm thinking we should open it first to see what it is."

"Okay, you do it."

Elizabeth gingerly picked the envelope up by the tip of a corner and carried it to the table. Sally followed her and hovered while she laid it face down. The flap had been tucked inside rather than glued. Elizabeth held it down by the corner and worked the flap out. Inside was a folded piece of paper. Elizabeth pulled it out by the edge and opened it.

STAY AWAY AND LEAVE THINGS ALONE

was written in black crayon.

* * *

"Stay away from whom and leave what alone?" Constable Black asked.

"We're not sure," Sally said.

She and Elizabeth had taken the note and envelope to the RCMP detachment to show it to the constables working on Bonnie's death. They had decided that Sally would do the talking since she had been the one who had spoken with Michael and Kat Mac.

Constable Black looked at Sally and then back to Elizabeth. "Would one of you like to explain."

Sally took a deep breath. She was so nervous. It was important that she explain everything in the order it had happened, and what she had talked about and with whom.

"And you think this note has something to do with Bonnie Stone's death," Black said, when she had finished.

"We don't know," Sally said. "It just seems strange that

after I talked with Michael and Kat Mac, we would receive this."

Black looked at Elizabeth. "Or maybe you could have sent it to yourselves?"

"What?" Elizabeth gasped. "Why would we do that?"

"Well, it seems to me that you get a kick out of pretending to be a detective and trying to solve murders. This could just be your way of getting the attention of the police and the media."

"That's ridiculous," Elizabeth sputtered.

"Is it? Why would someone threaten you?"

"Maybe we're getting too close to the person who killed Sylvia Bush and Bonnie Stone."

Black shook his head. "No one killed Sylvia Bush."

"Well, someone did murder Bonnie. We know that Bonnie's Angel cards were thrown on her," Elizabeth said.

Constable Black stood and hustled them out of the room. "I think you should take your misguided talents and go back to Edmonton," he said, handing the note and envelope back to Sally. "I'm sure we will be able to stumble through this on our own."

"Now what do we do?" Sally asked, as they walked to the Tracker.

"Well, we know this threat is real so we have to take better measures to protect ourselves." Elizabeth opened the driver's door, picked up an excited Chevy off the seat, and climbed in.

"Right. No going out at night even together," Sally said, getting into the passenger's seat.

"Chevy will still need to be walked before bed, but we can do that just up and down the street. And I will drive you to class every morning and pick you up afterwards."

"But that leaves you alone all morning." She didn't like that.

"Again, I have Chevy for protection."

"What if this is a joke?" Sally asked.

"But who would send it to us?"

"Well, everyone in my class knows what Bonnie was doing and that she had asked us to help. Maybe someone from the retreat put it there as a joke."

"Someone like Daryl?"

"If he did than it would explain how it got there without Beverly seeing someone."

"Maybe we should ask him."

They went back to the bed and breakfast. Elizabeth put Chevy on his leash as they went up the stairs and knocked on Daryl's door.

Daryl groaned when he saw them. "What do you want now?"

All the niceties that Sally had thought about starting with vanished and she got right to the reason they were there. "Did you shove an envelope under our door today?"

"What?" Daryl asked, confused.

"We found an envelope on our floor when we returned to our suite late this afternoon," Sally said. "We've been trying to figure out who left it."

"What makes you think I would do something like that?" Daryl demanded.

"We're talking to everyone in my class," Sally said. "You just happen to be the first because you're staying here."

"Well, it wasn't me," Daryl stepped back into his room.

"Did you see anyone go up to our suite today?" Elizabeth asked, before he could close the door.

"What makes you think I would be paying attention to something like that?"

"Why do you answer every question with a question?" Elizabeth asked angrily.

"Because I'm getting tired of you two and your stupid questions. Who do you think you are, anyway, expecting me to answer your questions as if you are the police?"

Sally sighed. "Look, you know Bonnie asked us to help her find out if her cousin was murdered. Now she's dead and we are just trying discover what happened to both of them."

"Well, I had nothing to do with it. I've been in my room all afternoon working on my novel, like you should be." He looked meaningfully at Sally, who blushed. "I didn't leave an envelope under your door and I wouldn't have seen Big Bird if he had come down the hall."

"Okay, thank you," Elizabeth said, turning away.

"So, what was in this envelope?" Daryl asked.

Elizabeth and Sally looked at each other. Sally pulled the envelope from her jean's pocket and handed it to him.

He took out the note and read it. "I'm assuming you are supposed to stay away from Bonnie's death," he said, stuffing the paper back in the envelope.

"That's what we are assuming, also," Sally said. "But we don't know who we've scared enough to send it to us."

"Have you taken it to the police?" Daryl handed the envelope back to Sally.

Sally snorted. "They think we sent it to ourselves for the publicity."

"And did you?"

"Of course not," Sally said, indignantly.

"So what are you going to do about it?"

Boy, he asked a lot of questions, Sally thought. Kind of like us. "We really don't know," she admitted. "We're wondering if someone from our class may have sent it as a joke."

Daryl started "You thought I would do it as a joke?"

Sally shook her head. "We're trying to think of every possible scenario."

"Yes," Elizabeth said. "We really hate to think someone would be threatening us."

"Well, it wasn't me and now I have to get back to work." Daryl closed the door in their faces.

They paused at their door and Elizabeth opened it slowly. It was dark inside and she flipped on the switch. Nothing on the floor. They entered and she undid Chevy's leash.

Sally threw herself on the couch. "I'm still hungry," she said.

"Do you want to go get something?" Elizabeth asked.

"No, I don't feel like going out. Let's see what we have here."

Elizabeth turned on the television while Sally rummaged through their meagre supply of food. "We have a can of beans, one of spaghetti sauce with meat and a box of spaghetti."

"Well, I guess it's spaghetti and meat sauce," Elizabeth said, flipping to the Vancouver news channel.

While Sally made supper, Elizabeth fed Chevy, then set out the plates and cutlery. They seldom sat at the table preferring to watch television while they ate.

Elizabeth hated to admit it but she was frightened. Nothing like this had happened to her before and she didn't know how to deal with it. She knew they should heed the note and head home immediately. She would bring up the subject later, after they both had had a chance to think it over.

"Spaghetti's ready," Sally called.

They dished up and sat on the couch.

The news anchor finished giving the Vancouver news and turned to what was happening in the rest of the province.

"I met a woman named Polly McNeil this morning," Elizabeth said, as she wound some spaghetti around her fork. "She's here looking for the mother of her grandchild."

"That sounds a little complicated." Sally was cutting her spaghetti into bite sized pieces.

"Apparently Polly's son was dating a girl but when she got pregnant the son didn't want to be a father and dropped her. She ran off and hasn't been seen since."

"So why is she here? Shouldn't it be the girl's parents?"

"They're in Europe so the police contacted Polly. Her son was an only child and was killed a few months ago. Now, she and her husband want to find their grandchild because it will be the only one they ever have."

"There sure are a lot of disheartening stories, aren't there," Sally said.

They concentrated on eating while listening to the news anchor.

"It seems there may now be two Whistler's Murders," the anchor said. "The police say that the autopsy of the woman found laying on a street in Whistler has shown that she died from a blunt force trauma to her head that would not have been caused from being hit by a car. The police are asking for tips from anyone who may have seen Bonnie Stone the afternoon or evening of July 17."

A picture of Bonnie flashed up on the screen.

"And now for an update on the discovery of the body during the demolition of a house in Whistler. Police have found a piece of jewellery that they think may have belonged to the victim. They are encouraging anyone who had come to see them about the young woman to contact them if she had been wearing jewellery when she was last seen."

The anchor then continued with other news.

"Maybe that's the break the police need," Elizabeth said, gathering up the plates. She ran some water into the sink and put the plates in to soak. She was scraping the last of the spaghetti from the pan into the garbage when there was a knock at their door. Chevy ran to it barking.

"Don't answer it," Elizabeth said quickly, as Sally started towards the door. The nearest thing she could find for a weapon was a white ceramic pitcher with blue and red polka dots on it. She grabbed it.

"What's that for?' Sally whispered.

"It's the best I can do," Elizabeth whispered back, as she tip toed to the door. "Damn," she muttered, just noticing that there was no peep hole.

The knock sounded again. "Hello?" a woman's voice called.

Chevy's bark grew louder.

The voice sounded familiar to Elizabeth. She looked at Sally.

"Don't know," Sally mouthed. She picked up Chevy who finally quit barking.

Elizabeth raised the pitcher over her shoulder and motioned for Sally to open the door.

"Why me?" Sally shook her head. "Let's ignore it."

Elizabeth waved her back and undid the lock. She slowly opened the door and peeked through the crack.

"Elizabeth?"

"Oh, hi, Polly," Elizabeth hid the pitcher behind her back as she pulled the door wider. "Come in."

Elizabeth backed into the living room as she introduced

Polly to Sally who put Chevy down on the floor. She set the pitcher on the coffee table as the two women shook hands.

"I'm sorry to disturb you," Polly said. "But you seemed very sympathetic this morning and since I am here alone I was wondering if you would mind coming with me to the police detachment."

It was getting late and Elizabeth wasn't enthused about going to the detachment again. "What do you have to go for?"

"I saw the news tonight. I gave Leslie a necklace and I want to find out if that's what the police found."

Well, in the interest of solving a murder, she was certainly willing to do anything. "Sure, I'll go with you," Elizabeth said. "But, I'd like Sally to come with us," she added. She wasn't about to leave her best friend here alone after the note they'd received that afternoon.

Polly looked a little taken aback but agreed. "I'm staying here like you suggested," Polly said. "So we can all travel in the same vehicle."

"We'll take mine," Elizabeth said. "Chevy will wait for me quietly in my Tracker."

They climbed out of the vehicle at the station. There were a number of cars there and when they got inside it was crowded with people.

"Are all these people here about the jewellery?" Sally asked.

"It looks like it," Polly said. "I saw some of them here when I came to tell my story."

They found a place to sit and waited their turn. After a few minutes Polly began to talk.

"When Leslie told me she was pregnant with my grandchild, I was so happy. Even though they weren't engaged I gave her a locket that my mother had given me when I was pregnant with my son. Then I found out that my husband had been talking with my son, telling him that he was too young to be saddled with having to look after or pay support for a baby. I suggested that we take in the baby and raise it, but my husband blew up saying he didn't want to be encumbered with a baby either. My son listened to him and broke off their relationship, even going so far as to state that he wasn't even sure the baby was his. That hurt Leslie's feelings and I believe that's why she left."

"And you've never heard from her since."

Polly shook her head. "I've been waiting for the past four years for her whereabouts to be discovered. I never thought she was dead just that she had decided to get away from the boy who hurt her so much."

"How does your husband feel about you looking for Leslie and the baby?"

"He didn't like it at first, but now with our son gone, he's changed his mind."

The crowd began to thin as people explained a piece of jewellery their loved one had possessed and were turned away. Some left with a look of hope, while other's expression was of resignation.

Polly went up to the desk and described the locket she had given Leslie. The officer behind the desk left for a moment. Polly glanced over at Elizabeth and Sally, a stricken look on her face. When the officer returned Constable Black was with him.

"Mrs. McNeil, would you come with me, please," Black said. He saw Elizabeth and Sally and his lips formed a thin line.

"We gave Mrs. McNeil a ride," Elizabeth explained.

"Doesn't look good," Sally said, as they watched Polly walk away with the constable.

"No, it doesn't," Elizabeth agreed.

It was half an hour before Polly returned, wiping her eyes. They walked in silence to the Tracker where Chevy waited.

"It was the locket I gave Leslie," Polly said.

Elizabeth let her breath out. "So the body belongs to Leslie?"

"The police aren't exactly saying that," Polly said. "They still want to wait for the DNA confirmation, which should be back any day now."

"So really nothing has been settled yet," Sally said.

"Well, we know that Leslie was here." Polly blew her nose. "And that she probably sold my grandchild to strangers."

Oh, man, what a terrible thing to have to live with.

* * *

The next morning Elizabeth drove Sally to class. "Now make sure you don't go anywhere until I'm with you," Sally said, getting out of the vehicle."

"Okay," Elizabeth agreed. "But I don't think you're that safe here with Kat Mac and Michael."

"There are the rest of the students," Sally said. "I'll make sure I'm always with one of them until you come and get me."

They had discussed the note after getting back to their suite last night. Sally had opted to stay the rest of the week. "If we continue to be careful, we'll be okay."

After transcribing the tape from the Peak 2 Peak Gondola, Elizabeth changed into the bathing suite and headed to the pool again. She could get used to this, she thought as she laid on the lounge chair. Chevy curled up in his spot under the chair.

She was tired from the late night and found herself dozing in the warm sun. She heard a noise and quickly opened her eyes. Chevy, who had curled up under the chair, growled. A woman, wearing a two piece bathing suit, stopped in mid stride and stared at the dog. Elizabeth smiled.

"He's just a little protective. He won't do anything unless he thinks I'm in danger." Might was well let people know that he was on guard.

The woman continued to another chair and sat down. Elizabeth recognized her as Jessica Smallwood. Her daughter was the Penny, Cynthia had met.

Elizabeth watched and when Jessica didn't seem to want to talk, she lay back. She didn't close her eyes this time. Not that she was paranoid but she didn't want to take a chance. She also decided that she didn't want to get into the pool either. She'd seen enough crime shows where people were drowned by their attackers. She wasn't giving anyone a chance to do that.

Boy, how her attitude had changed about being involved in a murder mystery. In past years she'd thought it was exciting and fun, and never once had she felt afraid. Now she was aware that her actions could affect her well-being.

She noticed that Jessica kept looking towards the lot next door, not that she could see much because of the bushes. Had she been told about the identification of the necklace last night?

Elizabeth couldn't help herself. "I saw you on the news a couple of nights ago. I'm sorry about your daughter."

Jessica looked at her. She took a bottle of sun tan lotion out of her bag.

Well, that didn't work. "My name is Elizabeth Oliver. My friend and I are staying here in the suite on the top floor."

"I'm on the second floor," Jessica said, rubbing some lotion on her arms.

Bonnie's old room. Beverly sure was doing a booming business because of the body discovered next door. As family members were leaving after finding out the young woman wasn't related to them, others were showing up to take their place. Did Jessica know the history of the room she was staying in? Elizabeth wasn't about to tell her.

"Did the police tell you that the jewellery has been identified?" Elizabeth asked.

"How do you know so much about it? I was just told this morning."

"I went with the woman who identified it."

"But it doesn't prove yet whose body it is."

"Yes, you're right," Elizabeth nodded. "In the interview, you said that you lived in Vancouver and that Penny went to an abortion clinic there."

Jessica looked at her. "Yes. So?"

"Did Penny know that she would be given the choice of putting her child up for adoption before she went there?"

"How would she know that?" Jessica demanded.

"Maybe a friend of a friend told her. Maybe she learned about it on the Internet."

"Well, I have no idea." Jessica put the lotion away.

"Do you think the body is hers?"

"You sure are nosy, aren't you."

Elizabeth felt herself blush. "I have been told that," she admitted. She didn't say anything about why she was nosy. Instead she gave her another reason. "I have written some articles about true crime. I guess I'm just wondering if your story would make a saleable article."

"Would I get paid for it?" Jessica asked. "I've heard that some of the magazines offer one hundred thousand dollars for some stories."

"I don't write for those types of magazines," Elizabeth said.

"Oh." Jessica was quiet.

Elizabeth waited while Jessica made up her mind if she wanted to talk.

"To answer your question," Jessica said. "I don't know if the body is Penny's yet and I'm not going to put myself though the agony of speculating." Jessica lay back on the lounge chair and closed her eyes.

Obviously, she wasn't worried about someone attacking her. Maybe that's her way of trying to make me feel comfortable and so I'll let my guard down. Well, it's not going to work.

Elizabeth stood and went into the bed and breakfast. She could enjoy the sun from their balcony without the worry. But she realized that she had lost some of her sense of freedom and that bothered her.

Instead of sunbathing, Elizabeth dressed and got herself a Pepsi. She sat on the couch. One thing had been nagging at her all morning. There was the chance that Cynthia may have dropped the note off. She seemed to like the idea of hiring a private investigator. And Elizabeth hadn't made a report to Cynthia, hadn't seen her for while. Maybe Elizabeth wasn't keeping her in the loop as much as she would like. Maybe she wanted more excitement. Sneaking in here could have given it to her.

She wanted to go and see Cynthia about the note but had promised Sally that she would stay at the bed and breakfast until time to pick her up. Now was not the time to do anything stupid. She looked at the clock. Still an hour to go. Damn, she didn't know if it was better to be behind on her research and article or ahead. Being behind meant that she always had something to do with any free time. Of course, she really couldn't blame her boredom on her finished research. It was the killer in this town that kept her inside.

She turned on the television and flipped through the channels. Again, she settled on the all news station. As pictures of the crowd at the RCMP detachment last night ran the news anchor was saying. "The piece of jewellery has been identified as belonging to Leslie Borden. She was a young girl who got pregnant by her boyfriend. Her boyfriend's mother, Polly NcNeil, gave her the necklace. When her boyfriend, Perry, rejected her she left home. She has not been seen since. The police have not confirmed that the body is that of Leslie Borden, though. They are still waiting for the DNA testing."

"Nothing new there," Elizabeth said. She turned to a comedy show and slouched on the couch watching it.

At last the time was up. She grabbed Chevy and went out to her vehicle.

* * *

Kat Mac began the morning by telling everyone about Bonnie's murder. "I'm not sure how many of you take the time to watch television so I'm just letting you know that the police now think Bonnie was murdered."

Everyone was silent watching her. She looked over the students, nodded, and got on with her lecture. But she didn't have the usual drive behind her words. It was obvious that the news had affected her especially when, just after the break, she announced that the class was going to end early. She left the room. Everyone rose slowly and gathered their things. They filed out.

Sally joined her usual group in the lunch room. They were discussing Bonnie's murder.

"Didn't Bonnie ask you to look into her cousin's murder?" Lisa asked Sally.

"She thought her cousin had been murdered and she did ask my friend, Elizabeth, and I to see if we could prove it."

"Why you two?" Reggie asked.

"Bonnie found out that Elizabeth has a knack for

discovering murderers."

"And from what she said on her last day, she seemed convinced that Sylvia had been murdered," Kirk said. "Do you think her death is connected with Sylvia's?"

Sally wasn't sure how much to say about it. After all, one of these people could be a killer. They had all been there when Bonnie had said she was looking for Sylvia's murderer. Although, why any of these people, who had been strangers just two weeks ago, would kill her was a mystery in itself. "The police are still saying Sylvia's death was accidental so I don't know what to think."

"Well, I think we should all be careful," Reggie said. "It could be that Bonnie's death had nothing to do with Sylvia's and something to do with the retreat or our class."

"What do you mean?" Lisa gasped.

Sally felt her nerves tingle. This could be something. She listened to what the others had say.

Reggie looked around. "I know it sounds silly," he said, lowering his voice and leaning in. "But Daryl was not happy with the way Bonnie conducted herself here. Maybe his anger got the better of him."

"I know he is taking this course very seriously but do you think he's that obsessed that he would kill her?" Kirk asked.

Reggie shrugged. "It's just a thought."

"Well, the rest of us have been working hard so if that's what happened, then we are safe," Lisa said.

"And speaking of work," Kirk said, rising. "I have to get back to my room. See you tomorrow."

Lisa stood also. "Yes. I have to finish my costume for Saturday night."

That left Sally and Reggie. Sally watched as Daryl and his two buddies, Luke Johnson and Henry Freisen, walked by. They didn't even look in their direction.

"Do you believe your theory about Daryl?" Sally asked, when they had left the room.

"Not really," Reggie said.

"So you don't have anything to base it on?"

"No, but I don't want to talk about him. Tell me more about yourself."

Sally smiled and told him about her life in Edmonton. Then she listened to a quick rundown of the places he had lived when growing up before his family settled in Hinton. "Now, I work in the town office there as a planner."

"Why did you take this retreat?" Sally asked.

"Like everyone else I want to be a writer. I just don't know what type yet. So, so far, I've taken a mystery writing course, a romance writing course, and a non-fiction writing course.

Sally grinned. "Are you eliminating them off your Bucket List or waiting to complete this one to decide which genre is right for you?"

"A bit of both, I guess. I think what I should do is write something and then figure out where it fits."

Sally looked at her watch. "Oh, I have to go. My ride is probably outside."

Reggie put his hand over hers. "I'll see you tomorrow. Don't do anything foolish with this investigation you and your friend are doing."

"We won't," Sally said, hating that she had to go.

* * *

On the way back to the bed and breakfast Sally and Elizabeth saw John out in his yard.

"Let's stop and talk with him," Sally said. "I've been wondering if he's experiencing elder abuse."

Elizabeth parked sideways behind John's car. She wanted to be able to get out of there fast if his daughter came back. She didn't trust or like Wendy.

"Whatever my daughter told you about me isn't true," John said, when he saw them. "I know she tells people lies about me to keep them away."

"Why does she do that?" Sally asked.

John shrugged. "I think she's afraid I might find someone to start a relationship with and that person will try to take advantage of me because I have money."

"What happened to your wife?" Elizabeth asked.

"She died just before I won the lottery." His voice caught. "We'd been picking the same numbers for years and when it finally paid off she wasn't here to share it with me."

Elizabeth wasn't sure how to comfort the man. After what his daughter had said she was afraid to do anything that may be misconstrued as an advance.

"What types of lies does your daughter tell?" That would take his mind off his late wife.

"That I've make advances to younger women, and that I'm getting dementia and forgetting things or remembering things that didn't happen."

"How do you know she says those things?" Sally asked.

"Because she tells them to me, too." He looked affronted. "She says that I've tried to kiss a neighbour, that I've told people things that never happened." He was beginning to get distraught. "I don't know why she would try to ruin my life like that. People are avoiding me, like I'm a leper or something."

A van sped up as it came along the road. Elizabeth looked up and saw Wendy glaring at them through the windshield.

Sally leaned forward. "Does Wendy ever hit you or push you?" she asked quietly.

John looked shocked. "Oh, no. She's never hit me."

"But she doesn't let you do much and she seems mad when you talk with us."

"I know." John bowed his head.

"John," Sally said quickly. "If you think you are being abused by your daughter, we can help you."

"What can you do?" John asked dully.

"We could report her to the authorities. Elder abuse is a crime just like any other abuse."

The vehicle stopped and Wendy jumped out. "Dad, I told you to stay in the house while I was gone. What are you doing out here?"

"I wanted to clean the pond again." John's voice was subdued. "It needs to be done every couple of days."

Wendy looked at Elizabeth and Sally. "Didn't I tell you to leave my father alone? He's not in very good health."

"Yes, I am," John said defensively. "I'm fine."

"We're just talking with him," Elizabeth said. "We enjoy his company."

"I warned you about him and what he does when young women are around."

"I don't do anything," John said, his voice rising. "Why do you keep telling people that?"

"Because it's true." Wendy grabbed his arm and steered him towards the house. "You just don't remember." She looked back over her shoulder. "Stay away from him."

Elizabeth and Sally slowly climbed into the Tracker. "Now what do we do?" Sally asked.

"We can't report this until we know which one is telling the truth."

"Well, I'm opting for John."

"There is another scenario," Elizabeth said slowly. She hated to mention it because she liked the man. "Maybe Sylvia went for a walk and met John out in his yard just like you did. What if they struck up a conversation and she came back over and over again. What if he thought she was interested in him and he made advances to her. What if she rejected him and in his anger he killed her."

Elizabeth held her breath letting Sally think it over.

"How would he get the body to the Upper Village?" Sally asked, sceptically.

"Maybe he met her there so his daughter wouldn't know about it."

"Oh god, I hope that's not how it happened." Sally groaned. "I just can't see him doing that, though. He seems so gentle."

"We should get that picture of Sylvia and take it to him. See what his reaction is."

"If his daughter will let us."

Back in their suite Sally went to her bedroom and looked up elder abuse on the Internet. She found the Canadian Network for the Prevention of Elder Abuse, a national non-profit organization.

"So, what are you learning?" Elizabeth asked, bringing them each a drink.

"Well, this group wants to make sure the elder people are able to live independently, safely and without fear of abuse, neglect, or exploitation."

"What do we do if we suspect someone is abused?"

Sally clicked on Find Help and then on the icon of the province of B.C. The only thing that came up was a map of the province in the upper left hand corner. She went back and then tried again. Still only the map. She tried some sections and was told that the site was under construction. In one, though, they read that the abused person may be ashamed of what their family member was doing to them or they could even be frightened of them.

"Sometimes the abused victim doesn't know they were being abused," Elizabeth read over Sally's shoulder. "That sounds like John's situation. He doesn't know it's happening to him."

"We've got to do something," Sally said, shutting down her computer. "We can't leave him to suffer at her hands."

"Yeah, let's get him away from her so we can prove that he killed a woman," Elizabeth said grimly, as they walked to the living room.

Chapter 20

"So nothing has changed." Elizabeth was sitting in one of the stuffed chairs. "We have Kat Mac who may have stolen Sylvia's manuscript so she could get a book published after seven years of nothing. Then we have Michael who may have killed her because he liked her story idea and wanted very badly to get published. Each of them would then have killed Bonnie because she found out the truth." She looked at Sally.

"And then there's John who may have killed Sylvia because she resisted his advances," Sally took up the conjecture. "If he did murder Sylvia then why would he kill Bonnie? As far as I know she never met him."

"Maybe she figured it out and talked with him. He hit her with something as they were walking down the street."

"But Wendy hardly lets him out of her sight," Sally pointed out.

"She may have helped him knowing that Bonnie could expose him as a killer. That could be why she gives him those so-called vitamins that make him black out. To keep control of him."

"So what do we do?" Sally asked, in exasperation. "Try to get him away from the daughter who is abusing him or from the daughter who is protecting him?"

"Let's have something to eat and figure out what to do," Elizabeth suggested.

"We'll have to go shopping first. There isn't anything left here except Chevy's food."

"Okay, but we have to walk Chevy first, then we'll go to one of the restaurants in the village."

"Works for me," Sally said getting up.

Chevy wasn't impressed with his short walk, just down to the end of the block and back.

"Sorry, Bud," Elizabeth said, rubbing his ears. "But we don't feel safe going on one of the trails in the bush."

They drove to the village and found an empty table at a

café. After ordering they looked around. "I wonder if we should be checking to see if anyone is following us," Sally said.

"The two of us being together is probably keeping anyone at bay," Elizabeth said. "I just wish there were more clues or that I could arrange the clues we have into some sort of pattern."

"Yes, because we are leaving early Saturday morning," Sally said.

"You're not staying for the dress-up party?"

"No," Sally said. "I don't have a costume and I really can't get into the party mood. I think I just want to go home and relax a couple of days before going back to work."

"Yeah, I just have to do the WildPlay Elements Park and I'm finished."

"Do you want to do it tomorrow after I get out of class?"

"Sure. Then my article will actually be done before I leave here."

"That will be a first," Sally smiled.

After a few moments silence Elizabeth said. "I was thinking today that maybe Cynthia brought us that note."

Sally thought about it. "She could have. But why?"

"Maybe just hiring a private detective wasn't enough of a thrill for her."

"Do you want to go ask Cynthia about it?"

"I think we should. But first let's stop in and confront Wendy about the abuse." Elizabeth said.

Sally hesitated. "I'm not sure if I want to be in their house if either one of them is a murderer like you suggested." She looked at Elizabeth. "How have you done this so many times? Haven't you ever felt scared?"

"Not as much as I've been here. Maybe the other killers felt safe when I was investigating, like they felt I couldn't do anything against them. No one ever sent me a threatening note like what happened here. We could always ask John and Wendy to come outside and talk."

"It won't hurt to try."

They paid the bill and got in the Tracker. When they reached the house, the lights were out and Wendy's van was gone.

"Well, that settles that," Elizabeth said, as she drove to the bed and breakfast. With Chevy at their side they went across the street and rang the bell.

"Come in," Cynthia said, when she saw them. "We don't want Alison and Rick to see you here."

"Uh, no," Elizabeth said. "We'd rather talk outside."

"Okay," Cynthia said, puzzled. She stepped out onto the porch and led them over to a table and chairs. "Have you come to report?" she whispered.

"We've come to show you this," Elizabeth handed her the note and watched her reaction.

"You received this?" Cynthia asked, excitement in her eyes. "Did you take it to the police? Did they check it for fingerprints?"

Elizabeth hesitated then said. "There were no prints on it."

Cynthia nodded. "The person must have used gloves. Did they try for a DNA sample on the glue?"

"The envelope wasn't sealed. The flap was just tucked in."

"Smart," Cynthia said. She held onto the note. "I would think Rick and Alison sent it to you."

"Why would they have done that?"

"Maybe they found out about me hiring you. They might be trying to scare you off."

Elizabeth couldn't think of a way to ask Cynthia if she herself had pushed it under their door. "That could be but someone else could have done it, too."

"Who? Is there someone else involved? Did you learn something in Vancouver?"

"Did you know the woman who was killed here last week?" Elizabeth asked.

"The one that the police had originally thought was run over?" Cynthia asked.

"Yes."

"I know she was staying at the Snowbound Bed and Breakfast and going to the writer's retreat." Cynthia said. "But I never met her. Why do you ask?"

"We're just wondering if her death and the body being found in the demolished house are related." Elizabeth ignored

Sally's look of amazement.

"Do the police think they are?" Cynthia asked,

"I don't know but it seems strange that there would be two bodies found in the same town within a week of each other."

"Yes, you are right," Cynthia said. "I never thought about it that way."

"So that's why we showed you the note," Elizabeth said, taking the envelope from Cynthia. "You've lived here a long time. We were hoping you could give us an idea as to how the two bodies and the note might be related." Elizabeth stood. "We don't need an answer right now. We just want you to think about it."

"Why did you say that?" Sally asked, as soon as they were out of Cynthia's earshot.

"I couldn't answer her questions so I had to throw that in to keep her occupied."

"Well, I think it worked," Sally laughed.

* * *

"We have breaking news," the anchor of the twenty-four hour news channel announced.

"The police have busted an alleged baby ring in Vancouver that paid unwed mothers to put their babies up for adoption and then charged the adoptive parents thousands of dollars for the child. They rented three houses in Whistler. The demolished house in Whistler where the body of a young woman was found last week was one such house.

"The police have charged a man, who told the adoptive couples that he was a lawyer, with being part of the alleged gang. Our reporter, Les Hargrave, was outside the downtown Vancouver police station when the man was released on bail."

The picture switched to the front of a police station where Les Hargrave was one of a number of reporters surrounding a man and holding their microphones in front of his face.

"Is it true that you drew up the adoption papers for the baby ring?" one of the reporters asked.

"No comment."

"Do you know anything about the body found in the demolished house? Was she one of the unwed mothers?"

The man kept walking, ignoring the group.

"How did you recruit the mothers? How did you find the prospective parents?"

The man reached his car and climbed in. The cameraman kept the camera on the car until it turned a corner and disappeared.

"Looks like you're out of a job," Sally said.

"The police now say that the body found in the demolished house is not that of Leslie Brown, but it is that of Penny Smallwood," the anchor continued. "Even though the necklace found belonged to Ms Brown the police are speculating that she either lost or forgot the necklace when she left the house after her baby was born. It could have been that Ms Smallwood found it and was wearing it when she died. The killer may have busted it while burying her and just tossed it aside. That would explain why it wasn't found near the body."

The picture cut away to show a woman sitting waiting to be interviewed.

"We now have Nancy Williams, author of the book titled *Babies for Sale*," the anchor woman continued. "Thank you, Ms. Williams for speaking with us. You did a lot of research about children who have been sold by family members. Now can you tell us some of the reasons why babies or children have been sold?"

Nancy Williams smiled at the camera. "Well, one stripper mom sold her twins for two glasses of beer. There was a fortune teller sold her six year old grandson for nine thousand dollars and a dad sold his son for five thousand dollars so he could buy a truck."

"Those are shocking stories. Did you find anything out about any baby rings such as was busted in Vancouver?"

"There was one baby ring similar to this discovered in 1984 in Naples, Italy. They ran an abortion clinic and when the unwed mothers came in for an abortion they were told it was too late, the baby was too big. They were then offered one thousand dollars for their baby when it was born. Many were poor and needed the money so they accepted. The prospective mother was alerted and she immediately began to wear a pillow under her clothes, telling everyone she was pregnant. When the baby was due both the unwed mother and adoptive mother entered the clinic at the same time. After a week, they both left but only one had a child."

"Maybe the people who ran that ring started this one," the anchor said, in closing.

"I wonder how Alison and Rick fit into the picture," Elizabeth said. "Or if they fit into the picture at all."

"What if Cynthia was part of the baby ring," Sally said. "What if Cynthia was surprised when Penny showed up again and began to ask questions. Maybe she told Cynthia that she was going to go to the police about how she was approached about selling her baby, that she didn't know how else to find her son."

"Then why did Cynthia want to hire me?"

"That's a question only Cynthia can answer."

"Penny's mother, Jessica, is staying here," Elizabeth said. "I talked with her by the pool. At the time she still didn't know if the body was Penny's. I wonder how she feels now. Maybe I should go see her."

"Which room is she in?"

"Bonnie's room."

"Oh." Sally stood. "I'll go with you."

Elizabeth knocked on Jessica's door. No answer. Elizabeth was about to knock again when the door opened. Jessica swayed slightly, a glass in her hand.

"What?" Jessica asked.

"I met you this morning at the pool," Elizabeth said. "This is my friend Sally Matthews. We just heard about Penny on the news and we've come to offer our condolences."

Jessica stood back. "Come in," she said, sweeping her hand into the room.

The weird feeling Elizabeth had expected as she stepped into the room that Bonnie had occupied just last week didn't materialize. That was mainly because of the clothes strewn on the bed and on the two chairs and the almost empty bottle of vodka beside the pizza carton on the small table.

"Move some clothes and sit down," Jessica pointed to the chairs. It was obvious she was on her way to getting drunk.

Elizabeth and Sally picked up the slacks and blouses from the chairs and set them on the bed.

"When did you find out?" Elizabeth asked, as they sat down. She felt sorry for Jessica. She seemed to be taking the news hard.

"The police told me this morning," Jessica said. "I've been hiding here from the reporters ever since."

"Yes, they can be quite pushy," Elizabeth said. "Do the police think that someone from the baby ring killed her?"

"I don't know what the police think." Jessica stopped prowling around the room and took a healthy drink from her glass. "And I really don't care."

That was strange but then again, she had just received a shock. She'd be thinking clearer later. "Are you going to look for her son?"

"No." Jessica looked surprised. "Why should I do that?"

"Uh," Elizabeth was the one caught off guard this time. "I just thought that you might carry on with what Penny was doing when she died."

"That was Penny's desire, not mine," Jessica said, topping up her glass. "I don't want to raise a kid at my age. The little guy is better off where he is."

"What are you going to do now?" Sally asked.

Jessica looked down at her glass and a tear rolled down her cheek. "Plan my daughter's funeral."

* * *

The next morning Elizabeth took Sally to the retreat, both checking John's yard to see if he was out.

"I doubt she will let him out of the house until the retreat is over," Sally said, when they saw the yard was empty.

Elizabeth dropped Sally off then went and bought some groceries. She also picked up a *Vancouver Sun* newspaper before going back to the bed and breakfast. They may have more in there about the baby ring. She was putting the groceries away when there was a knock at their door.

Elizabeth looked at the polka-dotted pitcher that was sitting on the table. She decided against it and went to the door. No one would try to kill her here.

"I saw the news last night," Cynthia said, as she entered the room. "I knew it was Penny who had been killed."

"Yes, you were right," Elizabeth said, motioning Cynthia to sit down. "So you've come to discuss the ending of our agreement."

"Oh, no. You still have to find out how Rick and Alison are associated with it."

"Maybe they aren't part of it. Maybe there is a different explanation for their change of names."

"I have thought of that and I've been trying to figure out what it could be. So far nothing reasonable has come to mind."

"Do you want to go over there and ask them outright?"

"Oh, I've been tempted to many times but I never had the guts to do it. I've been watching their house, though, for any suspicious actions."

"Have you seen any?"

"Actually the only thing that is suspicious is that they've been keeping to themselves recently. They leave the house, go to their vehicle and when they return they go straight into the house. They don't sit outside anymore, almost as if they are hiding."

"Have the police been to see them?"

"Not that I've seen since that first visit when the body was discovered. Which, to me, means that they are not suspects. So it's up to you to get the evidence to convict them."

Cynthia's throwing out of police terms was wearing thin on Elizabeth. "Well, I'm still checking a few leads," Elizabeth said, standing. She was lying but it was for a good cause. "In fact, I was just going to the library to look up some old newspapers articles."

"Good," Cynthia said, rising and heading for the door. "Let me know what you learn."

"Will do."

Elizabeth turned on the television and finished putting the groceries away. There was mention of wars and earthquakes and then an interview with a lawyer who drew up the paperwork for legal adoptions came on.

"We would like to make it clear that Mr. Bendix is not part of the baby ring," the news anchor said. "We have asked him to comment on what is involved in the adoption of a child."

"It can cost up to $15,000 to adopt privately in British Columbia," the lawyer said. "There is also a long wait as few newborns are being placed for adoption. To go through a public adoption agency the cost is minimal but they have older children, some with special needs and sometimes there are siblings."

"Are you saying that most couples want babies rather than older children?" the anchor asked.

"Yes, that way it feels like your own child. You don't have to undo learned behaviours as you would in a child who is older."

"So, how do you think this ring would have operated?"

"This is just hypothetical," Mr Bendix said. "It may not have had anything to do with this particular baby ring, but from what I have read about the group there probably were at least three partners, maybe four. One would have worked in the abortion clinic. One could have met couples through her job at an adoption agency who were looking for a newborn baby. She would put both the prospective parents and the mother in contact with a lawyer who would draw up the necessary papers. Then just before the baby is due they would send the pregnant mother to stay at one of the houses they rented for this purpose. They may even have rented out a second house to the prospective parents. This way the parents could be in the hospital when the child was born. The attending doctor would probably have also been involved. After the birth the new parents would return to their own home and after a few days recuperating at the rental house the mother would also leave."

"Isn't it illegal for a lawyer to do that?"

"Chances are he wasn't a real lawyer. He probably just rented office space in Vancouver as he needed it and put up a few degrees on the wall."

"How much would they have charged for their services?"

"Fifty to 100,000 dollars."

"And people paid that amount?" the news anchor was astonished.

"Yes."

"Why?"

"Either because they had been turned down through regular channels or because they didn't want to wait. They may even have been given their preference of a boy or girl. Each mother could have gone through an ultrasound to determine the sex of the baby."

"And how much would the mothers have received?"

"Probably five to ten thousand dollars."

"So everyone would have been happy with the arrangement, the girls because they received cash, the parents because they had a baby."

"Right."

Elizabeth shut off the television and she and Chevy headed to her vehicle to pick up Sally. She wondered how many baby adoption rings were operating throughout the country.

She was early and waited a few minutes. Soon there were students coming out fumbling in their pockets or purses for their cigarettes. Others hurried to their cars. Sally came over to the Tracker.

"Well, how did your class go today?" Elizabeth asked.

"Better," Sally said. "Everyone was more relaxed. What did you do this morning?"

"Bought groceries and talked with Cynthia. She heard that Penny was the one who was under the house. She has also been spying on Rick and Alison. She still thinks they had something to do with the death."

They drove by John's house. It still appeared empty. "I wonder if Wendy's taken him some place until after we are gone." Sally said.

"I wouldn't be surprised."

"So are we going to the WildPlay Elements Park?" Sally asked.

"Yes. Let's just grab a lunch and go."

After they'd eaten a canned salmon sandwich, Elizabeth put Chevy in the vehicle. "There's lots of shade there and it only takes a couple of hours to do the course," Elizabeth explained.

They handed in their waivers and lined up to step into their harnesses. After the instructions they climbed up the ladder up to the first element, a walk across a narrow wooden bridge. As long as Elizabeth concentrated on crossing the swinging logs or the moving steps and joking and laughing with Sally, she was okay. It was when she had to climb higher up a tree to cross the longest zip line that her fear of heights insinuated itself into her consciousness. She looked down at the ground way below and felt herself freezing. She wasn't sure if she could go further.

She looked back at the people behind them. She couldn't go back and there was no way for her to get to the ground. She could let the others go ahead but she couldn't stay up there all day.

"Are you okay?" Sally asked.

"That's so far to go and so high up," Elizabeth said.

"You can do it. Just don't look down."

"Too late," Elizabeth said. She took a deep breath and moved her zip line pulley from her belt to the wire and attached it. She undid one karabiner and hooked it on the line and then did the same with the second. She worked slowly telling herself that she had nothing to fear. She wouldn't fall.

"I could have just stood on the ground and took pictures," she muttered, as she sat down in the harness. All she had to do was raise her feet and she would be off but every time she went to lift her feet off the platform, her stomach did a flip and her feet wouldn't move.

"You have to do this," she whispered to herself. "You can't let this rule you." Elizabeth swallowed twice, counted to three, and with a lurch deep in her stomach, finally set off. The ride seemed to take forever. A couple of times her feet swayed to the right and she had to adjust her karabiner to keep them lined up with the painted footprints at the other end. She breathed a sigh of relief when her feet smacked the mat and she grabbed the padded end of the line. Once she had her feet firmly on the platform she felt a surge of power. She'd just conquered her fear again.

She was able to relax and enjoy the rest of the course and they progressed through the ever increasingly difficult sections of swinging logs, zip lines, hanging stirrups, a barrel, and cargo net with abandonment.

"That was fun," Sally said, when they had walked across their last wire and reached the final steps down. "Thanks for waiting until I could do it with you."

"Thank you for your support."

* * *

Back at the bed and breakfast they had just climbed out of the Tracker when Cynthia ran over.

"I'm so glad you finally got here," Cynthia said. "You have to stop them."

"Stop who?"

"Rick and Alison. I just saw them sneaking boxes into their house. They're packing and are going to fly the coop now that the police have busted the baby ring."

Elizabeth glanced at Sally. Now what did they do?

"You have to go and catch them in the act," Cynthia said urgently.

Elizabeth put Chevy on his leash and she and Sally headed across the street, Cynthia right behind them. She had no idea of what to do now. She didn't like the idea of going to Alison and Rick's place but she couldn't think of a way to get out of it, short of telling Cynthia that her hiring of Elizabeth was all a fraud.

They climbed the steps and Elizabeth knocked on the door. Rick opened it and stared at them.

"Sorry to bother you," Elizabeth said. "But we noticed that you brought some boxes home and we were wondering if you needed help packing." Boy, that even sounded stupid in her ears but that was all she could think of on such short notice.

Rick stood with his mouth open. It must have sounded stupid to him as well. "Uh, thank you, but we're doing okay ourselves."

"Who is it?" Alison asked, peering around his shoulder.

"I believe it is the packing committee of Ambassador Crescent," Rick said.

"What?"

"Hi, Alison," Cynthia said. "We've come to see if you need

help packing."

"How did you know we were packing?" Alison asked.

"I saw you carrying boxes into your house."

"Well, thank you, but we're capable of doing it by ourselves." Rick began to close the door.

"You both lived in Whistler about two years ago," Elizabeth said. "That would be about the same time that the young woman was murdered across the street."

"What are you talking about?" Alison asked.

"Nothing, but it just seems suspicious that you left here after she died and then came back just before her body was found, almost like you wanted to keep an eye on the investigation."

"What are you suggesting?" Rick demanded. "We had nothing to do with her death."

"Then why did you move back here?" Cynthia asked. "You lived on Fitzsimmons Road North over two years ago."

Alison and Rick exchanged looks. "So you did recognize us," Alison said.

"Not at first," Cynthia admitted. "Your hair is different and Rick, you've lost a few pounds."

"We knew we were taking a chance moving so close to where we'd lived before but when nothing was said we thought we were safe."

"So why did you leave and then why come back?" Elizabeth asked.

"Ah, that's right," Alison said. "You're an amateur detective. Are you working on the death of that young girl?"

Elizabeth suspected that Cynthia would know all about investigator/client confidentially. "Yes," she said. "I'm curious about it."

"And because we moved away and then came back, that made you think we had something to do with it."

"I'm sure you have a good reason for it," Elizabeth said, quietly, certain now that she and Cynthia had been wrong.

"And you would like to hear it, I suppose," Alison smiled.

Elizabeth took that as a good sign. "It would put my, and a few other's, minds at rest."

"Come in, then, and we'll tell you."

"Are you sure?" Rick asked.

"I'd rather them know the truth than suspect us of murder."

Elizabeth picked Chevy up and carried him into the house behind Alison and Rick. There were taped boxes labelled with the words kitchen or den on them piled in one corner and a bunch of empty boxes waiting for be filled.

Elizabeth took a chair closest to the door and noticed that Sally did the same.

"Two and a half years ago we won five point six million dollars in the lottery. We decided not to cash it in or tell anyone, not even our children, about it until we knew exactly what we were going to do with it. So we sold our house here and moved to Kamloops. We collected our money, gave our children a share, donated some to charity and gave some to close relatives. Then we decided we wanted to come back here. We bought a lot in a new development and hired a contractor to build us a house. We wanted to be close to keep an eye on the construction so we moved in here until it was completed. It's now done and we're packing to move in."

"Why all the secrecy?" Cynthia asked.

"We've heard about winners who have be hounded by charities and relatives and friends for money once they win. We didn't want that to happen."

So these were the lottery winners the woman at the visitor information had talked about. After hearing their story Elizabeth doubted that she would get an interview with them.

"Did you change your names?" Elizabeth asked.

They looked surprised. "No," Alison said. "Why would we do that?"

Elizabeth shrugged. "I just thought that if you were afraid of people finding out about your winnings, you might have." Boy did that sound lame.

"I'm sure, that after this length of time, we are old news."

"Thank you for clearing that up," Elizabeth said, standing. "We'll let you get back to your packing."

"Well, that's solved," Sally said, when they were out on the street.

"Yes." Cynthia sounded a little disappointed that it was such a nondescript explanation.

"So now our agreement is fulfilled," Elizabeth said.

"You haven't found out who did kill Penny," Cynthia pointed out.

"You hired me to find out if Alison and Rick had anything to do with Penny's death, not find the actual killer."

"Okay, I'll mail a cheque to the SPCA in Squamish tomorrow."

Elizabeth held out her hand. "Our contract is now formally over," she said, as Cynthia shook her hand.

Cynthia started to walk away then turned back. "Could I hire you to find the killer?" she asked.

"It would be a waste of your money," Elizabeth said. "I think the police are close to solving her murder. Besides we're leaving on Saturday to go home."

"Oh." Was all Cynthia said.

"So what are the chances of meeting two people who have won the lottery in less than a week?" Sally asked, as they entered their suite.

"Probably pretty slim anywhere else, but it makes you wonder how many past winners have bought condo's or homes here. It is a beautiful, popular resort town."

Chapter 21

"It's really bothering me about John and his daughter," Sally said, as they were eating supper. "I can't, in good conscience, leave here without doing something for him."

"What do you want to do?"

"I found the B.C. Centre for Elder Advocacy Support web site. I then went into the Senior's Advocacy Information Line which has a toll free number that John can phone between 9:00am and 1:00pm. There is also a Victim's Services Program which he can access. I would like to get this information to him."

"That's going to be tough after yesterday. What if we gave it to both of them, let Wendy know that we are worried about the way she treats him. That might be enough to make her be nicer to him."

"Yes, we could let her know that we will go to the police, or register a complaint with the authorities."

"Okay, it's still daylight. Let's go now."

Sally grabbed the paper with the information on it and the two of them walked with Chevy out to the Tracker. Elizabeth pulled into the driveway behind Wendy's van.

"Oh, this is scary," Sally said, as they climbed out.

"You don't have to come," Elizabeth said, trying to keep the butterflies quiet in her stomach. She put the leash on Chevy. He was small but his bark would alert someone if something happened.

"I'm not letting you go alone," Sally said.

"Go away," Wendy said, through the screen door.

"We have some information on elder abuse we would like to give to John," Sally said before Wendy could close the inside door.

"What elder abuse?" Wendy demanded. "Are you threatening me?"

"We just think John should know what resources are out there for him."

"Dad doesn't need any resources."

"We think that the way you treat him is not healthy for him or for you."

"I don't care what you think. Now, go away."

"We'll phone the Victim Services Program ourselves if you don't let us give John the information."

Wendy looked over her shoulder, then back at them. "Dad's asleep."

"We'll wait."

Wendy seemed uncertain as to what to do. "Look, why don't you tell me what this is all about?"

"We think you are drugging your father. He seems sharp when we talk with him when you are not around. And we only have your word that he has dementia."

Wendy bit her lip. "Is that why you've been hassling us, because you think I'm abusing him?"

Sally held her hand up and began counting her fingers. "You try to keep him from talking with us, you hustle him into the house when you do see us talking, you dragged him out of the village even though he wanted to stay, you are giving him drugs that he doesn't want to take, you are telling terrible lies about him that are cutting him off from the rest of the community. What does that sound like to you?"

"You've known us less than a week and yet you judge me just like that." Wendy snapped her fingers. "Do you know anything about dementia, about how hard it is to look after someone you love as they deal with the disease?"

"We work with people with dementia and Alzheimer," Sally said. "That's why we know he doesn't have the symptoms. His loss of memory and confusion is from the so-called vitamins you give him."

"You don't get it, do you?" Wendy lowered her voice. "Dad is very sick. He doesn't know it though. His doctor told me and we decided that it wouldn't do Dad any good to tell him. Those vitamins are his medicines. They are strong and one of the side affects is that he temporarily loses his memory about what has happened."

"But don't you see that you are causing him more harm by making him think things happened when they didn't or vice versa," Elizabeth said. "It would be better for him to know the truth. That way he could decide what to do with his life."

Wendy looked down at her hands. "You don't know how many times I've come close to doing that." She raised her head. "Thank you for coming, but Dad is in bed for the night."

Elizabeth and Sally stepped off the veranda and walked to the Tracker. "What do you think?" Elizabeth asked.

"Well, it wasn't something I expected, but it does explain some things."

"Yeah, but only some things. It doesn't explain why she didn't want him talking with us or why he has to sneak away from her."

"He did tell us that she's afraid someone will try to take advantage of him because he has money."

"But he denies that he makes advances to younger women," Sally said. "And he knows that she says that about him. To me that's not dementia or illness. To me that's direct mental abuse."

* * *

The next morning Elizabeth and Sally discussed Bonnie's murder. "If we believe Wendy, we can eliminate the theory that John killed Sylvia because she resisted his advances," Elizabeth said. "And then neither he nor Wendy murdered Bonnie to keep her quiet about Sylvia's murder."

"Then we are left with Kat Mac or Michael," Sally said. "Maybe I should confront them this morning about it."

"Not alone," Elizabeth said quickly. "We'll do it when I pick you up."

Elizabeth dropped Sally off then cleaned the suite and washed some of her clothes. She phoned her dad to forestall his own call, then talked with Paul. Jared was still in the hospital but was making progress. He expected him to be let out by the weekend. Elizabeth was torn. She should be there with him, not spending her time trying to chase down some killer. But she was stuck in Whistler because she couldn't leave Sally.

At noon she drove to pick Sally up hoping that she hadn't already talked with Kat Mac and Michael. She left Chevy in the vehicle, hurried into the building, and to Sally's classroom. The door was closed, the class still in session. Elizabeth leaned against the wall and waited.

Eventually the door opened and the students filed out. Some glanced at her, some didn't even see her. When no more came out, Elizabeth stuck her head around the door and saw Sally standing in front of the teacher's desk. She entered the room.

Sally introduced her to Kat Mac. "We are looking into Bonnie Stone's death," Sally said.

Elizabeth was glad she was getting right to the point. Sometimes that was the best way.

"Why?" Kat Mac asked.

"Because we had promised her that we would help her find out who murdered her cousin, Sylvia, and now we're wondering if that same person killed Bonnie."

Kat Mac sighed. "Why do you keep saying that Sylvia was murdered? It was an accident."

"Bonnie didn't believe it was and now she's dead. That makes us think she may have been right."

"So what does this have to do with me?"

"Sylvia sent Bonnie some texts saying that you liked her manuscript," Elizabeth said. "Is that true?"

"I don't remember. That was two years ago and I've been busy since then."

"Did you ever see Sylvia's manuscript?"

"I really don't remember. I've been teaching this course for years and I've read lots of manuscripts."

"You helped Michael Wolf get published two years ago. He was in the same class as Sylvia."

"I merely put in a good word for him with the publisher who came to talk with the students. His idea did the rest."

"Did he have a complete manuscript when he came here?"

Kat Mac stood. "I really don't understand what these questions have to do with either Sylvia or Bonnie and I'm not going to answer any more."

"We've heard a rumour that you steal student's ideas and try to get them published," Elizabeth said. "Is that where your new book came from, a student, say Sylvia, and that's why she is dead?"

"How dare you!" Kat Mac exclaimed. She raised her hand and pointed to the door. "Get out of my classroom now!"

"We'd like to ask a few more questions," Elizabeth said.

"Get out!" Kat Mac shouted, her face turning red.

Elizabeth and Sally did as they were told.

"Phew," Sally said, when she'd closed the door.

"Yeah. She didn't take that very well. I don't think you'll be welcomed back in her class for the last day tomorrow."

"It doesn't matter if I'm not," Sally said. "I'm not getting much more out of it. What I really have to do is go home and write my story and see what happens."

"That's what writing is all about," Elizabeth smiled.

"I don't know if Michael will be in his classroom but we can try," Sally said, as she led the way upstairs.

They walked through the open door. Michael was the only one there.

He looked up when they stopped beside him. "Hello," he said to Sally, then looked at Elizabeth.

"I'm Elizabeth Oliver," she said, holding out her hand.

"Michael Wolf. And you two must be here about Bonnie and Sylvia."

Sally nodded. "You must have heard that Bonnie was murdered."

"Yes, but the only thing said about Sylvia was her death was accidental."

"I think we are the only ones who think Sylvia may have been murdered," Elizabeth admitted. "And since we did promise Bonnie we would look into it, we are."

"Oh, oh. This sounds ominous." Michael leaned back in his chair and linked his fingers behind his head. He looked at them.

"You said that there was a rumour that Kat Mac stole students ideas," Elizabeth began. "We went to her and told her about it."

"And what did she say?" Michael asked.

"She kicked us out of her room."

"Why did you tell her about it?"

"Because we wanted to know if she had taken Sylvia's manuscript and turned it into the new book that she has coming out."

"You think she killed Sylvia and stole her manuscript?" Michael asked, incredulously.

"That was one idea that we came up with," Sally said.

"And what was another?"

"Well, you got a book published after taking the class with Sylvia."

Michael laughed out loud. "Are you serious? Are you accusing me of killing Sylvia and then Bonnie?"

"Not really," Sally said. "But you were the one who told me about the rumour and it just carried on from there."

"Well," Michael sobered quickly and leaned forward. "Carry it on somewhere else because I had nothing to do with either of their deaths." He went back to his computer.

* * *

Elizabeth and Sally walked slowly to the Tracker. "I think we'll just have to leave this for the police," Elizabeth said. "Two women are dead and no one we've talked to seems to know anything about their deaths."

"Daryl asked me if we'd learned anything about who sent the note," Sally said, as they drove to the bed and breakfast.

Elizabeth raised her eyebrows. "He's worried about you?"

"I doubt it. He's probably just curious."

As they pulled into the parking lot they saw Jessica stagger down the path to her car. She was wearing the same clothes she'd had on the night before and her hair hadn't been combed. She leaned against her car as she searched through her purse finally coming up with a set of keys.

Elizabeth and Sally climbed out of the Tracker and went

over to her just as she pushed away from the car, lurching to the side. Elizabeth caught her and leaned her against the car again.

"Hey, what are you doing?" Jessica slurred, slapping ineffectively at Elizabeth's hands.

"Where are you going?" Elizabeth raised her hands in the air and stepped back.

"I need more vodka," Jessica said. She bent over and tried to fit a key in the door lock.

"I don't think you should be driving," Elizabeth said.

"I'm fine," Jessica said, turning the key in the lock and pulling it out.

Elizabeth didn't like the idea of letting her drive in her condition. She stepped between Jessica and the car. "Why don't you come to our room for a drink? We have some vodka coolers."

Jessica wrinkled her nose. "Thoth are for kids."

"Then let's go together," Sally said. "We were just on our way to the liquor store ourselves."

"You were?"

"Yes." She deftly took the keys out of Jessica's hand, while Elizabeth manoeuvred her around to the passenger's side.

Elizabeth opened the door and helped Jessica get in, no mean feat since she kept listing to the left and almost falling. After doing up her seatbelt Elizabeth climbed into the back seat. Sally started the car and they drove the nearest liquor store.

"You two stay here and I'll get the vodka," Elizabeth said, jumping out of the car.

"Here, take this." Jessica fumbled in her purse finally finding her wallet and handing Elizabeth a fifty dollar bill through the window.

Elizabeth tried to remember the label on the vodka bottle she'd seen in Jessica's room but it wouldn't come to mind. So she just grabbed the first one she saw and paid for it. She handed it and the change to Jessica when she got to the car.

Sally drove back to the bed and breakfast and they helped Jessica along the path and up the steps.

"Why don't you join us in our suite?" Elizabeth said. They had nothing else to do and it seemed that Jessica could use the company.

"Sure," Jessica held up her bottle. "Ash long ash I have this it doeshn't matter where I drink it."

Elizabeth set a glass on the table for Jessica, who immediately opened the cap and poured some vodka into it. Sally got a cooler and divided it into two glasses for her and Elizabeth.

"Help yourself," Jessica said, banging the bottle on the table top. She took a healthy drink.

"Thank you, but we'll stick to this," Sally said. "Do you want some mix for that. We have Pepsi and orange juice."

"Got any ice?"

"Yes, we do." Sally went to the refrigerator and got one of the ice trays she'd filled when they'd first arrived at the bed and breakfast. She emptied the ice into a bowl and set it beside the bottle.

Jessica grabbed three cubes and plunked them in her glass. She took another drink then weaved her way over to the couch and sat down. She sipped on the vodka as she watched Elizabeth and Sally join her in the chairs.

"Do you want to tell us about Penny?" Elizabeth asked. Maybe talking about her daughter might make her feel better.

"Penny wash a good baby," Jessica began. "But it washn't long before she changed."

"Changed? How?" Elizabeth asked.

Jessica stood and poured herself another glassful of vodka. She brought the bottle back and set it on the coffee table.

"Penny wash the first and only grandchild born to my parents. They doted on her, shpoiling her terribly. When she was young, every time she came home from visiting them she had a pile of toys and ash she got older they began giving her money. She never had to baby sit or do chores to learn the value of earning her own money and how to shave it. Every time she needed money she just went to shee them and they gladly handed it over. I kept asking them not to but it wash ash if they were trying to buy her love."

"Some grandparents are like that," Sally said.

"But they weren't like that with me when I wash growing

up," Jessica said, bitterly. She was leaning precariously to one side, almost spilling her drink. "They made me clean my room and vacuum the floor for my allowance and they never gave me any extra spending money. I had to baby sit and get a part time job for my money."

Sounds like there was a lot of resentment there, Elizabeth thought. "Do you have any siblings?"

"I had a brother who died when he was shmall. My parents blamed me because I was shupposed to be looking after him in the yard. Instead I went to watch my favourite television program. He ran out into the street and was hit by a car."

Oh, the poor woman, the poor family. That would be hard to get over. Maybe that was why Jessica seemed to drink a lot.

Sally got up and went to the kitchen where she made a pot of coffee. While it dripped she sliced some cheese and ham onto the plate.

"When my father died, my mother moved in with us," Jessica continued. "She and Penny became even closer. When Penny got pregnant my mother blamed me, said I had been an unfit mother who hadn't taught her any values. She kept saying that I had been a bad child who hadn't learned a thing she had tried to teach me."

Jessica took a gulp of her drink. "I just couldn't do anything right ash a kid or ash an adult."

Sally set some napkins on the coffee table then brought the plate with the ham and cheese and a bowl with some crackers to the living room. She held them in front of Jessica. Jessica seemed to think it over before taking a napkin and piling some of the food on it. Elizabeth was glad to see Jessica eat something. She didn't know how long the woman had been drinking but if she'd needed a new bottle of vodka it meant that the one from last night was gone. When Sally offered Elizabeth the snacks she took some. Sally set the plate and napkins on the table in front of Jessica before helping herself.

"So why did your mother leave Penny her estate and not you?" Elizabeth asked.

Jessica's top lip curled. "She shaid that I didn't know how

to look after money, that I would blow it in a year. She gave the bulk of it to Penny, almost a million dollars. She left me a meashly hundred thousand dollars. That kid didn't deserve all that money. She didn't look after the old bat like I did. She didn't cook for her or bathe her or changed her stinky diaper when she was dying of cancer. I did all those things and more and still that old bat left her money to my daughter." Jessica shook her head. "It just wasn't fair," she said quietly, slumping over against the arm of the couch. "It just wasn't fair."

Sally jumped up and grabbed her glass before it spilled just as there was a knock at the door.

Chevy began barking as Elizabeth and Sally looked at each other. Elizabeth stood and went over to the door, Chevy at her heels. She picked him up and opened it.

Constables Black and Pierce stood in the hall. "We're looking for Jessica Smallwood and we were told that she may be with you."

Elizabeth stood back and let them enter. Black and Pierce immediately went over to Jessica. Black shook her shoulder. Jessica opened her eyes and looked up at him.

"Jessica Smallwood, we are arresting you for the murder of your daughter Penny Smallwood."

"I didn't kill Penny," Jessica sputtered, trying to stand. "You can't arrest me."

Black helped her up and then handcuffed her hands behind her. "We have just talked with your husband," he said, as he and Pierce led her out of the room. "And he told us the whole story."

Chapter 22

"Wow," Sally said, after she had shut the door. "We were pretty close to getting her to confess. Do you think she would have?"

"It's hard to say. The vodka was making her talk easily but she was almost passed out. It's probably a good thing the police came when they did or we may have had her sleeping on our couch."

"Well, that's one down and one to go." Sally paused a moment. "I'm still not sure if I believe what Wendy told us yesterday. I still want to know the real truth about John."

"We don't have much time left," Elizabeth said. "Let's try to see him one more time and if we can't talk with him then we will contact the authorities. Let them sort out whether he is really sick and she is lovingly caring for him or if she is abusing him."

"And we'll take Sylvia's picture with us in case John did meet her while she was here."

They walked up the steps, crossed the veranda, and knocked on the door. Wendy opened the inside door, then started to close it when she saw who it was.

"We're here to talk with your father about Sylvia," Elizabeth said, quickly. Nothing else had seemed to faze her. Maybe this would work.

Wendy stopped. Elizabeth wasn't sure but she thought Wendy paled a little. "Don't know her."

"Who's there, Wendy?" John called from the background.

"Hi, John," Sally lifted her voice. She tried to look around Wendy. "We've come to see you."

"Why won't you leave him alone," Wendy hissed. "I told you he's a sick man."

"We just want to ask him about a woman he may have met two years ago," Elizabeth said.

"He may have met...." Wendy repeated.

"Hello," John said, coming up behind Wendy. "Come in."

"It's such a nice evening, why don't we visit outside," Elizabeth said, backing up and taking one step down.

Sally did the same.

"Sure," John said jovially, coming out onto the veranda. "Wendy, could you get us some lemonade?"

"Dad, I don't think you should talk with them alone." Wendy held her ground. "You don't know them."

"Oh, yes I do. They're nice young women. Please get the lemonade. I'm thirsty."

They sat at the small table on the veranda. Elizabeth and Sally took the chairs closest to the steps. Wendy finally headed inside for the lemonade.

"What a cute little dog," John said, patting Chevy on the head. "I'm thinking about getting a dog."

"What type are you looking for?" Elizabeth asked.

"I've always liked collies, but Wendy doesn't want one. Too much trouble she says."

"Have you decided if you are going to take the science fiction course at the retreat?" Sally asked.

He looked at the half open door. "Yes," he whispered. "I'm going to start working on a manuscript this winter and enrol next year. I just haven't told Wendy, yet."

"Good for you," Sally grinned. "I'm sure you'll like it."

"Thank you."

"You said you talked with other students attending the retreat over the years," Sally said.

"A few, but it's surprising how many of them drove from the bed and breakfasts to the retreat. And the ones who walked usually had an Ipod headphone stuck in their ear."

Sally took the picture of Sylvia out of her pocket. "Could this woman have been one of the ones you saw or spoke to?"

He stared at it. Then he rubbed his hand over it.

"She was here two years ago," Sally prompted.

He had tears in his eyes. "That's Sylvia, my daughter. Where did you get this?"

"Sylvia was your daughter?" Elizabeth looked at Sally. So many things fell into place with that statement.

"Yes. From my first marriage." He leaned forward eagerly "Where is she? Is she here? Did she come back? Can I see her?"

He didn't know? Elizabeth was at a loss. How did she answer those questions? To put off an answer she asked. "When did you see her last?"

"Two years ago. She came here to see me.

"Dad, are you telling that story about Sylvia again?" Wendy appeared at his side with a tray of lemonade in glasses. She looked venomously at Elizabeth and Sally. "I've told you that my father has dementia. His mind doesn't always work right."

Elizabeth didn't think it was appropriate that Wendy should talk like that in front of her father.

"But Sylvia did come to visit us," John protested. "I introduced her to you."

"No, Dad, she didn't," Wendy said firmly. She set the tray on the table and put her hand on his shoulder. "You dreamed it or it was a side effect of your meds. It took a while to get the dosage right."

John shook his head. "But I wasn't on meds then."

"Yes, you were. You had just started them." Wendy looked at Elizabeth and Sally. "The visit is over."

"Oh, please, Wendy," John pleaded. "Let them stay and talk about Sylvia. I want to know more about her. I want to know where she is."

"No," Wendy yelled. She turned to Elizabeth and Sally. "Leave now."

Chevy jumped up and barked, startling Wendy. Elizabeth stood and faced her. "We will go to the police if you don't let us talk with him."

Wendy crossed her arms and stood glaring at them. Elizabeth leaned against the railing, watching her. She was glad that the veranda was clearly visible from the street. Chevy laid back down but kept alert as if he knew there could be trouble.

"Have you found Sylvia?" John asked hopefully. "Is she coming to see me again?"

Elizabeth hated that he didn't know the truth and she could see no reason to withhold it any longer. "She died in an accident here two years ago?" she said gently.

"Sylvia's dead?" His voice cracked. He looked from Sally

to Elizabeth, his eyes pleading. "But she can't be. She said she was going to come back and see me. That we had a lot of catching up to do. I told her how sorry I was that we lost contact. I said it wouldn't happen again."

"I'm afraid that she is dead," Sally confirmed. "She must have died shortly after meeting you. It was deemed an accident but still something should have appeared in the local newspaper. Didn't you hear about it or read in the papers?"

"No, I never saw or heard anything."

"Did you hear about it?" Elizabeth asked Wendy.

"No," Wendy said. "And no one by the name of Sylvia came here to see Dad."

"Yes, she did," John said emphatically. "You know she did. It wasn't my imagination like you keep saying."

"If Sylvia never came here then it seems strange that your father would recognize a picture of her as an adult," Elizabeth said. "You'd think he would only remember her as a child of eight when he last saw here."

"Okay," Wendy finally conceded. "She came here. But only once and it was a short visit."

"It was short because you asked her to leave," John said. "You told her that I was sick and that I tired easily. But Sylvia whispered to me that she was coming back."

"Well, she never and that should tell you something about what type of person she was. I've been trying to spare you the hurt of her not coming back to see you."

"How did Sylvia happen to meet you here?" Elizabeth asked, wondering if it had been a coincidence that Sylvia had picked a retreat in the town where her father lived.

"Sylvia said she'd gone on the Internet and had found out where I lived. She used the retreat as a reason to come here. She said she walked past here twice before getting up the nerve to come and visit me." John wiped his eyes on his sleeve.

"That must have been a surprise."

"It was but I recognized her immediately. She looks so much like her mother."

"It must have been a surprise for you, too." Elizabeth said, looking at Wendy.

Wendy averted her gaze.

"I had told Wendy about her half sister years ago. After I won the money I wanted to locate Sylvia and share it with her. Wendy tried looking for her but couldn't find her."

Elizabeth doubted that Wendy had tried very hard. "So you finally found each other and then she dies."

John took a shuddering breath. "It can't be true. It just can't be true."

"How did it happen?" Wendy asked.

"She fell down some concrete steps and banged her head. She died from her injuries."

"Oh, my poor Sylvia," John cried.

"Do you know a Bonnie Stone?" Elizabeth asked Wendy. She was trying to get the message across to John.

"No," Wendy shook her head.

"You haven't heard about her being killed near here?"

"Oh, yes, I heard about that woman but I didn't remember her name."

"Do you know that she was your half-cousin?"

"I don't have a cousin named Bonnie."

"I have a niece named Bonnie," John spoke up. "but I haven't seen her since my divorce. Her last name wasn't Stone, though."

"That was her married name." Elizabeth waited until he put two and two together.

"Bonnie's dead, too," he said, with resignation. "My god, what have I done." He stood and went into the house.

"I think you've done enough damage," Wendy snarled. "You can go now."

Sally picked up the picture of Sylvia and they left.

* * *

"If we can believe Wendy, she didn't know about Sylvia dying here," Sally said. They had taken two coolers and gone down to the pool to enjoy some relaxing before supper.

"I don't think we can believe much that Wendy says. It took a lot just to get her to admit that Sylvia had actually been there at all."

"We certainly can eliminate the theory that John killed Sylvia because she resisted his advances. And so neither he nor Wendy murdered Bonnie to keep her quiet about Sylvia's murder."

"So Sylvia was the daughter he had been talking about at the bar that night," Elizabeth said.

"And Madeline is his first wife. It's strange to think that she was just down the street from him a few days ago."

"No wonder Bonnie had said he reminded her of someone," Sally said. "I wonder if that's what Bonnie remembered when she was talking with Michael. Who John reminded her of. And so she went there to see him."

"But he didn't act like she had seen him," Elizabeth said. "Maybe they weren't home."

"What if he was drugged and she talked with Wendy?" Sally asked.

"You know," Elizabeth began thoughtfully. "Wendy was worried about John meeting someone who would take advantage of him because of his money. Then one day Sylvia shows up and wants to renew their father/daughter relationship. What if Wendy was afraid that she would want some of the money?"

"So she kills her," Sally said. "But how does she prevent John from hearing about it?"

"I don't know. But he talks about Sylvia, and Wendy thinks that he will tell someone so she begins to drug him and then makes up stories about his behaviour so people avoid him."

"Then two years later Bonnie comes to see him. She tells Wendy who she is and the fear starts all over again. And Bonnie dies."

"I wonder how we can prove it."

"You don't have to prove it," Wendy said, stepping through the bushes from the empty lot next door. In her hand was a gun.

Elizabeth's first thought was to wonder if the handgun was registered. Her second thought was that she was going to die all because she was too nosy. It took all her courage to say.

"You killed Sylvia and Bonnie."

"I thought you would eventually figure that out," Wendy said. 'That's why I've come to get you two. We're going for a drive." She waved the gun. "Stand up and walk normally to my vehicle. Carry your dog and keep him quiet."

Elizabeth and Sally did as they were told. They walked around the house and down the path to Wendy's van, not seeing anyone who could help them.

"The keys are in it," Wendy said. "You drive." She pointed to Sally.

"You get in the passenger's side," she said to Elizabeth.

Elizabeth looked around as she climbed in, hoping someone would come along. But since the young woman's body had been identified, most of the guests had left. The only one remaining was Daryl and he was probably slaving over his computer.

Sally started the van. "Where are we going?" she asked, her voice shaking.

"Just get out to the highway and turn right."

"You must have been scared when Sylvia showed up," Elizabeth said, as they headed north towards Pemberton. She needed something to keep her mind off their predicament. "She must have been happy to see her father"

"He's my father," Wendy said. "She came here because she had tracked Dad down on the Internet. As soon as Dad saw her he started to cry. He knew her the moment he saw her. They only talked a little bit and he was already wanting her move in with us. He wanted her to be part of our family. He thought we should get along like sisters."

"And you didn't want to."

"Of course not," Wendy sneered. "I knew from the start that she had only come because of the money that he had won. She could have found him anytime but no, she waited until he was rich, then came forward. And I couldn't let her get her greedy hands on our money."

"So what did you do?"

"I slipped some sleeping pills into Dad's coffee and when

he got tired I helped him to bed. I then told her that he did that a lot and offered to buy her supper. We talked and I let her think I was okay with everything. She kept telling me she was so happy to have found her dad and then to have the bonus of a sister on top of that. Then I said that I had to go somewhere for a few hours but would meet her again at eleven fifteen at the Upper Village."

"Where did you have to go?"

"Back to check on Dad and give him some more pills to keep him quiet."

"And Sylvia agreed to meet you there even though it was late?" Elizabeth asked.

"Oh, not immediately, but I told her it would be a quiet, peaceful place where we could sit for hours and talk. I think she was just so eager to get to know her sister that she agreed."

"So what did you do?"

"Well, I didn't show up. Instead I stayed in the dark and watched her go from being eager to worried to scared. Finally, she decided to leave and I jumped her when she got to the steps. I hit her with a rock then pushed her down them and when that didn't kill her I banged her head on the corner of one of them. That worked."

The coldness in her voice sent shivers down Elizabeth's spine. She looked at Sally who was concentrating on her driving on the curving road. She was going slow, probably trying to postpone the end event as long as possible.

"How did you keep him from hearing about her death?" She hugged Chevy sorry that she had got him into this.

"I unplugged the television and told him it was broken. Plus, we went on a trip to Sparwood to see some friends."

"Very smart."

"Thank you," Wendy said smugly.

"Where are we going?" Sally asked for the second time.

"There are lots of old roads north of Pemberton," Wendy said. "Keep driving. We'll find one of them."

"And then Bonnie comes to visit last week," Elizabeth continued.

"Bonnie showed up at our door one morning. Luckily I had

found a photo of her in Sylvia's stuff so I recognized her. I told her Dad was sick and still asleep but she insisted on coming in and talking with me. She told me all about her and Sylvia's childhood, how Dad had left her aunt, and how they hadn't seen him in years. Then she showed me her Angel cards and explained how Bridgette had warned her to use caution. She said she had thought it was something at the retreat that she had to worry about. And she turned up Adriana saying that the card meant that she was going to help Bonnie find the answer. Bonnie was so excited when she told me that, stating that Adriana's prediction had come true when she recognized her Uncle John." Wendy laughed. "And she was right. It brought her right to me. But she should have paid more attention to Bridgette's warning. It might have saved her life."

They passed the turn into the parking lot for Nairn Falls and soon reached Pemberton.

"Just follow this road through town," Wendy said.

"So how did you kill Bonnie?"

"She wanted to come back the next day to see Dad. I didn't want her to but like her cousin she was insistent. I drugged Dad and kept her at the house till dark, just giving Dad enough medicine to keep him sleeping all day. When she finally left I crept out after her hit her on the head with a rock. I loaded her into my van and drove to near the retreat and dumped her out. I then found her precious Angel cards and threw them on her."

"Did you unplug the television this time to keep your dad from hearing about Bonnie and the fact that she was Sylvia's cousin."

"Don't mess with something that works, is my motto," Wendy gloated.

They were driving through the native reserve.

"Turn right here and head towards Lillooet," Wendy said. She began to watch out the windshield looking for a suitable road. The native reserve carried on for quite a few miles.

Elizabeth searched her mind for something more to talk about. "Bonnie said that Sylvia had sent a text that she had something exciting to tell her. Finding her, ah, your father must have been it."

Wendy didn't answer.

"Why did you send us the note?"

"I thought I'd try to scare you away. But you were too stupid to heed it and now you have to pay." She spotted a road. "There, that one, turn down it."

Elizabeth's stomach clenched. She felt as if she was going to be sick. She'd been trying to think about what she could do to prevent Wendy from killing them but nothing had come to mind. She didn't know any self defence, she was limber but doubted that she had the coordination to spin around, fling out her leg, and kick the gun out of Wendy's hand with her foot.

The road was gravel and as they drove the tires created a cloud of dust behind them. After a couple of kilometres Wendy told Sally to turn down a narrow lane. It curved to the left and ended in a gravel pit.

"Well, this is perfect, better than I had hoped for," Wendy said. "Now undo your seat belts and climb out slowly. Don't try anything fancy."

I don't have anything fancy to try, Elizabeth thought. She wished that she had listened to her father and stayed out of other people's business. She wished that she had phoned her father and her siblings and Jared more while she was here. She wished a lot of things.

"Now turn and walk into the trees. No use you lying out where you could be found easily."

Elizabeth hugged Chevy to her. Tears fell at the thought that he had always been so trusting, following her where ever she went and now he was going to die because of her. Sally put her arm around Elizabeth's waist as they walked towards the bush.

"I'm so sorry," Elizabeth whispered to Sally.

"It's not your fault. I was the one who got us into this."

Suddenly there was a cry behind them and a gun shot. They both turned in time to see John with his arms wrapped around Wendy. He was shaking her back and forth while she was shrieking and trying to point the gun at him. Elizabeth dropped Chevy and she and Sally ran over to help. Elizabeth grabbed Wendy's hand holding the gun and wrestled it out of her grasp.

She threw it away.

John let Wendy go. Sally pushed her face down on the ground and sat on her back.

Wendy turned her head to see who it was. "Dad!" She struggled to free herself. "What did you do that for? We have to stop them. They killed Sylvia and Bonnie."

Sally grabbed Wendy's wrists and held them behind her to stop her from trying to turn over.

"No, you killed them," John said sadly. "I knew it as soon as I saw that you had taken my gun."

"Dad, listen to me." Wendy strained to see him better.

John turned away.

"Dad, I did it for us," Wendy cried. "Sylvia would have wanted your money. I had to stop that."

John refused to answer her and, as if realizing it was over, she finally quit her struggles.

Elizabeth was so relieved that she couldn't speak for a few moments. She couldn't believe how close they had come to dying. "Let's tie her up," she said. "John, do you have some rope so we can tie her hands and feet?"

John hurried to his car, which he'd left around the curve, and drove it up beside the van. He opened the trunk and rummaged around. "I have some duct tape," he said.

"That will work," Elizabeth said. Sally still held Wendy's hands behind her so Elizabeth wrapped the tape around her wrists. Now they could relax. "We'll do her feet once she's in the van."

"What are you doing here?" She asked John. "How did you find us?"

John's hands were shaking as he ran them through his hair. "Yesterday, I decided to quit taking the pills Wendy kept giving me to see for myself what was happening to my memory. I had to pretend though because I didn't want her to know so I feigned sleep when she gave them to me with lunch. When she left the house I got up and as I walked by her bedroom, I saw the box that holds my gun lying on her bed. I went in to check and the gun was gone. I jumped in my car. I didn't know where she would have gone but I spotted the van turning onto the highway. I saw that you two were in it and that Sally was driving. I knew something was wrong."

"Thank you for following," Sally said.

"Yes, thank you for saving our lives," Elizabeth agreed. It must have been hard to choose them over his daughter.

"What are you going to do with her?" John asked.

"She confessed to killing Sylvia and Bonnie so we have to take her to the RCMP," Elizabeth said.

Elizabeth and Sally pulled Wendy up and walked her over to the passenger's side of the van. Once she was seated Elizabeth wrapped the tape around her ankles.

"I'll drive and Sally you sit in the backseat so that you can keep an eye on her. John, are you going to be okay driving back alone?"

"Yes. I'll meet you at the detachment."

Before getting in the van Elizabeth went and retrieved the gun. She put it in the back of the van.

Elizabeth drove straight to the RCMP detachment in Whistler and went in to find Constable Black. Wendy was taken into custody and Elizabeth, Sally, and John gave their statements.

When John dropped them off at the bed and breakfast Sally dug the photograph of Sylvia out of her pocket. She turned it over and handed it to John.

"Madeline gave me this photo when she came to pack Bonnie's clothes. She put her phone number and address on the back. I'll leave it with you."

"Thank you."

Elizabeth and Sally climbed the stairs to their room. After the close call they had just had neither felt like talking. They collapsed on the couch, drained. Finally Elizabeth said.

"Don't ever tell Dad or Terry or Sherry what happened today."

Sally shook her head. "If I did Phil would never let you go out anywhere and I'd have no one to do things with."

Elizabeth reached over and picked up the remote turning on the television. It was on the news channel. After a few minutes of talking about world crises, the anchor person announced that

Jessica Smallwood had been arrested for her daughter's murder.

"According to sources, Ms. Smallwood followed her daughter here. During an argument she killed her, then buried her body under the house, which was empty at the time."

* * *

On Friday morning Elizabeth drove Sally to the retreat so she could say goodbye to her classmates.

"So, did you get Reggie's email address?" Elizabeth asked, when Sally climbed back in the Tracker.

Sally grinned. "I sure did."

Elizabeth drove to Alta Lake where they loaded Chevy into a canoe and they headed out on the leisurely, three hour paddle down the River of Golden Dreams to Green Lake. After their near miss yesterday, it felt so good to relax, to feel the sunshine, to just be alive. Even Chevy seemed to sense that life was good. He spent much of the time looking over the edge of the canoe at the water.

They spent the afternoon packing then went for supper in the Village.

The next morning they rose early and loaded their things into the Tracker. They paid their bill then went across the road to see Cynthia.

"I sent the SPCA a thousand dollars because you did find Penny's murderer," Cynthia said. "Plus, I heard you discovered who had killed the two other women who had gone to the retreat."

Elizabeth didn't want to even think about that. "It was nice meeting you."

"Do you want a reference from me?"

"I have your address. If I need one I'll contact you."

They stopped in to see John. He was very subdued when he spoke but his voice got a little energized when he told them that he had called Madeline and she was coming to Whistler on Sunday to see him.

Elizabeth followed Nancy Greene Way to Highway 99. She turned left, drove through Whistler and they were on their way home.

* * *

The auras I have been seeing before receiving Mikks and Gwins stories are bothering me so I phone my mother. She is silent for a moment after I explain them then says.

"When you were little you used to see colours and shapes and then you would tell me about the strange people you had met and what they had told you. I took you to a doctor who told me these were called silent migraines or migraine auras without the headache. When you turned five they quit. Maybe you should go see your doctor about them if they have returned."

I am relieved. I have an explanation for them. I guess I didn't have to worry about being thought of as crazy by Kat Mac or the rest of the class.

But even if Mikk and Gwin are not real aliens from another planet and even if my story is all fiction, everything has worked out the way the Angel cards said it would. I had my meeting with the publisher and Kat Mac surprised me by attending. She told him how great she thought my manuscript was and the publisher agreed right there to read it. I gave him the hard copy I had brought with me. Since then I've been spending my time visualizing the front cover, writing up my bio, and picturing my book on a shelf in a book store: Crybaby by Lisa Zhang.

Kat Mac and I are going together to the party tonight to celebrate, both the good news about my manuscript and our meeting.

ABOUT THE AUTHOR

Joan was born in New Westminster, B.C. and raised in Edmonton, Alberta. She has worked as a bartender, hotel maid, cashier, bank teller, bookkeeper, printing press operator, meat wrapper, gold prospector, warehouse shipper, house renovator and nursing attendant. During that time she raised two children and helped raise three step-children. She has had travel and historical articles published in magazines. Between 1990 and 2000 she researched and wrote seven Backroads Series books about Alberta, B.C., the Yukon and Alaska that were published by Lone Pine Publishing in Edmonton, AB.

Joan love change and has moved over thirty times in her life living on acreages and farms and in small towns and cities throughout Alberta and B.C. She now lives on an acreage in the Port Alberni Valley on Vancouver Island with her husband, five cats and four chickens. She currently works in a group home doing one-on-one support with a mentally and physically challenged man.

Joan belongs to the Crime Writers of Canada, the International Association of Crime Writers/North American Branch, the Vancouver International Writers Festival, the Writers

Guild of Alberta, the Federation of B.C. Writers, and the Port Alberni Arts Council. Her short story *A Capital Offence* received *Ascent Aspirations First* Prize for Flash Fiction.

The Only Shadow in the House,
Sumach Press, Oct 2010, Toronto, ON.

A Capital Offence, Short story, Ascent Aspirations Magazine
Anthology Eight Winter 2010

Illegally Dead,
Sumach Press, 2008, Toronto, ON.

NOTE FROM THE PUBLISHER:

Thank you for purchasing and reading this BWLPP. We hope you have enjoyed your reading experience. BWLPP and the author would very much appreciate you returning to the online retailer where you purchased this book and leaving a review for the author.
Best Regards and Happy Reading, Jamie and Jude

BWLPP and BWLPP Spice
The Beverly Hills Boutique of eBook publishers.
Vintage and New from award winning authors.
Top quality books loved by readers,
Romance, Mystery, Fantasy, Young Adult
Vampires, Werewolves, Cops, Lovers.
Looking for Something Spicier
for Sexy Spicy Selections
Try BWLPP Spice